"Hi, Jax," Mia said.

Her voice sent a shiver down his spine.

"Hey, it's nice to see you again." He kept his voice light and friendly, even though everything inside him hummed and buzzed. He dropped a quick peck on her cheek to keep up appearances, but her heady scent and soft skin had him lingering longer than he should have.

"You do know that's my sister." Shane's voice boomed in his ears.

Jax froze like a deer caught in car headlights.

Mia was still off-limits. That much hadn't changed.

He wasn't about to screw up again. He valued Shane's friendship. Jax would lose that if he messed with Shane's sister.

Mia smiled at something one of the women said. It was like the sun coming out on a dark, rainy day.

Why the hell was he thinking about Mia's smile? Why was he thinking about her at all? Nothing good could come of it.

He needed to stop. Now.

Why wouldn't his brain get the message?

Dear Reader,

Newly divorced Mia Kavanaugh is *off-limits*. Her brother is Jax Rawlins's best friend. Still...Jax can't help falling for this kind, sweet, sexy, loving woman. She and her three daughters have captured his heart. But a relationship with Mia means returning to his hometown of New Suffolk, Massachusetts. Something Jax swore he'd never do.

Thank you for picking up this copy of *The Last Time We Kissed*—book three in my Sisterhood of Chocolate & Wine series! For those who don't know me, I'm Anna James. I write contemporary romance, and although I've been writing for years, this is my first series with Harlequin. I hope you enjoy reading *The Last Time We Kissed* as much as I enjoyed writing it. I'd love to hear what you think of Jax and Mia's story. Please share your thoughts with me on Facebook (annajames.author) and X (@authorannajames), or drop me a line through my website, authorannajames.com.

Happy reading,

Anna James

PS: If you haven't read book one or book two in my Sisterhood series yet, you can pick up a copy of *A Taste of Home*, Layla and Shane's story, and *A Deal with Mr. Wrong*, Piper and Cooper's story, at Harlequin.com.

THE LAST TIME
WE KISSED

ANNA JAMES

SPECIAL EDITION

ISBN-13: 978-1-335-40213-4

The Last Time We Kissed

Harlequin Enterprises ULC
22 Adelaide St. West, 41st Floor
Toronto, Ontario M5H 4E3, Canada
www.Harlequin.com

Printed in Lithuania

Recycling programs for this product may not exist in your area.

MIX
Paper | Supporting responsible forestry
FSC® C021394

Anna James writes contemporary romance novels with strong, confident heroes and heroines who conquer life's trials and find their happily-ever-afters.

Want to learn more about Anna and her books?

Sign up for her newsletter: authorannajames.com.

Follow her on Instagram: @author_anna_james.

Books by Anna James

Harlequin Special Edition

Sisterhood of Chocolate & Wine

A Taste of Home
A Deal with Mr. Wrong
The Last Time We Kissed

Visit the Author Profile page at Harlequin.com.

For my editor, Susan. Thanks for all you do
for my books and for making me a better writer!

All my best,

Anna

Chapter One

Jax Rawlins stood in the corner of the Manhattan gallery, studying the people milling about the space. It seemed more people were gazing out the floor-to-ceiling windows at the gorgeous skyline than viewing the images that hung on the wall.

That wasn't good.

His cell buzzed. Jax extracted it from the pocket of his trousers and glanced at the caller ID. His mother. Again. He couldn't deal with her right now. He had more important issues that needed his immediate attention—the sales, or lack thereof, of his photographs at this show. He declined the call.

As he lowered his hand to return the phone to his pocket, it buzzed again.

This time his dad's number flashed across the screen. *Dammit.* It was bad enough that they were arguing—again—but why did they each insist he take their side in the dispute of the day? Why couldn't they just leave him out of it?

Not that they'd ever been able to do that. They'd dragged him into their disagreements for as long as he could remember.

Jax ignored the call and shoved the phone in his pocket. Something he could do with a couple of hundred miles between his loft here in Manhattan and his parents' home in New Suffolk, Massachusetts.

Cate Endsley, his agent, approached with a tight smile.

"Would you just shut the damned thing off," she growled in a hushed voice.

Hell, she must have noticed him fiddling with his cell.

"You need to focus on what's important," Cate continued. "The turnout tonight is…disappointing. Again."

"Sorry." Cate was right. Tonight's crowd was definitely not what he'd hoped for. "Maybe people are just running late?" Oh, who was he kidding? Not Cate, if the look on her face was anything to go by. Jax's shoulders slumped. They were two hours into this evening's event, and he'd seen maybe fifty people, tops, come through the gallery. A far cry from the hundreds who usually attended one of his shows.

People loved to see the images he captured of the struggles of wild animals in their natural habitats. At least, they used to, but lately…all he had to do was look at this small gathering to see how the winds had changed.

His phone buzzed again. He reached in his pocket and grabbed the device.

"Leave it," Cate demanded. "Your flavor of the week is just going to have to wait until after the show to talk to you."

"You wound me." Jax gave a soft chuckle and pressed a hand to his heart. "You know you're my one and only."

Cate rolled her eyes skyward. "You're not my type." She eyed him up and down. "You're the wrong gender, for one thing. But even if you were someone I found attractive, I'd stay as far away from you as possible." Cate let out something between a snort and a laugh. "Your reputation with the ladies precedes you."

So he wasn't ready to settle down yet. He was only thirty. Way too young to be tied down. *Like Dad had been when he met Mom.*

Jax wasn't interested in *until death do us part.*

His phone buzzed yet again. Definitely not interested in forever. *No way. No how.* All anyone needed to do was look at his parents to see why. Married thirty-one years and miserable for each and every one of them. Lord only knew why they didn't just divorce. It was as if they'd rather be miserable together than happy apart. *Like that makes any sense.*

Cate shook her head. "Seriously?"

He held his hands up in front of him. "You asked me to leave it and I will."

His parents would just have to learn how to communicate with each other. He wouldn't take sides in whatever war they were waging against each other today.

"Go mingle," Cate demanded. "You need to drum up more interest in the photos on display." She gestured to the number of prints still hanging on the wall.

He nodded and walked over to a thirtysomething couple standing a few feet away, in front of his portrait of a lone wolf.

"It's the same thing over and over." The woman gave a discreet gesture with her hand that encompassed several images hanging on the wall in front of them. "An animal, cold and alone. Struggling to survive."

Yes. It's what people expected from a Jax Rawlins photo.

"Agreed." The man nodded his head. "It's rather depressing, if you ask me."

Jax's jaw nearly hit the ground. No one had ever described his photos as depressing before. *Edgy. Raw. Fascinating.* Those were words he was used to hearing.

"Maybe it's some kind of metaphor? You know, individuals struggling to survive in this crazy world we live in?" the woman suggested.

The man chuckled. "Maybe."

The woman turned to Jax. "What do you think?" She didn't seem to recognize him.

"Art is subjective." Jax made sure to keep his tone conversational. People were entitled to their own opinions. "The same image speaks to people in different ways."

"Still, I'd love to know what inspired the photographer to capture the wolf at this particular moment in time." The man gestured to the picture in front of them.

Jax wasn't thinking about society norms, that's for sure.

"I see stark vulnerability in the wolf's eyes," the woman said. "She'd rather be part of the pack than alone."

Jax smiled. "It's what resonates with you."

"Shall I have this put aside for you?" Cate appeared by his side.

"Not right now." The woman offered a polite smile. "I want to see the rest of this collection." She tugged on the man's arm, and they moved on.

"They've already viewed the rest of your images," Cate said under her breath.

Jax exhaled sharply. "I know." He'd seen them milling about the room for some time now. What the hell was going on? A few short months ago, everything had been going great. He scrubbed his palms over his face.

"I think it's time to face facts. This subject matter isn't cutting it anymore. You need to move in a different direction."

That was easier said than done. His head started to throb. He'd spent the last ten years honing *this* direction. It's what worked—he peered around the room again at the dwindling crowd and the number of photos still hanging on the wall— at least, it had until recently. What had happened to change things?

"There's something else you should know." Cate sounded… worried.

"What's that?" He tried to keep his tone light. Conversational. But inside, bile roiled around in his gut.

She exhaled a heavy sigh. "The show you have booked for this weekend is canceled."

He jerked his attention to her, and his mouth fell open. "When did this happen?"

"This afternoon," Cate admitted.

"Why?" he asked.

"The gallery said they needed to close for the week to make some minor repairs," Cate said.

"That's not so bad." Why was she making such a big deal of it? Jax wasn't thrilled with the delay, but he didn't see a problem with it.

"The cancelation is not the bad part."

Jax's brow furrowed. "Then what is?"

"They declined to rebook."

Jax shook his head. "That doesn't make any sense. I've done dozens of exhibits at the Arte Loft over the years. They always beg me to come back."

Cate ran her fingers through her hair. "I don't know what to say."

The fact that she didn't spoke volumes.

Jax rubbed at his temples. "It's not like Arte Loft is the Breitenberg gallery." He could almost understand the rejection if it were. Almost, because he still didn't understand why Gunter Breitenberg wasn't interested in his work. Jax had exhibited at some of the most prominent galleries around the globe.

"Forget Breitenberg," Cate said.

He gawked at her. "Are you kidding? That's been the ultimate goal all along." Ever since he'd started his career. "It's one of the most prestigious galleries in the world. An exhibition there would be a major coup for us. You said so yourself."

"If an establishment who loves your work is no longer interested in showcasing your photos anymore, what hope do we have for a gallery that's never been on board?" Her frustration came through loud and clear, and her blunt—as always—tone drove home her message with stunning clarity.

Jax's stomach pitched and rolled.

"You need to find something that will captivate people again."

Something...but what?

He wasn't sure, but he needed to figure it out. Fast.

Jax walked into his loft shortly after midnight. He shrugged off the jacket he was wearing and draped it over one of the leather club chairs in his living room.

He walked into the kitchen, then opened the fridge and grabbed a beer off the shelf.

He needed one after tonight. The evening never improved and he was sure that Cate would get an earful from the gallery owner regarding the lack of sales.

He removed the twist-off top and walked back to the living room while he drank.

Jax dropped down on the sofa. He set the beer on a glass-and-chrome side table, and pulled out his phone to check his messages.

Scrolling, he saw a bunch of notifications filling the screen. Including more calls from his parents. Maybe he should deal with them later?

No, he might as well get this over with.

He opened the calls in visual voice mail. After such a crappy night, he wasn't up for hearing their voices.

He read a message from Dad, who was complaining about an argument he'd had with Jax's mother and how Dad was right and Mom was wrong.

He ignored it and scrolled to the next. Mom's rebuttal on the argument.

Next.

Mom: You know, you really disappointed me, Jackie, when you didn't show up at my last book club meeting. I was hurt and embarrassed.

Jax's hands curled into tight fists. He'd told her he couldn't make her meeting. He'd been in Madagascar on a photo shoot, for crying out loud.

Hurt and disappointed. How many of his elementary school performances and art shows had she missed over the years? He could count the number of times she did attend on one hand. And she hadn't even had a good excuse for missing them. She'd been busy with golf and lunches with friends at the club. How pathetic was that?

Dad wasn't any better when it came to attending school functions, but he'd had work as an excuse.

At least Pops had been there for him. His former neighbor wasn't blood-related, but he was the closest thing to a grandparent that Jax had.

He adored the man. Would do anything for him.

Jax scrolled to the next message.

Jackie, I forgot to tell you, Mom began.

His hand fisted around his phone. He hated when she called him Jackie. Why did she continue when she knew how much it bothered him?

He sucked in some much-needed oxygen and read the rest of her message.

I've already told the group you'll be at the next meeting, in two weeks. Don't let me down again.

His jaw tightened. She'd committed him to attending a meeting that was two hours away, with no traffic, in the middle of the week without bothering to check with him. Did she really expect him to be at her beck and call.

Obviously, she did.

Stop it. Why are you letting this get to you? The behavior is nothing new.

Jax closed his eyes and focused on slow, deep breaths.

A few minutes later, he opened his eyes and rose from the sofa.

He had other priorities to deal with right now. He needed a plan to salvage his career before it completely tanked and he became yesterdays' news.

Jax strode into his study. He powered up his computer and got to work.

A few hours later, a loud noise startled Jax awake. His eyes darted around the room, trying to focus. His study. And he was still sitting in the leather chair in front of his desk. Had he fallen asleep going through his unpublished pictures from his last shoot? Jax glanced at his computer. Yeah. That's exactly what he'd done.

What time was it? He glanced at the Mission mantel clock he and Pops had made together when Jax was a kid. Seven in the morning. Jax scrubbed his hands over his face. Lord, he needed a coffee. Standing, he was about to head into the kitchen when his cell buzzed. That must have been what woke him in the first place.

Who the hell was calling him this early in the morning?

His brain snapped to the tirade of angry messages left by his parents last night. Grabbing the phone off the desk, Jax was about to decline the call, but stopped when his best friend's number flashed across the screen.

He connected the call. "What's wrong?" Something must be, for Shane Kavanaugh to call this early.

"Got a 911 call this morning. Duncan Cruz and I responded. It's Alex Papadopoulos," Shane said.

His heart hammered so hard Jax thought he might crack a rib. What had happened to his beloved Pops? *What if...* No. He couldn't even imagine such an outcome.

"He fell down the stairs this morning." Shane's voice pulled him from his dark thoughts.

Jax exhaled a sharp breath. "How bad?"

"Hit his head pretty hard. Messed up his right leg some, but I don't think it's broken. We brought him to the hospital. Doctor's examining him now. I thought you'd want to know."

He dragged his free hand through his hair. "I do. Thanks. Any idea how long he'll be there?"

"Not sure, but I'm guessing they'll want to keep him overnight for observation. Like I said, he smacked his head pretty hard."

Bile roiled in his gut. "Okay. I'll head to New Suffolk as soon as I can." He'd planned to spend the day reviewing more of his unpublished photos, but that would have to wait. "Thanks again for calling me."

"You're welcome. Talk soon. Bye." Shane disconnected the call.

Jax headed for the shower. He needed to get on the road quickly—and get to Pops as fast as he could.

Jax arrived at New Suffolk General Hospital five hours later. He'd made great time, considering he'd hit rush hour traffic.

After a quick stop at the information desk, he took the elevator to the eighth floor and strode to Pops's room. When he arrived, the door was partially closed, but he could hear voices inside.

"Please, Mr. Papadopoulos. You have to listen to reason," a very frustrated female voice said.

"Hello?" Jax knocked on the door and pushed it open at the same time.

"Jax." Pops gave him a warm smile. "What are you doing here?" To the young woman dressed in light blue hospital scrubs, he said, "This is my grandson. He's single. Very handsome, too—right?" He winked.

Jax chuckled. At least he didn't have to worry about Pops having a concussion. His brain was one hundred percent engaged to come up with that.

The woman flashed a charming smile at him. "It's nice to meet you. I'm Rena, your grandfather's nurse."

He shook her outstretched hand. "Jax Rawlins. It's nice to meet you, too." Turning his attention to Pops, he added, "Shane called me. He was one of the paramedics who answered your 911 call."

"I thought I recognized him. You two are still friendly?"

Jax smiled. "Have been since kindergarten." Like Pops, Shane's friendship had been one of the constants in his life. Even if they couldn't get together all the time, when they did, it was like old times. "I see you're feeling better after your little spill this morning."

"I'm right as rain," Pops said. "I'm going home tomorrow."

"That's not a good idea, Mr. Papadopoulos," Rena said. "You dislocated your right shoulder, and your right ankle is badly sprained. You need to stay off it for at least four weeks. Doctor's orders."

Pops pulled a face and waved off her concern. "I'll be fine. Don't worry."

Jax stepped closer to the bed. "You should do what the doctor says."

Pops crossed his arms over his chest. "They want to send me to some rehab facility. It's bad enough I have to stay here today. I just want to go home."

"You need help, Mr. Papadopoulos," Rena insisted. "You just told me you live alone. A rehabilitation facility is your best option. Your insurance should cover most of the cost."

Pops glared at his nurse. "I'm going home. I can take care of myself."

Rena looked at Jax as if to say, *Please talk some sense into this man.*

The trouble was, Pops was stubborn, and he wouldn't do anything he didn't want to. They needed an alternative. One that worked for Pops and provided the care the doctor had ordered. "What about home care?"

"Yes," Alex blurted before Rena could reply. "I want to stay in my own house."

Rena cocked her head to the side. "It's an option, but it's expensive, and insurance won't cover the full cost."

"Let's not worry about that now." He'd cover the extra cost, if Pops couldn't. It was the least he could do after everything Pops had done for him. The man had opened his heart and his home to Jax. He'd been the family Jax had desperately wanted—desperately needed—when he was younger. "What else do we need to consider to make home care work?"

"He'll need round the clock help for the duration of his recovery," Rena said. "Are you prepared for that kind of commitment?"

Jax's eyes widened. He hadn't planned on staying more than a day or two at the most. He certainly couldn't stay in New Suffolk for the next month. "I'd need to hire someone." He turned his attention to Pops. "Would that be okay with you? They'd have to live with you temporarily."

The older man nodded. "As long as I get to stay in my house."

"Is the home set up for first-floor living?" Rena asked. "That includes a bathroom and a place to sleep. It would be difficult, if not impossible, for your grandfather to navigate stairs in his current condition."

A mutinous expression crossed Pops's face. "I can navigate the stairs just fine," he insisted.

"First-floor living won't be an issue," Jax said to Rena. Turning to Pops, he added, "You can use the downstairs spare bedroom and main bath." Before Pops could protest further, he said, "It's only for a month. You're going to have to make some compromises if you want to recuperate at home."

Pops narrowed his gaze. "Fine. I'll stay downstairs."

Jax squeezed Pops's hand. "Good." He turned to Rena. "When can we set this up?"

"I'll contact the patient advocate and have her come in and discuss some options with you later today." Rena headed toward the door.

"Perfect." With any luck, he'd have the care Pops needed in place in a day or two. Then Jax could return to Manhattan.

Mia Kavanaugh stood in the upstairs hall of her home and watched the plumber who squatted over the pipe where her toilet once stood. "I had the septic tank emptied last week, but we're still having issues."

Please don't say I need a new septic system. Please don't say I need a new septic system. No way did she have the fifteen thousand dollars required for a new install lying around. She'd just replaced the air-conditioning unit last month, and her savings account was in the red.

"Mommy, Mommy, I gotta go, and Aurora is in the bathroom downstairs." Brooke, her seven-year-old daughter, raced up the stairs with a pained expression on her face. "When is the man going to be done?"

"Use my bathroom," Mia pointed across the hall to her bedroom with the en suite.

"I get to use Mommy's bathroom," Brooke gloated to her younger sister, Kiera.

"That's not fair," Kiera protested. "You said we're not allowed to use yours."

"This is an emergency," Brooke said.

Kiera started arguing and Brooke continued to gloat, which meant Brooke's need wasn't as dire as Mia had assumed.

"Stop it, girls," Mia commanded.

Her daughters continued as if Mia hadn't spoken.

She rubbed at her temples. Mia heard the muffled snicker of the plumber. She so didn't need this right now. "Both of you." She pointed to each of her daughters. "To your room. Stay there until I say you can come out."

Kiera stuck her tongue out at Brooke and marched down the hall.

"But, Mommy," Brooke protested. "I still gotta go."

Mia flashed her don't-mess-with-me glare at Brooke and pointed to her bedroom. "You have two minutes. Then go to your room."

The plumber turned to her a moment later holding a small wet Sqishmallow. "Here's your problem, ma'am."

Mia wasn't sure what she was more annoyed with: the fact that one of her girls had flushed a toy down the toilet, or the fact that the plumber had just called her *ma'am*. At thirty-one, she wasn't old enough to be considered a *ma'am*. Her mother… yes, but not her. Right?

Mia pulled a face when the plumber tried to hand her the toy. "You can toss it in there." She pointed to the trash. She wasn't going to try to save it.

He pressed the lid open on the small silver canister and tossed the Sqishmallow in. The lid closed with a loud clang. "I'll have this put back together for you in a few minutes. Just gotta grab a new wax ring for the toilet from my truck. Be back in a jiffy."

She stepped aside to allow him room to exit.

Mia breathed out a sigh of relief. She wouldn't need a new septic in the foreseeable future. *Thank God for small mercies.* The roof, however, was a different story. She'd need to replace it within the next four months—before winter hit—for sure.

It's not like she didn't know the house had problems— those issues had made it possible to buy her ex out when they split four months ago, instead of having to sell the place and uproot the girls—but she hadn't expected to replace every-thing at once. She was going to need another job to earn the extra cash. Her salary as an elementary school teacher wasn't going to cut it.

"Mommy. Daddy is on the phone." Aurora, her oldest, handed Mia her cell.

"Thanks, sweetie." Mia pressed the mute button. "Tell the plumber I'll be right back."

Aurora smiled. "Okay, Mom."

Mia unmuted the call. "Hello, Kyle." Stepping into her bedroom, she shut the door. "You'd better not be calling to cancel on me." As he'd done three times in the last month. "The girls are looking forward to seeing you."

"I'm not going to cancel," Kyle said.

Relief flooded through her. She was sick and tired of explaining to their daughters why Daddy couldn't come and see them when he was supposed to.

"As a matter of fact, I'm calling to see if I can pick them up a little early. I'm taking them to Chuck E. Cheese tonight for dinner, and I wanted to give them time to play at the arcade for a while before the place gets slammed."

"Sure. No problem." The truth was, she could use the respite. Being a single mom with three active kids was challenging, to say the least. Soccer practice, piano lessons, swim lessons. That was just Aurora's schedule. Add in Brooke and Kiera and the Mom taxi ran from first thing in the morning until just before bed most days, transporting her daughters to their various activities.

"What time are you coming?" she asked.

"I'm leaving work now. I should be there in fifteen minutes."

"Okay. I'll have them ready."

"Mia," Kyle began.

"Yes?"

"One more thing."

Her brow furrowed. What more could her ex possibly want? "What is it?"

"Would you like to join us tonight?" Kyle asked.

Mia's jaw dropped. No. She couldn't have heard him right. "Could you repeat that, please?"

Kyle chuckled. "I thought it would be nice if we took the girls out together. Like old times. It'll be fun for them to have us both there."

None of what he said made sense. He didn't want to be with her anymore. It's why he'd left. "I don't think Oriana would appreciate me coming."

"That won't be a problem. We're, ah…not together anymore."

No surprise there. The shocker was that they'd stayed together after Oriana had declined Kyle's marriage proposal a few months ago.

"So, did you want to join us?" Kyle asked again.

Her mind whirled. "Forgive me, but why are you asking? You must see that this has come as a huge surprise to me given everything you've said and done over the last couple of years." He'd made it abundantly clear he wasn't interested in working through their problems.

"It's not that big a deal." Kyle sounded frustrated. "I just thought we could show a united front to the girls, that's all."

Okay. That made sense, and it would be good for the girls if they could do as he suggested. If he was willing to make the effort, she would, too. "I can't tonight. I already have plans." Today was her last day of school for the year, and she planned to celebrate. It had been a long year. The New Suffolk public school would still hold classes, but the private school she taught at was D. O. N. E. *Hallelujah.* "Maybe next time."

"You have other plans?"

Mia couldn't miss the hint of disapproval in Kyle's voice. She sucked in a deep breath and blew it out slowly. "Yes. I'm going out with my sister and some other friends." Not that she needed to explain.

"I would think your daughters' welfare would be a priority for you."

Was he kidding? Aurora, Brooke and Kiera were her top priority. How dare he challenge her on that. He'd ditched the girls three weeks in a row, for goodness' sake. "I think we're done here. The girls will be ready when you arrive. No need to get out of your car." She didn't want to see him. "I'll send them out."

"Wait. I'm sorry. I shouldn't have snapped at you that way. I know how important the girls' well-being is to you. And of course your sister and your friends are important, too."

Damned straight. Mia didn't know what she'd do without all of them. Their friendship and support had gotten her through her divorce. And Piper... Her baby sister meant the world to her.

"I should never have implied otherwise. Can you forgive me?" Kyle sounded genuinely sorry.

Mia lowered the phone and stared at it. *Who are you and what have you done with my ex?* She raised the phone to her ear again. "Fine." She didn't want to fight anymore. They'd done enough of that, especially over the last two years. "I'll see you when you get here." Mia didn't wait for his response before ending the call.

Shoving her phone into the back pocket of her shorts, she stepped out into the hall.

"You're all set." The plumber handed her an invoice. "I take cash or credit." He grinned.

Mia glanced at the paper in her hand. Her eyes bugged out at the figure she owed at the bottom of the page.

Crap. More debt, and not enough money to cover it. Her shoulders slumped.

She needed that second job. *Fast.*

Chapter Two

"Bye, girls." Mia dropped a kiss on each of her daughters' heads. "Have fun at Chuck E. Cheese tonight. I'll see you soon. Grammy will be here when you get home later."

"Bye, Mommy," they said in unison as they slid into Kyle's Audi Q7.

"Are you sure you don't want to come with us?" Kyle winked at her and flashed what Mia used to think of as his best sexy grin.

Was he kidding? Bile burned in her belly. He. Didn't. Want. Her. Anymore. He'd made that fact abundantly clear when he walked out on her almost a year and a half ago. When he'd signed their divorce decree earlier this year. So what was up with him now?

"Yay! Mommy's coming with us," Kiera cheered.

"Woo-hoo." Brooke pumped her hand in the air.

"No. I'm not." Mia glared at Kyle for opening his mouth in front of their daughters, when she'd already told him no. Now she was the bad guy for disappointing her girls.

"What?" He acted as if he had no idea why she was angry with him.

He could play the wounded party all he wanted. He didn't fool her. She'd caught his smug little smile before he placed the innocent expression on his face.

"I'm sorry, girls. I can't tonight."

"Okay, Mommy." Kiera gave a little wave. "Bye-bye."

"Bye-bye, sweetie. Have fun with Daddy." Mia blew a kiss to each of her girls.

She was happy Kyle's little stunt hadn't upset their daughters. Not if their smiling faces were anything to go by.

Kyle scowled and rolled up the front and rear car windows without another word. He backed out of the driveway and drove down the street, disappearing a minute later.

Alone at last. Mia grinned. She turned and walked to the front door.

Her cell chimed as she stepped inside, indicating she'd received a text message from Piper.

Heading to Donahue's pub in a few. Want a ride?

Mia texted her sister back. No. Kids just left. I still need to shower and change. I'll meet you there. Let everyone know I'm going to be a little late.

Mia's phone dinged again. She smiled at Piper's thumbs-up emoji.

She climbed the stairs, walked into her bedroom and stripped off her clothes. In the bathroom, she turned on the shower and waited for the water to heat.

Mia gazed at herself in the bathroom mirror.

She ran a hand over her not-so-flat stomach. Yes, after three pregnancies, her body was a little worse for wear. Who had time to hone their muscles at the gym? Not her, that's for sure.

And her hair. Mia sighed. The unruly mass of dark curls that touched the top of her shoulders was as far from sexy and sophisticated as one could get.

The come-hither grin Kyle had tossed at her earlier flashed through her mind. He hadn't done that in—too long to remember. The last few years they were married... Her stomach churned. Sure, they'd had sex, but the truth was, he hadn't found her attractive in a long, long time.

So what had tonight been about?

Did she care?

For the first time in a long time, the answer was no.

Kyle didn't matter anymore.

Mia yawned as she pulled into the parking lot at Donahue's pub an hour later. It had been a long day with very little sleep the night before. Kiera had woken in the middle of the night from a bad dream and crawled into bed with Mia.

Kiera might have fallen back to sleep immediately, but with all of her tossing and turning, Mia remained wide awake.

At least she didn't have to get up and go to school tomorrow. She would, however, need to start her summer job hunt. Now was the time to find something. Memorial Day was a week and a half away, the unofficial kickoff of the tourist season. New Suffolk's population would almost triple in the coming weeks. People came from all over the East Coast to enjoy the sun and surf during the summer months.

Mia hurried inside and found her besties at a table in the rear of the bar. "Hi, ladies." She grabbed the empty seat next to her sister. "Sorry I'm late."

"No worries," Layla Williams said. "You didn't miss much."

A server stopped by the table. "What can I get you?" she asked Mia.

"Ginger ale, please." A glass of wine would put her to sleep, and a Coke would keep her awake all night.

The server nodded and moved to another table.

Four pairs of stunned eyes stared at her.

"What?" she asked.

"Do you have something you want to share with the class?" Elle Patterson asked. "Like why you're not drinking at girls' night out?"

"It *is* a curious turn of events." Piper aimed an inquiring gaze in Mia's direction.

Understanding dawned. Mia rolled her eyes. "Oh, please. It's not what you think. I'm just tired, that's all."

"That can be a sign of pregnancy." Layla's gaze danced with mischief.

Mia folded her hands across her chest. "Says the woman who is having sex on a regular basis. Some of us aren't that lucky." Certainly not her. She hadn't had any since…her evening with Jax.

Four *long* months ago.

And they'd used protection. Each and every incredible, glorious time they'd come together that fantastic evening.

"Been a long time, huh?" Piper mock-punched her in the arm.

"That's a shame." Layla grinned.

"Oh, sure," Elle scoffed. "Rub it in."

They all laughed.

"Seriously, guys. I'm not pregnant." She was one hundred percent sure of that. "Thank God. I mean I can't even imagine…" Mia shuddered.

"Would it be so bad if you were?" Abby Phillips sighed wistfully.

Ah, hell. Abby wanted kids, but the chances of her conceiving were slim. And here Mia was droning on like it was a fate worse than death.

"I'm sorry," Mia draped her arm around Abby's shoulder and gave her a gentle squeeze. "That was an insensitive thing to say. Forgive me?"

"There's nothing to forgive." She flashed a rueful smile. "I'm the one who should apologize. It was a silly thing to say to a single mother who already has three kids."

"It's all good," Mia said.

Abby let out a soft chuckle. "It is."

Mia breathed a sigh of relief. "So, what were you talking about before I came in?"

"We were boring Abby and Elle with wedding details." Piper grinned and pointed to Layla and herself.

Mia sighed. Her brother, Shane, was marrying Layla. Her sister, Piper, was marrying Cooper Turner, whose father co-owned TK Construction, with her mother.

It wasn't like she begrudged her sister and friend their happiness. She *was* happy for them. Thrilled, even. Her brother was a great guy, and so was Cooper Turner.

But given her failed marriage and recent divorce, their news was...bittersweet.

"And I was telling these three hopeless romantics—" Elle pointed to Piper, Abby, and Layla "—how I've sworn off men."

Abby snickered. "We all know that won't last."

"I'm serious," Elle insisted. "I've had it. The last four guys I've dated have been complete duds. Only interested in what *they* want. Why should I waste my time? I'm going to focus on finishing up my business administration degree." She winked at her cousin. "I can't work at the Coffee Palace for the rest of my life, Abby. Although I do appreciate the employment for the last six years."

"Why not? I like having you around." Abby grinned.

The server placed Mia's order in front of her. She also set down a glass of wine the size of a goblet in front of Elle.

"I didn't order that," Elle said.

"It's from him." The server pointed to a good-looking man with long blond hair who sat at the bar.

Elle placed the glass back on the tray. "Please tell him thanks. I appreciate the gesture, but I can't accept."

The server nodded and disappeared.

"Are you crazy?" Layla said. "He's gorgeous."

"He is," Elle agreed. "But I'm not interested."

"Amen to that." Mia raised her glass and touched Elle's.

"Oh, come on," Piper protested. "Not all guys are duds.

You two have just had bad experiences. You have to get back on the horse, so to speak, and try again."

"She's right," Layla agreed. "Trust me. I wasn't looking to fall in love again after Antoine, and then I found Shane, and I've never been happier. I can't wait to walk down the aisle."

Elle snorted, and Mia rolled her eyes skyward.

"What? Have you sworn off men, too?" Piper asked her.

"Hell, yes." If Mia nodded any faster, someone might mistake her for a bobblehead. "Definitely."

Piper's gaze went wide. "You're really not interested in finding love again?"

"Oh my. How times have changed." Mia arched her brow. "It wasn't that long ago you were in the same camp."

"I know." Piper chuckled. "And now Cooper and I are together. He changed everything."

"Good for you." Mia pointed to Piper. "And you." She pointed to Layla. "I, however, am not the least bit interested." The truth was, she wasn't sure she could survive another broken heart.

"So you don't care that Jax Rawlins is in town?" Abby asked.

"He is?" Her pulse kicked up a notch. *Dammit.*

Mia sighed. She supposed her body's reaction was natural. This was Jax Rawlins they were talking about. He was every schoolgirl fantasy she'd ever had come true, and then some. Just the thought of what he'd done to her, *all night long…* Mia shivered.

Yes, she missed the physical part of a relationship, all right. *But not the emotional part.* She wanted nothing to do with that.

Abby nodded. "He stopped by the Coffee Palace this afternoon. Said he was in town for the weekend visiting a friend."

Her mind snapped back to the last time she'd seen Jax. The day she and Kyle had finalized their divorce…

"Hold up, Mia." Kyle called to her as she strode toward the courthouse exit. *"I need to talk to you."*

She kept walking. What more could he have to say? He'd gotten what he wanted. The judge had signed the paperwork a few minutes ago, making him a free man.

"Please, Mia. It's important."

She stopped. Turning, she spotted Oriana by his side.

Tall, stylishly dressed head to toe in designer clothes, she walked with poise and confidence. Her long, thick, glossy hair swished from side to side.

Mia glanced at her own outfit. Standard black pants with a casual blouse. Runway ready, she wasn't.

The couple stopped when they reached her.

"I'll wait for you outside," Oriana said.

"Thanks, darling." Kyle smiled and kissed her cheek. "I won't be long."

Her gut twisted, because yeah, seeing him with Oriana...

Mia sucked in a deep, steadying breath. She straightened her shoulders and held her head high. "You wanted to speak with me?"

"Yes. I'm going to ask Oriana to marry me tonight."

Mia almost doubled over from the verbal blow.

"What do you think about that?" Piper asked.

Mia blinked. "Huh?"

"Jax. Here. In New Suffolk." Layla grinned and gave her a playful nudge. "Any chance for a repeat performance?"

Her eyes bugged out. "Shush. You know I told all of you about that in confidence." Mia darted her gaze around to see if anyone was listening. "I trusted you guys to keep my secret." New Suffolk was a small town. She didn't want to be gossiped about anymore. Kyle's cheating, their split, and their subsequent divorce had fueled the gossips for months. Mia closed her eyes for a moment. She couldn't even imagine what would happen if news of her indiscretion got out. She shook her head.

"You're right." Layla gave her a quick hug. "I wasn't thinking. I'm sorry."

"Still..." Elle leaned closer to the table, and the rest of them copied her. In a hushed voice she added, "It could be an opportunity to counter that, um, drought you've been experiencing lately."

Delightful tingles trickled down her spine at the idea. What the man could do with his hands and that mouth...

"You're considering the idea. That's good." Piper grinned.

"No." Mia denied the claim. Their one night together had been about her needing to prove she was still...desirable. *Wanted.* A moment of vulnerability thanks to Kyle and his proposal plans that evening. And the way Jax had looked at her, with such heat in his gaze, had been a balm to her wounded soul.

"We'll see." Her sister smirked.

No way. Not gonna happen.

A lick of heat roared through her.

Oh, crap. She was in trouble now.

His cell pinged as Jax walked into Donahue's pub. He pulled the phone from his pocket and unlocked the screen.

Running late. Just got off shift. Leaving the EMS building now. Should be there in less than ten.

Jax answered Shane, No problem. I'll grab a pool table. He shoved the phone back in his pocket and peered around the room. He spotted Mia Kavanaugh at a table a few feet away. His mind flashed back to the last time he'd seen her here, four months ago.

Don't go in. Don't go in. *Jax repeated the silent mantra as the black ball skittered across the pool table at Donahue's pub. It teetered on the edge of the pocket and dropped in.*

"I win," Shane Kavanaugh crowed as he clapped him on the back. "You lose, buddy. Again."

Shane was right. He'd lost both games tonight. Still, it was the most fun he'd had in months. Years, if he was being honest.

Traveling around the world left little time for enjoying the simple pleasures in life. Like a couple of beers and a game of pool with an old friend.

"Next time," he vowed.

Shane just snorted. "I gotta go. My shift starts in thirty minutes." He swallowed the last of his Coke and set the empty glass down on the table next to him. "Good seeing you again." Shane headed toward the exit.

Two women walked in as Shane exited.

He recognized Piper, Shane's sister, but who was the beauty standing next to her? He didn't recognize her. It couldn't be their sister, Mia—she was cute, he remembered, but she'd never taken his breath away. At least...not before. It didn't matter, though. He wasn't interested in either of Shane's sisters. Wouldn't pursue either of them even if he was. It was an unwritten rule. No hitting on your best friend's sister. They were off-limits. Which was fine with him. There were plenty of other fish in the sea.

"Hi, Jax," the woman said.

He jerked his head toward her. Recognition hit him like a punch in the gut. "Mia." Jax sucked in a quick breath. When had she developed all of those glorious curves? When had she gone from cute to... Jax swallowed hard. With her shoulder length brown hair and eyes the color of sapphires, she was drop-dead gorgeous "It's great to see you again."

He leaned in to kiss her hello. Just an innocent kiss on the cheek. No problem.

Jax lowered his head. A hint of vanilla and fresh-cut flowers flooded his senses. He breathed in the heady scent. His pulse pounded. Blood roared in his ears.

He pressed his lips to her cheek, luxuriating in her supple skin.

*Her soft, almost imperceptible sigh was almost his undoing.
What the hell was wrong with him tonight? This was Mia.*
Off-limits. Off-limits. OFF-LIMITS.

*He repeated the mantra, hoping his brain and body would
get the message.*

Now Jax strode to the table—to speak with Piper. Not her
sister. Not the woman who'd sent his heart into overdrive with
just a glimpse of her. Definitely not her—Piper had called a
few weeks ago, asking if he wanted to do another show at her
gallery. She wouldn't draw the kind of crowds a well-known
gallery would for him—the kind of crowds a well-known gallery *used* to draw for him, he mentally corrected himself—
but she'd done well since she opened last February, and he
wouldn't risk offending her by not even saying hello.

Yeah, right, his brain sneered. *You want to see Mia.*

No, dammit. He needed to ignore Mia.

Jax sucked in a lungful of much-needed air and approached
the table.

Piper jumped up and hugged him. She said something, and
he responded—appropriately, he hoped, because he wasn't
paying attention. He couldn't take his gaze off Mia.

"Hi, Jax," Mia said.

Her voice sent a shiver down his spine.

"Hey, it's nice to see you again." He kept his voice light
and friendly, even though everything inside him hummed and
buzzed. He dropped a quick peck on her cheek to keep up appearances, but her heady scent and soft skin had him lingering longer than he should have.

"Hey. You do know that's my sister." Shane's voice boomed
in his ears.

Jax froze like a deer caught in headlights. *Shit.*

Mia was still off-limits. That much hadn't changed.

He wasn't about to screw up again. He valued Shane's

friendship. Shane would lose it if he found out Jax had messed with his sister.

Piper chuckled. "You know he flirts with us because it drives you crazy, right?"

Shane rolled his eyes skyward. "We still playing tonight?" He gestured to the pool tables.

Jax nodded. "It was nice seeing you all again. We'll leave you to your girls' night out." He waved and followed Shane to a free table.

"So, how's Alex doing?" Shane grabbed the triangle frame and set it on the table. He lined up the balls inside.

"Okay." Jax grabbed the cue ball and placed it in the center of the table opposite the other balls. "He's coming home tomorrow." He aimed his pool stick and made a shot. The balls scattered, with the number two landing in the right corner pocket. "Looks like I've got solids." He lined up his next shot and missed.

"Were you able to hire someone to stay with him?" Shane asked. "Ten ball, left center pocket." He lined up the shot and sank the ball.

"We found someone who can stay with him during the evenings, but that person isn't available days, so I'll take that shift until I can find someone else. I'm hoping it'll only be a few days." He needed to get back to New York—to fixing his career—soon. "How about you? How are things with you and Layla? Any wedding plans yet?"

"No plans yet." Shane sank another ball. "We're enjoying just being engaged right now."

"How about your sisters?" Jax's gaze jerked to the table where Mia sat. "How are they doing?"

Mia smiled at something one of the women said. It was like the sun coming out on a dark, rainy day.

Why the hell was he thinking about Mia's smile? Why was he thinking about her at all? Nothing good could come of it.

He needed to stop. Now.

Why wouldn't his brain get the message?

Chapter Three

Mia walked into the Coffee Palace early the next morning. She'd wanted to talk to Abby last night about getting her old job back for the summer, but the opportunity to be alone with her hadn't materialized, and it wasn't something she wanted to discuss with everyone else around. Hence her visit here this morning.

She peered around the room. As usual, the place was packed. Servers flitted about the space, delivering orders and refilling coffee.

"Hey, Mia." Elle walked in from the kitchen with a tray of pastries in her hands. "Give me a minute and I'll grab you a coffee."

"Sure. No problem. Those smell delicious, by the way."

Elle waggled her brows. "They're chocolate toffee biscuits. Want one with your coffee?"

"Absolutely. Hey, is your cousin around?" Mia asked.

Elle slotted the tray into the metal slats in the display case. Turning her attention back to Mia, she said, "Not right now. She needed to take off for a little while."

That wasn't like Abby. She'd never run out of the Coffee Palace unless there was an emergency. "Is everything okay?" Mia asked.

Elle stepped closer to the display case and motioned for Mia to do the same. In a hushed voice, she said, "Abbs got a call from her mom. She's been really sick all morning. They went out for seafood last night, and Aunt Mary thinks she might have food poisoning."

"Oh no!" Mia said.

"Needless to say, Abbs went to check on her."

"I hope Mrs. Phillips is okay."

"Me, too," Elle agreed. "Have you got a few minutes? I could use a break."

"Sure." Mia smiled.

"Great. I'll have someone in back cover for me. Why don't you grab a table. We can chat for a while."

"Perfect. Maybe you could bring me two of those chocolate toffee biscuits instead of one?"

Elle's brows winged up.

"What?" Mia grinned. "I haven't had breakfast yet. And they are kind of small."

Elle let out something between a snort and a laugh. "Sure. No problem."

Mia walked to an empty table and waited for Elle.

"Here we go. Two biscuits and a black coffee for you, and a red velvet cupcake and an espresso for me." Elle placed the items on the table and sat down to join her.

"Boy, it sure is busy in here today," Mia said.

"It's always busy, especially now that the weather is warmer. More people are out and about."

"Has Abby—" Mia was about to ask if Abby had hired any summer help yet when Elle's phone rang.

Elle glanced at her cell. "This is Abby. Let me take this." She connected the call. "Hey, how's it going? Is Aunt Mary all right?"

Mia couldn't make out what Abby was saying, but Elle smiled, so she assumed everything was okay.

Elle disconnected the call. "Aunt Mary seems fine, but Abby is going to take her to her doctor just to make sure."

"That's a good idea," Mia said.

"Yeah. Although Abby isn't coming back today." Elle lifted the espresso to her lips and sipped. "Which means it's on me to train all of these new college kids." She gestured around the room. "Which also means my break is officially over. Sorry."

Mia sighed. It seemed like Abby wouldn't need any additional staff for the summer. "No problem. I should get going anyway." She'd need to see if any of the other local businesses were hiring. The trouble was, she was only available when her girls were in school, and summer camp after school ended. That was going to be a huge challenge.

"Take care." Elle gave a little wave.

"Wait. What do I owe you for the biscuits and coffee?" Mia asked.

"Nothing. It's on the house." She flagged down a young woman and said, "Sue, Mia needs a to-go coffee, black, no sugar, and a container for her biscuits."

"Where are the containers again?" Sue asked.

"In the back storage cabinet," Elle said.

"Right." Sue grinned and hurried off.

"It's going to be a long day." Elle shook her head and sighed. "Let me make sure she knows where the storage cabinet is." She waved and headed toward the kitchen.

Sue returned a few minutes later with Mia's coffee and a paper box. "Here you go."

"Thanks." Mia stood, grabbed her items and headed out. She'd spotted a few Help Wanted signs in some of the souvenir shops on Main Street last week when she'd taken the girls out for ice cream. She'd check them out before heading home.

Mia turned her Nissan Pathfinder into her driveway a few hours later. Sighing, she exited the car and walked into the kitchen. She'd talked to three shop owners and two local restaurants. She'd missed the boat for summer hires, by all accounts. Like Abby, the shop owners had already hired local college students who were home until the fall semester began, and although both restaurants were still looking for additional help, they needed her to commit to more hours than she could make work with the girls' schedules.

Her cell buzzed. Mia fished it out of her back pocket. Connecting the call, she said, "Hi, Mom. How are you?"

"I'm well, dear. How is your first official day of summer break going?"

If her mother knew how she'd spent the morning, she'd insist that Mia return to her former job as a project manager at TK Construction, the company her father and Ron Turner had started together over thirty-five years ago. That was something she wasn't prepared to do. At least not yet.

Working for TK required more hours a day than she could commit to. Construction project management wasn't a nine-to-five job, and you couldn't just up and leave a site because you had to pick up your kid from piano lessons or soccer practice.

Sure, she could bring her girls to the office and have them hang out there while she worked, like her parents had done with her and her siblings when they were kids.

But that wasn't what she wanted for her daughters. She wanted them to be able to come home after school and hang out, do their homework, and have friends over. Play outdoors.

She wanted to be able to spend time with them while they were growing up.

Something her mom couldn't do a lot of, especially after her father passed away.

Not that Mia was complaining. She adored her mother, but Mia wanted a different life for her girls.

Although she might not have a choice if she couldn't find a way to supplement her income soon.

Her gaze drifted to the laptop resting on the kitchen island and thought about the home design software she'd just installed.

She'd always wanted to start her own home design business.

Not gonna happen. Mia closed her eyes for a moment and exhaled a long breath.

Now was not the time to open a new business. She needed a job with a steady paycheck that allowed her to be home when her kids were home.

She loved children. Teaching had seemed like the perfect fit. She just needed a temporary income boost to pay her unexpected bills.

"It's going great, Mom. I stopped into the Coffee Palace and had a nice chat with Elle over coffee and some chocolate toffee biscuits."

"Sounds perfect," Mom replied.

They chatted for a few more minutes, and Mom said, "Oh, I've got to go. We have a client meeting in five minutes. I just wanted to say a quick hello and see how your day was going."

"Thanks, Mom. Love you."

"Love you, too, darling. Enjoy the rest of your day."

She'd try. But she'd be spending the next couple of hours, until the girls got home from school, looking for suitable temporary employment. "Will do."

"Bye now." Mom disconnected the call.

Mia shoved the phone in the back pocket of her jeans. Grabbing a glass from the cabinet, she glanced out her front kitchen window. A silver Porsche 911, with New York license plates, pulled into the driveway across the street.

Mia let loose a low whistle. "Nice car. Whoever you are, you've got great taste."

The driver's door opened, and a tall man with dark hair wearing a pair of jeans and a T-shirt slid out. With his back to her, she couldn't make out his features.

A black F-150 pulled in and parked behind the Porsche.

Mia frowned when her brother jumped out of the truck. She watched as Shane walked around to the back of his vehicle and lifted a wheelchair from the bed of the truck. What was going on at Alex Papadopoulos's house? Had something happened to her neighbor?

The stranger walked around to the passenger side of the Porsche.

Was that Jax Rawlins? She squinted as she peered out the window. With the glare from the sun, it was hard to tell, but... The man turned to face her brother, and yes, that was Jax, all right. Her pulse kicked up a notch.

What was Jax doing at Alex's house, and why was her brother with him?

Mia set the glass on the countertop without filling it. Grabbing her sunglasses from the console table that stood in the entry, she headed out the front door. The warm midday sun shone bright in the sky. She strode across the street with purpose. "Hey, guys." Mia gave a little wave as she approached. "What's going on?"

"Mia." Surprise flickered across Jax's handsome face. "What are you doing here?"

She pointed to the blue Cape-Cod-style home across the street. "I live there."

His brows knit together. "You do? I didn't know that."

How would he? He'd left New Suffolk twelve years ago, and their one night together last winter... She smiled to herself. They'd spent the night in a luxury hotel with phenomenal views of the city skyline and the Boston Harbor.

"I moved here right—" She was about to say right after she and Kyle married, but stopped herself. The point was moot now. "Almost nine years ago. I'm surprised we haven't run into each other before now."

"I don't get back to New Suffolk all that often." He walked

over to the passenger side of the Porsche. "Pops likes to visit Manhattan." He opened the door. Alex gave her a pained smile.

Mia rushed to his side. "What happened?"

"Took a little spill." Alex waved off her concern. "Nothing to worry about."

"I think your doctor would beg to differ." Her brother lifted a wheelchair from the bed of his truck and set it down on the driveway.

Mia's eyes widened. "I'll say. When did this happen?"

"Yesterday morning," Jax answered.

"Lost my balance when I was coming down the stairs," Alex grumbled.

"I'm so sorry. Is there anything I can do to help?"

"Thanks, but we're all set for now," Jax said. He motioned for Shane to bring the wheelchair over.

She watched while her brother and Jax helped Alex into the chair.

"If you're all set, Jax, I need to get going." Her brother gave her a quick hug and released her. "I need to run a couple of errands before I head in to work."

"We're good." Jax gave him a thumbs-up. "Thanks again for bringing the wheelchair." He flashed a sheepish grin. "It would have been a tight fit to get it in the Porsche."

Shane clapped Jax on the shoulder. "Anytime, man. Happy to help." Turning his attention to Alex, he said, "Take care."

"I will, and thanks again for helping me." Alex shook Shane's hand.

"You're welcome. See you later." Her brother gave a wave to the group. He hopped in his truck and pulled out of Alex's driveway a moment later.

"So…" Mia turned her attention to Jax. This close to him, she couldn't help but notice how his charcoal-colored T-shirt clung nicely to his broad shoulders. And those abs… She shoved her hands in her jeans pockets to stop her from acting on the sudden urge to slide her fingers under the soft material of his shirt and run her hands over the hard planes and solid muscles.

"So…" He stared at her, an enigmatic expression on his face.

Alex cleared his throat.

Jax blinked. "Right. I should help you inside so you can get some rest."

Heat crept up her face and flooded her cheeks. How could she have forgotten Alex was sitting there? In the blazing heat, no less. "Yes. Of course." Mia grasped Alex's hand. "I'll stop by soon and see how you're doing." With no family nearby, she'd made a point of checking in on him from time to time to make sure he was all right. "I'll bring some of my baked mac and cheese you like so much."

Alex's tired smile tore at her heart. "Sounds good."

"Feel better soon." She leaned down and kissed Alex's cheek.

"Take care, Mia. Thanks for stopping by." Jax pushed the wheelchair toward the front door.

"Bye." She gave a wistful sigh. Lord, what was wrong with her today?

Jax stopped halfway to the door and turned to face her. His lips curved into the most gorgeous smile. "It was great seeing you again."

Her heart hammered so loud she thought the entire neighborhood would hear it. "You too." Mia was pretty sure she was sporting a silly grin.

Soft, supple lips caressed his. Jax moaned as warm fingers traced lazy circles over his chest, his hips, his thighs.

A flirtatious laugh filled his ears.

"You're insatiable," he growled.

"I can't help it. I woke up thinking how good it would feel to have you inside me again."

He chuckled. "Who am I to deny your request?" He flipped their position and sank into her in one swift stroke. "Mia." Nothing had ever felt so good.

Jax jerked awake. A loud, obnoxious sound filled the room. He stared around the dark space. Nothing looked familiar. Where was he?

A beam of light sliced through the slight gap in the black-out shades, and he spotted his suitcase. The hotel room in New Suffolk.

Man, he'd been out cold and...he'd dreamed of Mia again. For the third night in a row. What the hell was wrong with him? Why couldn't he get her out of his mind? Sure, their one night together had been great. *Fantastic, pretty close to perfect.*

He scrubbed his hands over his face and uttered a frustrated grunt.

The annoying noise sounded again. Grabbing his cell, he canceled the alarm. Tossing back the comforter, he hopped out of bed. He needed to shower and arrive at Pops's house in thirty minutes. The overnight home health care worker's shift ended then.

Jax strode into the bathroom and turned on the *cold* water. It stung when he stepped beneath the steady stream, but it delivered the desired effect.

Shower complete, and a certain part of his anatomy now under control, Jax toweled dry and dressed in a pair of khaki cargo shorts and a navy T-shirt.

He checked his phone. Still no response from the home care company he'd contacted yesterday. Damn. The last two places he'd tried didn't have availability for a daytime person for three weeks. This was the last company in the area.

He glanced at his watch. It was still early. He wouldn't panic yet.

Jax drove down the street Pops lived on ten minutes later.

Classic New England Cape-Cod-style homes, colonials, and ranches lined the street with the typical near-the-seashore landscape of hydrangeas, rhododendrons, and beach plums dotting the sandy soil.

He'd never appreciated the natural beauty of his childhood neighborhood growing up, but now it appealed to his artistic side.

He spared a brief glance at the gray ranch-style home with the large front porch as he passed by. Two large topiaries flanked a lemon-yellow front door, and black bench swings hung at either end.

The home seemed…warm, welcoming. Words he never would have believed could describe the dwelling.

It had never felt anything of the kind to him growing up. That's why he'd spent as much time as possible out of it. Hanging out with Pops, with Shane. Playing after-school sports when he got older. Anything to delay returning home.

His parents… Being around them stressed him to the max. It's why he'd bolted from New Suffolk as soon as he'd graduated from high school.

Had they figured out he was here yet? Probably not. There'd been no phone calls. Surely they would have contacted him if they thought he was in town, right? Of course. Mom would get on his case for not staying with them, and Dad would call to tell him to ignore his mother.

And then the arguing would commence. The trouble was, they'd argue if he stayed with them or if he didn't.

Maybe they were out of town this week? He'd seen no movement there over the last three days.

He turned into Pops's driveway and parked beside the night caregiver's vehicle. Grabbing his laptop, he hopped out.

His gaze strayed to Mia's home.

Lord, what was he going to do about her? What was it about

that woman that had him thinking about her all the time? He'd never experienced that with any woman before.

Yes, sure, she had a great smile. A big heart.

Shane—he was a protector. He'd taken on that role when his father died sixteen years ago. He took that role very seriously, especially when it came to his two sisters and his mother.

Piper—the baby of the family. A little standoffish. At least, she used to be. He'd wager her detached aloofness was a coping mechanism. They might have different reasons, but neither she nor Shane had wanted long-term relationships. Except Piper seemed to have conquered her demons, if her recent engagement to Cooper Turner was anything to go by.

And Mia… She was the heart of her family. They meant everything to her. She loved them unconditionally and would be there for them no matter what. He'd seen it over and over again, firsthand, growing up.

Sweet, gorgeous, a smile that could light up the dreariest day, and sexy… And she had no idea how appealing she was.

No, dammit. He smacked the palm of his hand against his head. What was wrong with him this morning?

She's. Off. Limits. Get it through your thick head already.

He strode up the walkway and gave a brief knock on Pops's front door. Not waiting for someone to answer, he turned the knob and entered.

The sound of laughter filled the house.

Jax walked into the dining room and found Bill, the night caregiver, Pops, and Mia sitting at the dining room table, eating breakfast. What was she doing here?

"Good morning," he greeted them.

Mia's gaze jerked to his.

"Hey, Jax." Bill stood. "I guess it's time for me to get going. Thanks for letting me join you two." He nodded to Pops and Mia.

"You're welcome," Pops said. "See you tonight."

Bill walked over to Jax. "We had an uneventful night. He took his pain meds a few minutes ago."

Jax glanced at his watch. Five after eight. He could take another dose at four p.m. if he needed it. "Thanks, Bill." Jax shook his hand. "See you later."

Bill departed, and Jax walked over to the table.

"I should get going, too." Mia jumped up from her seat. She tried to grab her purse but ended up knocking it onto the floor.

Jax rushed over and picked it up for her. "Here you go." He sucked in some much-needed air. A hint of vanilla and fresh-cut flowers filled his nostrils. God, she smelled good.

Mia's gaze locked with his. "Thanks. Sorry to be so clumsy."

He wasn't sorry in the least. She'd given him an excuse to be close to her. His body hummed with anticipation. "Ah... no problem. Happy to assist."

Would her lips taste as good as he remembered?

Get a friggin' grip.

Mia moved away. "Take care, Alex."

"Do you have to leave so soon?" The words popped out of Jax's mouth before his brain could engage. *Idiot, idiot, idiot.*

"Yes," Pops agreed. "Please stay. I love your company."

"That's so sweet. Thank you." She returned to her seat. "I'm happy to visit for a little while."

Jax grinned. Because Pops was happy, not because Mia was staying.

Yeah, right.

"Perfect." Pops winked. "Now you can have one of these delicious blueberry muffins you made."

"You made the muffins?" he asked.

Mia nodded. "I thought Alex might enjoy them with his coffee in the morning."

"That was really nice of you." He admired her care and compassion. "Thanks."

Her smile lit up the room. "You're welcome."

"She made her famous mac and cheese, too. It's in the fridge." Pops shot him a sly grin. "If you're nice to me, I might share it with you."

Jax chuckled. "If by *nice*, you mean letting you do what you want, forget it. Doctor's orders stand."

"You need to focus on your pictures. You said so yourself. You can't do that if you're running around after me all day."

He sighed. Pops wasn't wrong. He'd made little progress with figuring out a path forward with his career. Which he needed to do sooner rather than later. "I'm fine for now. Don't worry about it."

"Listen to Jax." Mia grasped Pops's hand with hers. "He's right." She grabbed a deck of cards from her purse. "How about a game of rummy before I go home?" She glanced at Jax. "We can all play."

"You should hire Mia to watch me. She's a lot more fun than you." Pops stuck out his tongue at Jax. "A lot prettier, too."

Hire Mia? He'd get to see her every day. His heart beat rapidly.

No, no, no. That was the last thing he needed. He needed to return to Manhattan as soon as possible and come up with a plan for his career. "I'm sure Mia is busy. Like I said, you're stuck with boring old me until I can find someone else."

"What exactly would you need me to do?" Mia asked.

"Not much at all." Pops flashed an endearing grin. "Take me to physical therapy appointments, cook my meals, and maybe some light housekeeping."

Jax shook his head. "It's a little more than that. You need someone who can manage your pain medication. Assist you in getting to the bathroom, getting dressed, bathing. Make sure you stay off that ankle."

Pops crossed his arms across his chest and aimed a menacing glare at him. "I am *more than capable* of getting to the bathroom on my own, thank you very much. I can use my crutch. As for the other items you mentioned…" He gave a dismissive wave of his hand. "Bill helps me with those things before he leaves."

"How many hours a day do you need someone?" Mia asked.

Jax blinked. "Are you actually considering this?"

She nodded. "I was looking to pick up something part-time while the girls are at school. I'm free from nine in the morning until three in the afternoon."

"That won't work, unfortunately. I need someone for twelve hours a day. To cover the time when Bill isn't here."

His cell rang. Jax yanked it from his pocket. The home care company's name and number appeared on the screen. *Hallelujah.* "Excuse me. I need to take this." He stood and stepped outside. Connecting the call, he answered, "Jax Rawlins."

"Hello, Mr. Rawlins. This is Connie from SmartCare. I'm returning your call. Your message said you're looking for an aide who can help care for your grandfather for four weeks."

"Yes. I've already hired an overnight caregiver, but I need someone during the day. Just until his ankle heals."

"Starting when?" Connie asked.

"Today?" Jax crossed his fingers.

"I'm afraid that's not possible. We don't have anyone available."

"Not at all?" His shoulders sank.

"No. The earliest I might have someone is in a week and a half. We can set up an interview then to make sure he's a good match for your grandfather, if you're interested."

Jax dragged his free hand through his hair. "Okay. I'll make that work." It was better than nothing.

"Perfect. I'll send you the paperwork."

"Great." Jax gave her his email address. "Thank you."

"You're welcome. Bye." Connie ended the call.

Jax walked inside. Pops and Mia were in the middle of a card game.

"Everything okay?" Pops asked. "You don't look happy."

Understatement of the year. "Everything is fine."

His phone rang again. Mom's number appeared on the screen. *For crying out loud.* "It's all good." He flashed a tight smile and ignored the call.

Pops snorted. "If you say so."

"I do." Maybe if he kept repeating the words it might be true? *Ha.*

His cell buzzed. A message from Cate appeared on the screen.

Read this. It's the most favorable.

He clicked on the link she provided and read a review from his last exhibition. *Shit.* If this was the most favorable, he was in bigger trouble than he'd imagined.

"Are you sure everything is all right?" Mia asked.

No. His career was one step away from being flushed down the toilet, and he was running out of time to stop it. Not to mention his parents. If they spotted his car in Pops's driveway… Jax rubbed at his temples.

"I win." Mia's voice had him jerking his gaze in her direction. Her smile made his pulse kick up a notch. "I'm going to head out now."

"Do you have to go?" Pops looked disappointed.

Mia glanced at Jax. "Yes. I do." She kissed Pops's cheek. "Take care. I'll stop by again in a few days to see how you're doing." She strode out of the room, waving at him as she passed by.

His cell dinged again. Another message from Cate flashed on screen.

Please tell me you've come up with an idea for new pictures.

No, he hadn't, and he wasn't going to be able to for at least another week and a half. Until someone from SmartCare became available.

You should hire Mia. Pops's words flooded his brain.

He'd have time to concentrate on fixing his career if he did. At least for a few hours a day.

He needed all the time he could get.

"Mia, wait." Jax jumped up and ran after her.

Hand poised just above the doorknob, she turned her attention to him. "What is it?"

"Are you still interested in helping out with Pops?" He kept his voice low so Pops couldn't overhear. "I'll take whatever hours you can give me for the next week and a half."

"Are you sure?" Mia cast a wary glance in his direction.

No. His brain was screaming *bad idea, bad idea, bad idea.* But what choice did he have? He needed help caring for Pops so he could concentrate on fixing his career. Time was running out. "Yes. I'll make it worth your while." He named an hourly wage that made her eyes bug out.

"Okay. I'm all in." She smiled a mile-wide grin.

A lick of heat raced through him. *Shit.*

Having her around would be pure torture because he wanted her.

But he couldn't have her.

Chapter Four

"Everyone out." Mia stopped the Pathfinder at the drop-off spot in front of the school. Aurora and Brooke hopped out and headed for the school entrance. "Come on, Kiera. You don't want to be late." And she didn't want to be late for her first day taking care of Alex.

"I'm coming." Smiling, Kiera unfastened her seat belt and practically leaped out of the vehicle. She raced to catch up with her two older sisters.

"Have a great day," Mia called.

The sky opened up just as the girls walked inside. She flicked on the windshield wipers and pulled out of the parking lot and into traffic.

A few minutes later, Mia turned onto the street she lived on. As she drove, she noticed a woman who appeared to be in her late fifties standing in the driveway a few houses down from her own home. The woman was holding an umbrella and stared up the street. Mia slowed and did a double take. What was Francine Rawlins staring at?

She parked her car at home. Grabbing an umbrella and the plastic container containing the chocolate-chip cookies they'd made last night, she opened the door and raced across the street to Alex's house.

Mia rang the doorbell and waited.

Out of the corner of her eye, she saw Francine step out onto her lawn. Was she watching Mia?

Frowning, Mia gave a little wave.

Francine waved back.

What the heck?

Alex's front door jerked open.

Jax appeared in the entryway. "Hi, Mia."

"Hey." Mia gave one last look up the street.

"Are you coming in?" he asked. "I've got to get going."

"Yeah. Sure." Her brows drew together. Francine was definitely watching her.

"What are you doing out there?" Jax poked his head out the door. "You should come in now. It's starting to rain harder." He stepped to the side to allow her entry.

"Right. Of course." As Mia stepped inside, she cast one last glance up the street. Francine was gone.

"Boy, it's really coming down out there." Jax closed the door.

She nodded. "The good news is, it's supposed to clear up in a couple of hours. I'm hoping I can take Alex out for a walk in his wheelchair later. I mean, if he's comfortable with that."

"That's a great idea. Here. Let me take that for you." He gestured to her umbrella.

"Thank you." *Considerate.* She liked that.

Jax closed her umbrella and placed it in the stand by the door. "What have you got there?" He pointed to the container she held in her hand.

"A little treat for the patient. I thought chocolate-chip cookies might cheer him up."

"Thank you. That was very thoughtful. I'm sure he'll love them."

She smiled. "You're welcome. I had the girls help me, so they're actually from all of us."

"Would you like a cup of coffee?" Jax asked as he walked through the formal living room and into the kitchen.

"That sounds fantastic. I didn't have time to stop at the

Coffee Palace before I dropped the girls off at school. Between Kiera's lost backpack and Brooke forgetting her lunch, we left later than usual and…" She sounded like a bumbling fool. "You get the picture."

"I do." Jax chuckled as he walked through the living room and into the kitchen.

Mia glanced around the space as she followed him. Alex's house was a duplicate of hers—at least, it had been until she'd removed the common walls on her first floor, making the kitchen, living room and dining room one large open space.

She'd done the work herself. Right after she and Kyle had purchased the home.

"You like your coffee black—right?" Jax's words snapped her out of her musings.

He remembered? Mia smiled. "Yes, but I can get it." Setting the container of cookies on the table, she crossed to where the coffeepot sat on the counter near the sink. "I know you have to head out."

Jax came to stand by her with two mugs. "Actually, I've decided to work here today. That way I'll be around if any problems arise."

He was so close she could smell the subtle scent of whatever cologne he was wearing. Fresh and clean with hints of oak and sandalwood. *Delicious.*

"I hope that's okay with you." He flashed a devastating smile that sent a flurry of shivers skating down her spine.

Good grief, what was wrong with her this morning?

You can't stop thinking about the night you shared with him. That's what.

Mia couldn't deny it. That night together was all she'd been able to think about since she saw Jax at Donahue's. It was…

Fabulous, amazing, fantastic.

Probably the most uninhibited and incredibly satisfying sex she'd had.

Ever.

There went those shivers again.

Truth be told, regardless of how much she'd denied it to Piper, Elle, Abby and Layla, Mia wanted a repeat performance.

Several repeat performances.

No, no, no. Mia closed her eyes for a moment and tried to get her wayward thoughts under control. She needed to concentrate on taking care of Alex, not fantasizing about Jax.

Except it wasn't a fantasy. She'd already experienced the reality. That was the problem.

"Mia?" Jax frowned. "Will it be a problem for you if I work upstairs?"

"Absolutely not. No problem at all." Her words came out in a rush. She was a bumbling fool, all right, if the expression on Jax's face was anything to go by.

"Good," he said.

Mia filled each mug with the steaming brew and set the pot back on the warmer. "Tell me, how is our patient this morning?" She wandered over to the table and sat.

Jax joined her at the table. "He's pretty sore today."

"I'd expect as much. Sometimes injuries hurt worse after a couple of days," she said.

Jax's gaze strayed to the container of cookies. "He's resting now." He pointed in the direction of the den on the other side of the kitchen. "I tried to get him to lie down in his bed in the spare bedroom down here, but I lost that battle, so he's sleeping on the couch."

"Why wouldn't he go into the bedroom?" Mia asked.

"It's like a dungeon in there," Alex grumbled. "It's bad enough I've gotta sleep in there until my bum leg heals. I'm not going in there if I don't have to. The couch is fine."

Jax rolled his eyes skyward. "I guess he's not asleep after all."

"That's right," Alex agreed. "I'm not some baby who needs a nap."

Mia smiled. She couldn't help it. She stood and made her way to where Alex was propped against the wall between the kitchen and dining room. "Let's get you back to the couch so you can relax. Maybe we can watch a movie or some television together?"

"Okay." Leaning on his crutch, Pops started back to the den.

Jax rose. "I need to head upstairs. Work beckons."

Was that disappointment in his voice, or was she the one who didn't want him to leave?

Mia gave herself a mental shake. She couldn't care less if Jax wasn't around.

Liar.

Okay, yes. Maybe she'd hoped he'd join her and Alex in the den for a few minutes, but that was crazy. She was here to work, not socialize, for goodness' sake. "Have a good day." She gave a little wave and exited the room.

Sitting in the chair next to Alex, she asked, "Can I get you anything?"

"How about another cup of coffee and maybe one of the chocolate-chip cookies you brought me?" Alex grinned.

Mia burst out laughing. He'd heard her entire conversation with Jax from the moment she'd arrived.

Thank goodness he hadn't heard her thoughts.

"Coming right up," she said.

Mia jumped up and headed to the kitchen before Alex could spot the color staining her cheeks.

Jax rolled his shoulders and slumped against the slatted folding chair. He should have gone back to his hotel room. At least he'd be comfortable. But no. He'd seen his mother standing on her front porch when Mia had arrived, and he wasn't going to risk having her spot him. It's why he'd arrived early to Pops's house this morning and had parked his Porsche in the garage. He shook his head. The last thing he needed right now was to have to deal with his parents in real life.

He jumped when his phone rang. Reaching into his pocket, he grabbed it and connected the call. "Hey, Cate."

"How's it going?" The anticipation in her voice was mixed with a hint of dread. "I haven't heard from you in a few days. I'm hoping that's a good thing."

"Yeah." He rubbed his hand across the back of his neck. "I've been pretty busy." But not with matters that concerned her.

"That's great." Cate sounded relieved. He didn't have the nerve to burst her bubble. "Let's get together this evening, and you can show me what you're thinking."

"Can't tonight."

"Okay. Tomorrow then. I'm dying to see what you've come up with," she said.

Time to fess up. "I'm in New Suffolk. An emergency came up that I'm still dealing with."

"Jax…" she began.

"Cate." He cut her off before she could launch into a speech about how important it was for him to figure out his new "thing" and how both of their careers were riding on him getting things right. "I already know what you're going to say, and I'm working on it." He just wasn't making much progress. He'd found a couple of old photos he could use, but that wasn't going to cut it. He needed to shoot more images.

"Well, whatever it is, I hope you resolve it soon. I need you back in New York and one hundred percent focused on your career as soon as possible."

She didn't need to tell him. "I'll be back in the city in a couple of weeks."

"A couple of—" She stopped before finishing her sentence. "Stay in touch. I want to know how you're progressing."

No pressure there. Not for the first time today, he dragged his fingers through his hair. "Yeah. Sure. Talk later."

"Take care, Jax." Cate's words were filled with sincerity.

"Thanks." He cut the connection.

Shoving the phone back in his pocket, he glanced at his watch. Noon. He should go downstairs. To check on Pops.

Yeah right, his brain scoffed.

Mia was another problem he wasn't sure how to solve, and that was starting to worry him. It might have been better to just go it alone with Pops until the caregiver was available.

Nope.

Why he dismissed that thought immediately, he couldn't say. He only knew that he did.

Jax shook his head. Mia was a problem for another time.

Standing, he rolled his shoulders and walked downstairs. Finding no one in the kitchen or den, he called out, "Pops? Mia?"

"We're in the spare bedroom," Mia responded.

"Come on in. You gotta see this," Pops said.

Curious, he strode down the hall. He found Pops sitting in the rocking chair that stood in the right corner of the room.

Mia sat on the floor, leaning against the wall. Her long, shapely legs were stretched out in front of her.

An image of them wrapped around him flooded his brain. His pulse soared and his body... Jax walked around the room, his back to Pops and Mia, and tried like hell to get his anatomy under control before he made a complete fool of himself.

"What's this I need to see?" He breathed deep and peered around the room. The space looked the same as it had when he came in this morning.

"She's a genius," Pops said.

The sound of Mia's soft chuckle surrounded him like the slide of silk sheets against his naked skin. Jax swallowed hard.

The thought did nothing to help his present situation. In fact, it made his situation a hundred times worse.

Lord, what was it about this woman that had him reacting like a horny teenager every time he caught a glimpse of her?

"I wouldn't say that. I was just throwing out some ideas," Mia said.

"Brilliant ideas," Pops corrected her.

"Okay. I give up." Jax held his hands up as if surrendering. "I have no idea what either of you are talking about." He flopped down on the bed—it was the only thing he could think of to hide the massive bulge in his jeans—and propped himself up on his elbows.

Mia stood. She walked over to where Pops sat and motioned for him to join them.

Praying he wouldn't embarrass himself, Jax rolled over and hopped off the bed. He walked over and knelt on the other side of Pops.

Mia handed Pops an iPad. "What do you think?"

Jax stared at the computer-generated layout of a room that looked very similar to the one they were in, except three of the walls were painted a cool light gray and the last a dark gray.

"It's even better than I imagined." Pops's eyes lit with excitement. "I especially like the patterned wall in the darker shade. How would you do that?"

"It's just wood slats attached to the wall. If you don't like the diagonal layout, I can come up with something different," Mia said.

Pops shook his head. "No." He pointed to the screen. "I like the picture on your computer screen as is. That's a pretty cool program. Where'd you get it?"

"I bought a license for it through TK Construction. They use it to show their clients proposed renovations. You know, like the home renovation shows we were watching earlier."

"TK Construction?" Pops's brows drew together in a deep V.

Jax grinned. "Mia's mother co-owns TK with Ron Turner."

Mia nodded. "My dad and Ron started the company more than thirty-five years ago."

"I didn't know TK stood for Turner Kavanaugh," Pops said.

Mia smiled. "Most people don't."

"Will TK be able to do the work?" Pops asked.

Mia shook her head. "There's no major construction needed. I'll handle the little there is. It shouldn't take long." Her expression turned thoughtful. "Not more than a week, and I can do it during the hours I'm already here and make sure I'm available when you need me, too. There's not a lot of construction work involved, really. Just adding the wood slats to the feature wall." She pointed behind them. "The rest is just paint and a few decorations." She gave a swift nod of her head. "Piece of cake."

Pops sent a dubious glance in Mia's direction.

She laughed. The sweet melodious sound sent a frisson of pleasure skittering down Jax's spine.

"Don't worry. I know what I'm doing. My father made sure all three of his kids could swing a hammer. I even worked for TK for a few years after college."

"I remember your dad." Pops's voice came out a little gruff. "He was a good man."

A sad smile crossed Mia's face. Why Jax had the sudden urge to pull her into his arms and hold her tight, he couldn't say, but he did.

I'm losing my mind. It was the only explanation he could come up with for such crazy thoughts.

"He was the best dad a girl could ask for," Mia said. She straightened her shoulders. "So, what do you say? Do you want to do this?" She flashed a mile-wide grin.

"Absolutely." Pops gave her a thumbs-up. "When can you start?"

"I'll order the materials this afternoon, and hopefully I can start tomorrow. In the meantime, how about I fix you some lunch?"

"Sounds like a plan," Pops agreed.

"All righty. Let's get you settled in your recliner in the den until your meal is ready." Mia handed Pops his crutch.

"I don't mind cooking for all of us," Jax said.

"But I'm supposed to —" Mia started.

"I know, but I'm here today, and I need to eat, too."

"I don't know..." Pops eyed him warily.

He knew why. He'd burned the mac and cheese he'd heated up for dinner last night. They'd wound up eating pizza at eight p.m., which was fine for him, but he could tell Pops was pretty hungry when it finally arrived. Takeout should have been his first choice. It's what he did for himself if he wasn't going out. "I'll make sandwiches with chips." At least he knew how to do that.

Jax strode into the kitchen. Grabbing lunch meat, condiments, lettuce and tomato from the fridge, he placed the items on the counter and pulled the bread from the drawer.

"Need some help?" Mia asked as he spread the mayonnaise on the bread.

He looked up from his task. "Pops sent you in here, didn't he." It was a statement more than a question.

Mia tried but failed to hide a smile. "He told me about last night."

"I have a feeling that Pops is never going to let me live that down." Jax grabbed four more slices of bread. "Turkey with lettuce, tomato and mayo okay with you?"

"Sure." Mia nodded.

He lined up the slices and started making the sandwiches. "Thanks for coming up with that design for the spare bedroom. I wish I could convince him to move down here permanently, but he's being stubborn about it."

"What are his objections?" Mia walked to the fridge and pulled out a pitcher. "Iced tea for you?"

He nodded. "Yes, please. He says he doesn't want to share a bathroom with everyone."

"I can understand that. To be honest, I feel the same way." She looked at him and paused, as if deciding whether to say something or not. "I might have a solution for the problem."

That got his attention. "You're serious?" He'd feel much more comfortable going back to the city if the stairs were no longer an issue.

"Yes. It's something I'm looking at doing for my house in a few years, when the girls get older."

"Tell me more. Do you already have a design?"

"I do, but it requires moderate renovation—Alex would lose the den—and it would cost significantly more money and more time to complete than what I'm proposing for the bedroom."

"Don't worry about the cost. I'll cover that." If Pops agreed. Not that Pops didn't have the money, but Jax would love to be able to give him this gift. He'd done so much for him and Jax wanted the opportunity to repay that. "When can you show us?" he asked.

"I have the design on my tablet. We can talk about it during lunch."

He grinned. "Perfect."

Jax planned to give Mia a friendly hug and peck on the cheek, but somehow his mouth connected with hers.

Nothing ever tasted so good.

Chapter Five

Mia sank into Jax's kiss with a soft whimper. What was it about this man who could ignite such wanton need in her? She'd never felt anything like it with anyone. Not even her ex.

"So good." His hushed murmur in her ear sent her pulse soaring. Lifting her, he placed her on the island and devoured her mouth.

"Hey, what's going on in there?" Alex's voice thundered.

Mia froze. Had Alex figured out what they were doing?

"What was that loud noise?" Alex asked.

He'd heard them? Of course he had. He'd proved it earlier when he'd asked her for the chocolate-chip cookies. Heat scorched her cheeks.

What was she thinking behaving in such a manner? In someone else's house. *Oh dear Lord.* She needed to get out of here. Now.

Jax grasped her chin and lifted her gaze to meet his. With his free hand, he pressed his index finger to his lips. "Shh. It's okay," he whispered.

Was he crazy? Nothing about this situation was all right. They'd been about to… And Alex *knew*. Mia winced. How was she supposed to face him after such behavior?

"Don't move," he murmured in her ear. Jax leaned down and picked up a metal bowl from the floor. "This is what he heard."

She frowned. Where had it come from?

"Everything's fine, Pops," Jax called. "I accidently knocked over the bowl of fruit that was sitting on the island while I was making the sandwiches."

Mia peered down. Bananas, apples and oranges lay scattered on the floor. He must have sent it flying when he'd planted her on the island. She'd been so caught up in what they were doing, she hadn't heard it crash onto the floor.

"You really are hopeless in the kitchen. Do us all a favor and let Mia make my meal. She knows what she's doing," Alex retorted.

"I couldn't agree more." He punctuated the softly spoken comment with a kiss at the corner of her mouth. "I'd say you're an expert."

She was pretty sure her cheeks flamed even brighter. "I'm going back into the den now."

"Let me help you." Jax flashed a wicked grin. He lifted her as if she weighed nothing at all and set her on the floor. "Here." He handed her two plates. "One for you. One for Pops." Grabbing his sandwich, he followed her.

Mia exited the kitchen and walked into the den. "Here you go." She pasted a bright smile on her face and silently prayed Alex had no idea what was going on in his kitchen five minutes ago.

"Are you sure it's safe to eat?" Alex shot a wary glance at her.

Jax scowled. "It's fine, Pops."

"It is." Mia winked at Alex. "I watched him make it."

"Okay." Alex bit into his sandwich. "Not bad." Alex's surprised look made her smile.

Jax snorted. "Of course it's good. I'm not a complete moron when it comes to the kitchen. I've got some skills."

Oh yes you do, Mia silently agreed.

"So, Pops." Jax cleared his throat. "Mia has an idea she wants to share with you."

Her gaze shot to Jax's. What was he talking about?

"Go ahead," Jax encouraged her. "Tell him what you told me in the kitchen. About a first-floor master suite."

"Jax." Alex held up a hand.

"All I'm asking is that you listen, Pops. I worry about you having to do those stairs."

Alex opened his mouth as if he were going to say something, but didn't. A smile crossed his face. He glanced at Mia. "He's a good boy. Always wants what's best for me."

"I do, Pops." Jax came over and kneeled beside Alex's recliner. "I know how independent you are, and I'm not asking you to give that up. I just want to make sure you're safe."

Mia marveled at the kindness and compassion Jax showed Alex. It's not that she wouldn't have expected it from him— She'd always considered him a nice guy. From the first day she'd met him, when he'd come over to her childhood home to play with her brother after school one day—but he rarely showed it. He preferred people only see his roguish persona. She wondered why.

"Okay. What's your idea?" Alex's voice tugged her from her musings.

Mia cleared her throat and explained her plan. "I can show you the design I came up with for my house, and we can tweak it so you have exactly what you want."

"All right." Pops shot a look at Jax. "I'm willing to at least consider this, but it's not a done deal."

Jax grinned and clapped Alex on the shoulder. "That's all I can ask."

"Great. Let me grab my tablet. I can show you what I have now." Placing her plate on the side table beside her, she stood.

She walked into the spare bedroom and grabbed the tablet. She hit the power button and returned to the den.

"Here we are." Mia pulled up her program and loaded the design she'd created for her own house. "I'll walk you through it." Fingers crossed, he would like the concepts. Redoing his room was one thing, but converting the den to a bathroom… This job could give her the real-life experience she needed. She could use this job to start her portfolio. Solid proof that she had home design experience.

She might not be ready to give up the financial security of her full-time job, but that didn't mean she couldn't grab the opportunity if it came her way.

Mia spent the next thirty minutes walking Alex through her existing plan, making suggestions of where they could make changes to fit what Alex wanted.

"A soaker tub is not my style," Alex said.

"No problem." Mia smiled. "We can swap that out for a shower."

Alex nodded.

"We can use the layout I've already come up with, or I could come up with a whole new design."

"How much would something like this cost?" Alex pointed to the tablet.

"That's going to depend on what you want, Pops," Jax said. "High-end finishes versus standard fare."

"I'll tell you what." Mia knelt beside the recliner chair where Alex sat. "Let's talk some more over the next few days, and I'll work up a plan that includes costs. I can pick up some material samples at the home and garden center tonight so you can get a feel for what's available. Kyle has the kids for dinner." He'd already confirmed he'd pick up the girls at five and have them home by eight. "So I have some free time to work on this for you."

"Are you sure you don't mind?" Alex asked.

"Not at all. I love creating room designs." She meant every word.

"Okay." Alex nodded. "That sounds good. Jax will go with you."

Wait. What?

"What are you talking about, Pops?" Jax asked.

Mia was about to ask the same question.

"I want you to go with Mia to the home and garden center tonight. You know what I like. You can help her pick out the samples."

Oh crap. "That's not necessary." Mia waved off the idea. The last thing she needed was to spend one-on-one time with Jax. After what just happened in the kitchen, she needed to keep her distance.

"You need to get going." Pops jerked his head in the direction of Mia's house. "She's leaving for the home and garden store in fifteen minutes."

"I still don't think it's necessary for me to go. I'm sure Mia is more than capable of picking out samples without me. You two spent all afternoon going over things."

"I know, but I don't want to take any chances. She's never had another client before. I'm taking a big risk here."

Jax pulled a face. "How can there be any risk when you haven't even committed to anything yet?"

Pops didn't like his logic if the look on his face was anything to go by.

Jax heaved a sigh of relief. Finally, he'd gotten through to the man. Maybe now he'd stop pushing him. He needed to stay away from Mia, because he wanted her. Even more than before.

And she wanted him, too. She'd made that abundantly clear earlier today.

Shane would kill him if he knew what had happened between him and his sister four months ago. Worse, what was going on in his mind right now.

Off-limits. Off-limits. Off-limits. Why couldn't he get that through his thick head?

"You're right." Pops shrugged his good shoulder. "I was

crazy to even consider Mia's idea. I already have a perfectly good master suite *upstairs*."

Jax couldn't miss how Pops emphasized the word *upstairs*. He shook his head. "So that's how you're going to play this, huh?"

"I don't know what you're talking about."

Jax glared at Pops. "I'm not buying that innocent expression, old man. You're trying to manipulate me, and I don't like it. Why is it so important to you that I go with Mia?"

Pops sighed, and his shoulders slumped. "Okay. You're right about me moving downstairs. It's time. The stairs…they're not such a great thing for someone…" Pops gritted his teeth. "Of my age."

Jax blew out a breath. He knew how hard it was for Pops to admit.

"The thing is, the changes Mia talked about are going to cost a heck of a lot more money than the paint and the wood slats she'll need for the downstairs bedroom. Not that I don't have the money. I do. But I would feel better if I could go with her to make the material selections myself." Pops made a hand gesture that encompassed his injuries. "As you can see, I'm in no condition to do that."

No, he wasn't. A fact that frustrated Pops to no end. He valued his independence, and this fall had taken that away from him. It had also forced Pops to face some rather unpleasant facts. He needed to make some changes. Whether he wanted to or not.

"You've done so much for me already," Pops continued. "I hate to ask you to do more, but I'd feel a lot more confident if you were there to help with the selections. That way I know we'll have options I like."

When Pops put it like that, how could he say no?

"Hello, Alex? Jax?" Bill's voice boomed in the charged silence.

"We're in the den," Jax called.

The night caregiver appeared a moment later. "I hope you don't mind me coming in. I knocked a couple of times, but no one answered the door."

"Sorry," Pops said. "We didn't hear you."

Jax rose from his seat on the couch. "Thanks for coming in early today." He'd been ticked off when Pops took it upon himself to make the call earlier, although he understood now why he'd done it.

"It's no problem. Alex said you needed to run a few errands tonight."

Jax exhaled a resigned breath. "Yes. I do. There's a chicken and stuffing casserole in the fridge for dinner, along with some carrots."

"Mia made it for me this afternoon." A smug smile crossed Pops's face as he jerked his gaze to Jax. "She didn't want me to starve."

"Perfect," Bill said.

Jax just shook his head. Although he was thankful for Mia's foresight.

"Are you ready for dinner now, Alex?" Bill asked.

"Yes, please," Pops responded.

"I'll go and get that ready for you." Bill disappeared a moment later.

"I'm going to head over to Mia's now." Jax walked over to the recliner. "I'll stop in again to say good-night before I head to the hotel." He dropped a kiss on Pops's head. "Be good for Bill."

"I'm not a child." A petulant expression crossed Pops's face.

"Maybe not, but that doesn't mean you won't get into trouble while I'm gone." Jax gave Pops a knowing look. "Don't think I didn't hear about you trying to get up in the middle of last night by yourself. If you fall again, you might injure yourself worse this time."

Pops glowered and looked away.

"Have a good evening." Jax waved and walked out.

Jax jogged across the street and rang the front doorbell. He was taken aback when a little girl sporting brown curly pigtails and sapphire eyes, *Mia's eyes*, answered the door.

"Hello." He gave her a nervous smile. He didn't have a lot of experience with children. *Zero experience*. He had no idea how to act around them.

She crossed her arms over her chest and looked him up and down. "Who are you?" she demanded.

Jax flashed his best charming grin. The one he used with all the ladies. This little one was a female, after all. "My name is Jax. What's yours?"

"I'm not telling you." A mutinous expression crossed her round, freckled face.

He smiled to himself. Whatever he'd been expecting her to say, it wasn't that. He liked her attitude.

"Mommy says I'm not supposed to talk to strangers."

That made sense. Stranger danger was a real thing. "I'm not exactly a stranger," he said. "At least, not to your mommy. She's my, um…" Employee? *Nope.* Lover? *Definitely can't say that.* Jax cleared his throat. "Friend." Yes. He liked the sound of that. Very much. "Is she here?"

"What's going on?" Another girl appeared behind the first. The child had the same brown hair as the little spitfire, but it appeared longer, and it wasn't as curly as her sister's. At least, Jax assumed they were sisters. Mia's daughters.

Would the third one make an appearance?

He knew she had three, because Shane had told him.

She hadn't. The truth was, he didn't know that much about her these days. They'd lost touch twelve years ago, when he'd left for New York right after high school graduation.

Mia hadn't shared much about her current life the night they'd bumped into each other at Donahue's pub, other than that she was divorced, and she taught sixth grade at the private school the next town over.

Jax wanted to learn more about the woman she'd become. Which meant what?

Nothing. Absolutely nothing. He was curious. *That's all.*

"He says he's one of Mommy's friends," the little spitfire retorted. "But I don't know him. Do you?"

"Nope." The other girl shook her head.

The spitfire started to close the door.

Jax's eyes widened, and he laughed. A female who could resist his charms. Who knew such a creature existed? "Wait. I'm friends with your uncle Shane, too."

"You are?" The spitfire scrunched up her nose and stared at him again.

"Who's at the door, girls?" Mia's voice boomed from somewhere inside the house. She appeared a moment later. "Jax. Oh, jeez. I totally forgot you were supposed to come over."

"He says he's a friend of yours." Spitfire pointed at him. "Is that true?"

"Yes, sweetie." Mia smiled.

A rush of warmth flooded his chest at her confirmation.

"I've known Jax since I was a little kid. I was the same age as you are now."

"Wow," the spitfire said. "That's a long time."

"Yes. It is." Mia's sweet laughter sounded like a gentle rainfall on a warm summer day.

Funny, he was never interested in her when they were younger, but now...

Shane's sister. You need to remember that.

Besides, she didn't strike him as a fun-while-it-lasted kind of girl. She was more of a girl next door. Someone you went all-in with.

That's not going to happen. Ever.

That's why he needed to stay away from her. He didn't want to hurt her.

"Come in. Please." Mia motioned for her daughters to move out of the way.

Another girl appeared in the front entrance as he stepped inside. She was the spitting image of her mother except for her blond hair. She didn't say anything, but he could tell she was assessing him nonetheless.

"There's been a change in plans," Mia continued.

"Daddy had another work emergency," the spitfire said.

"That means he can't take us out to dinner. *Again*," the other brunette said.

"Yeah." The spitfire heaved a dramatic sigh.

He liked these kids. He really did.

"I'm sure Daddy is just as disappointed as you are, sweetheart." Mia placed her arm around the two brunettes and squeezed them tight. "He loves spending time with you girls, and he misses you when he can't be here."

There was that big heart again. Reassuring her daughters, and not making them feel worse by trash-talking their parent. Something Mia had every right to do, according to her brother. Kudos to her for taking the high road.

"My name is Kiera." The little spitfire pointed a thumb at herself. "This is my sister, Brooke." She pointed to the other brunette with straighter hair. "That's Aurora." She pointed to the blonde. "She's the oldest."

Jax felt as if he'd passed some kind of test as far as the little girl was concerned. "It's nice to meet you all." He extended his hand to Kiera. Her face scrunched up, and she stared at him as if he'd grown another head.

"You're supposed to shake it, silly." Brooke smirked and fastened her palm to his. "That's what adults do when they meet each other."

"You're not an adult," Kiera said.

"I'm older than you. That's how I know what you're supposed to do." Brooke straightened her shoulders and held her head high.

Kiera opened her mouth, but Mia cut her off before she could say anything.

"Don't start, girls," Mia warned. To him, she said, "Look, I need to feed these guys before I can go anywhere. And I need to bring them with me when I go to the home and garden store. I won't lie, it's going to be a little chaotic trying to select samples with the three of them in tow. I totally understand if you want to bail."

He should take the excuse she'd given him. Spending more time with her than required would only complicate matters.

Pops's words from earlier echoed in his brain. It's not like he was asking Jax to make a huge sacrifice. "No. That's okay. I'll come with you."

"Are you sure?" she asked. "I don't want you to feel obligated."

"Yes. It's what Pops wants."

Liar. You just want to spend time with her.

He knew it was true.

Chapter Six

He was coming with her. A delicious thrill ran through Mia.
No. No. No.

He was only coming because Alex wanted him to. And that
was fine. It was better than fine. It was the way it should be.
So why did she suddenly feel like a deflated balloon?

Foolish.

"Mommy." Kiera tugged at her arm.

Mia sucked in some much-needed air and blew it out slowly.
Pasting a smile in place, she looked down at her six-year-old
and asked, "What is it, sweetheart?"

"Is Jax talking about *our* Pops?" Kiera pointed to Alex's
house.

"Yes, I am," he answered. "Pops is like my grandfather,
but I'm not related to him."

Well that answered a few questions.

Kiera's gaze went wide. "He told me to call him Pops when
I was four, cuz I couldn't say his last name."

Mia smiled. She'd completely forgotten about that.

"You still can't," Brooke said.

"Can too." Kiera folded her arms across her chest and
glared at her sister.

"Stop picking on your sister, missy." Mia shot Brooke a
warning glance.

"Yeah." Kiera aimed a petulant look at her sister.

Jax's burst of laughter caught her by surprise. He patted the top of Kiera's head. "Don't worry about that, kiddo. I couldn't say Papadopoulos when I was young either. He told me to call him Pops for the same reason."

"He told me I could call him Pops, too," Brooke said.

"He must like you and your sisters a lot. He doesn't let everyone call him that."

"We're special. That's what Pops told me." Kiera puffed out her chest.

"You must be," Jax agreed. He peered over at Mia. "So, what's our plan for the evening?"

"Pizza," Aurora, Brooke and Kiera said at the same time.

"Pizza sounds great." Jax nodded.

"Are you sure?" she asked. "I know you and Alex had that last night." Mia couldn't hide her smile. For some reason, she found it endearing that he was just a little inept in the kitchen.

"I'm never going to live that down, am I?" he asked, an impish grin on his face.

"Nope. Come on, girls. Shoes, sweatshirts—it's going to cool down once the sun sets—then out to the car. Chop, chop!" She clapped her hands twice to emphasize her point. "We've got to get going so we can eat and get to the home and garden center before it closes tonight."

"Okay," the girls chorused together, and scattered to do her bidding.

"You're a take-charge kind of woman." Jax flashed a sexy smile that made her go weak in the knees. "I like that." He jerked his head toward her SUV. "Okay if I ride with you?"

Pulse racing, Mia picked her jaw up off the floor and stammered, "Umm… y-y-yeah. Sure."

"Great," he said.

"I'm ready, Mom." Brooke zipped by her and almost ran into Jax. He stepped out of the way just in time to avoid a collision. Without stopping, she raced out the door yelling, "Shotgun!"

"You're not old enough to sit in the front seat." Aurora followed her sister.

"Neither are you," Mia called. "And Jax is sitting in the front seat."

Kiera appeared with a frown on her face. "I can't find my other sneaker."

Mia's shoulders sagged. Turning to Jax, she said, "I'm sorry about this. I'll be right back."

"It's no problem. Do you need help looking?" he asked Mia.

"Yes." Kiera grabbed his hand. "Come with me."

Her daughter had dragged him halfway up the stairs before Mia could object. She raced up behind him, and couldn't help but admire the view. She remembered all too well what his backside looked like sans clothes. How his muscles bunched and flexed as she dragged her hands over every sculpted inch of him...

A groan almost escaped from her parted lips.

"Chop, chop, Jax," Kiera called as she continued to climb the stairs.

He turned around and flashed another sexy grin. "Like mother, like daughter." To Kiera, he said, "I'm right behind you."

When they all reached Kiera's bedroom, Mia asked, "Where did you find the shoe you have on?" The second one couldn't be far away.

"Right there." Kiera pointed to a spot at the foot of her bed.

"Did you check underneath?" Jax asked. Not waiting for Kiera's response, he got down on all fours and did just that. Reaching a hand into the dark space, he pulled out her lost shoe. "Here you go." He handed the matching sneaker to her daughter and stood.

"Thank you." Kiera launched herself at a surprised Jax and clamped her arms around his waist.

"You're, um, welcome."

Mia almost laughed at the expression on his face. He clearly didn't know how to react to her daughter's gesture.

"Okay, sweetie. You've got your sneaker. Put it on and let's get going. Your sisters are waiting in the car."

Kiera smiled. Slipping her foot into her shoe, she raced toward the stairs.

"Walk," Mia called as she headed toward the door.

A silent, bewildered-looking Jax followed.

Jax marveled at the warmth still radiating throughout his body as he walked to Mia's car. Who knew a guy could feel this great because a little spitfire had hugged him? Not him, that's for sure. He'd never felt anything like it in all of his life.

"You okay?" Mia asked him. "You look a little distracted."

He grinned. "I'm great."

"Good." She smiled at him. "Thanks for helping find Kiera's sneaker. You didn't have to do that."

"It's no problem. I didn't mind." That surprised him, too. He would never have believed he, a confirmed bachelor, would get down on his hands and knees to hunt for a kid's shoe, of all things. It was so…domestic.

And so not like him. He burned mac and cheese when he tried to heat it up, for crying out loud.

He hopped into the passenger seat of Mia's SUV, and she slid behind the wheel and started the engine.

"How is Alex doing tonight?" Mia asked. "He didn't rest a lot today."

"He's definitely tired, but he won't admit it."

Mia smiled. "He can be a bit stubborn."

"Ya think?" Jax let out a snort.

As they drove by the town soccer fields, Brooke asked, "Mommy, what time is my game on Saturday?"

"Two o'clock," Mia answered.

He swiveled around to face the back seat. "You play soccer?"

"Yep." Brooke nodded.

"I used to play soccer, too," he said.

"That's right," Mia said. "You played on the varsity team in high school. You made it all the way to the state finals and won your senior year."

He jerked his gaze to Mia. "You remember that?" She wasn't even around. She'd gone off to college by then.

Mia smiled. "How could I forget? It was all Shane talked about when I came home for Thanksgiving that year. He kicked the winning goal with an assist from you."

Jax snorted. "Shane's memory is a little off on that one. It was the other way around. *I* kicked the winning goal."

"Was Mommy on your team, too?" Kiera asked.

"No, sweetie," Mia said. "I played on the girls' team."

He jerked his gaze to Mia. "You did?"

"Yeah. Until sophomore year." A sad smile crossed her face.

The year her father passed away. He couldn't imagine what that had been like for her. As contentious as his relationship was with his parents, he couldn't conceive of losing either of them.

Why was he thinking about his relationship with his parents when that was the last thing he wanted to do right now? Jax gave himself a mental shake. "I don't remember you ever playing."

"Like I said, I'd stopped playing by the time you and Shane got to high school. Besides, even if I did play, I doubt you would have noticed. You barely talked to me in high school."

She was his best friend's sister, and off-limits. She still was.

Mia let loose a soft chuckle that sent a flood of desire rushing through him. "You were too busy chasing after the cheerleaders to notice anything I did."

"You wound me, woman." He thumped a fist to his heart.

Mia laughed even harder. "You've been saying that since high school. Once a Casanova, always a Casanova."

She was right. So why did that suddenly bother him?

"Do you want to play soccer with us when we get home?" Brooke asked him.

"Yeah," Kiera enthused. "That would be fun."

He wouldn't mind kicking the ball around for a few minutes. Heck, like the little spitfire had said, it would be fun.

"It's going to be dark by the time we get home," Mia said. "And you girls are going straight to bed. You've still got school tomorrow."

Jax glanced at the girls in the rearview mirror. He couldn't help but laugh at the mutinous expression on Kiera's face. She really was cute as a button.

Mia pulled the car into a parking spot in front of the pizza place, and everyone hopped out. He walked up to the little spitfire and ruffled her hair. "We can kick the ball around another time. Okay?"

The smile his spitfire flashed sent a rush of warmth flooding through him.

Mia pulled him aside and allowed the girls to get ahead of them. "Look, I know you mean well, and you don't have any experience with children, but they get disappointed when you promise them something and don't follow through."

He frowned. What was she talking about? *Ah, hell.* Their father had promised to have dinner with them and canceled at the last minute.

You'd think he'd know better. It sucked when people broke their promises, especially when you're a kid.

Jax knew that disappointment all too well. The trip to Disney World that never happened. The Bop It toy he'd never received. The dog he'd never gotten.

As annoyed as Brooke and Kiera had acted back at the house earlier, he knew how resentment and irritation could mask a wealth of hurt.

Jax shook his head. "I'm sorry. I wasn't thinking."

"I get it, believe me. But I don't want to see them upset again." Her head dropped, and a swath of curly hair fell across her beautiful face. "Can you understand that?"

Jax grasped her chin and lifted her head until her gaze met his. Tucking the curl behind her ear, he said, "Totally." Mama bear was fiercely protecting her cubs. It was another thing he admired about her. "Don't worry. I promise I'll make sure to say what I mean."

Mia's kids seemed great, but he wasn't planning on spending any significant time with them. Nor with Mia. From now on, he'd work back at the hotel while she watched Pops.

Yeah, right.

They walked into the pizzeria, and a hostess guided them to a table.

Jax peered around the room. He spotted Duncan Cruz in the takeout line. "I'll be right back," he said to Mia.

"Sure," she said.

He walked over to where Duncan stood. "Hey, man." Jax clapped him on the shoulder.

"Rawlins. Shane said you were in town. How's Alex doing?" He grabbed the pizza box the cashier handed him.

"He's doing okay. Hey, I want to say thank you for everything you did for him the day of his fall. I really appreciate you and Shane taking such good care of him and getting him to the hospital quickly."

"You're welcome," Duncan said. "Listen, I need to get going now, but let's get together for a beer while you're here, if you have time."

"Sounds good. I'll catch you later."

Duncan headed to the exit and Jax returned to the table.

"Sorry about that," he said to Mia. "Did you order?"

"Not yet." She gestured to her daughters. "We're still trying to decide."

"No problem."

Jax caught a glimpse of Brooke nudging Kiera in the ribs.

"Stop it," Brooke demanded.

"I can't." Kiera fidgeted in her seat.

"What's wrong, sweetie?" Mia asked.

"I have to go to the bathroom." A pained expression crossed her face. "Really bad."

Jax bit his lip to keep from smiling.

"Sorry." Mia stood. "Come on, girls." She motioned for all three to follow her.

"I don't have to go," Aurora said. "Can I stay here?"

Jax jerked his gaze to the little girl because that was the first thing she'd said since they'd all climbed into the car at Mia's house. And she still hadn't spoken directly to him yet.

"Is that okay with you?" Mia asked.

"Umm…yeah. Sure." He flashed a nervous grin.

"Thanks." Mia gave him a grateful smile, and his insides turned all soft and mushy, like a marshmallow. What the hell was up with that? "We'll be back in a few minutes."

Silence charged the air as soon as Mia, Brooke and Kiera disappeared. Jax pasted a grin on his face. He wasn't sure what else to do. Aurora just sat there, scrutinizing him.

Maybe she hadn't said anything to him because he hadn't introduced himself earlier? She wasn't at the door when he'd told the little spitfire his name. "So…my name is Jax."

Aurora flashed a you've-got-to-be-kidding-me expression at him and started to giggle.

Jax sighed. Of course she was laughing at him. He was making a complete idiot of himself. And this pint-size female was enjoying watching him squirm.

"I know who you are, silly," she finally said. "I recognized you at the house."

How could she have recognized him? They'd never met before today.

"I remember you from Auntie Piper's gallery. You were there the night it opened."

He vaguely recalled seeing kids that evening, but he'd been busy schmoozing and hadn't given it too much thought. He'd never actually met any of the children.

"Auntie Piper showed me your pictures. I liked the wolf."

He grinned. He couldn't help it. "How come?" He prayed she wasn't going to wax on about society's norms, or whatever that couple at his last showing had been talking about.

"She was so pretty." Aurora's voice was filled with awe and wonder. "I wished I could have seen her in person."

Funny how the kid had seen exactly what had made him want to capture the image in the first place—the raw beauty of an animal in its natural habitat. His pictures weren't meant to be a commentary on society.

"But I felt bad for her, too," Aurora continued.

"Why?" He cocked his head to the side. He was interested to hear what she had to say.

"Because she was all alone. She didn't have a family. All the animals in your pictures are like that."

Jax wasn't sure how to respond to Aurora's statement. He'd never thought about it before, but she'd made him think about it now.

He remembered what the woman at his last show had said about the wolf wanting to be part of the pack, rather than being alone.

"I would be sad if I was all alone and didn't have a family," Aurora added.

Yeah. A painful tightness settled in his chest, making it hard to breathe.

Mia, Brooke and Kiera returned to the table.

Jax shook off the sensation.

"I hope Aurora didn't talk your ear off about her pictures,"

Mia said when everyone was seated again. "I told her she wasn't allowed to bug you about them."

Jax's brows drew together. "Her pictures?"

Aurora shook her head. "I didn't, Mom."

"We talked about my photos." Jax waved off Mia's concern. "From my exhibit at Piper's gallery in February. When you say pictures, are you talking about photographs?"

"Yep." Brooke pointed to her older sister. "She's always running around taking pictures with the camera Auntie Piper gave her."

He turned his attention to Aurora. "You like to take pictures?"

"Sure do." Aurora's smile lit up her whole face.

"You know," Jax said, "I was around the same age as you when I got my first camera. Pops gave it to me."

"I didn't know that," Mia said.

Jax nodded. "He used to have his own photography business before he retired. One day I was over visiting him, he was showing me some of the pictures he had taken, and I was hooked. So he gave me a camera and taught me everything that he knew and—" he shrugged a shoulder "—the rest is history."

"That's so cool. I wish I had someone to teach me." Aurora gave a wistful sigh.

"We can look into classes," Mia said. "But don't be too disappointed if they don't offer anything for people your age. You're a little young."

Mia was right. Most children's photography classes were geared toward children older than Aurora.

"Okay, Mommy." Aurora's voice was full of disappointment.

I could do it.

Don't make promises you can't keep. Mia's words invaded his brain.

Jax glanced at Aurora. She had amazing insight for a kid, and her enthusiasm reminded him of himself at that age.

Where would he be today if Pops hadn't stepped up?

He wouldn't be a renowned photographer, that's for sure.

Who knew? Maybe Aurora would make a name for herself one day. She deserved the same chance Pops had given him.

Jax looked at Mia. "I'd be happy to spend some time with her while I'm here."

Aurora's mouth dropped open. "Oh my gosh. Yes. Absolutely yes. Please, please, please, Mommy," she pleaded.

Mia shot him a hesitant look. "Are you sure about this?"

Jax looked her in the eyes. "I wouldn't have mentioned it, if I wasn't."

Mia smiled. She seemed to understand that he'd keep the promises he made. "All right then."

He turned his attention back to Aurora. "I'm only in town for a couple of weeks, so I'm not sure how much I'll be able to teach you, but if it's okay with your mom, maybe you can come over after school one day this week for a couple of hours."

"Can we come too?" Brooke asked.

"Oh, honey." Mia's cheeks turned bright red. "That's—"

"A great idea," Jax finished. "Yes. You can all come over to Pops's house. For dinner." He grinned. It was the perfect solution. "I'll look at Aurora's photos, and we can even kick the ball around in Pops's backyard for a little while." And the best part… he'd get to see more of Mia.

Let's face it. That's what you really want, his brain taunted.

Yeah. It was.

Chapter Seven

*B*ad idea.

Bad idea.

Colossally bad idea.

There were hundreds, maybe even thousands of reasons why she should decline Jax's invitation to dinner, so why couldn't she think of a single one right now?

"Can we?" her girls chorused together. "Please?"

Aurora would truly benefit from Jax's professional photography experience.

Kiera and Brooke would benefit from kicking the soccer ball around with a former state champion.

She could…spend some extra time with Jax.

They were friends, after all.

He'd told her kids as much not more than thirty minutes ago.

Friends spent time together. They had dinner together.

Like they were doing now.

"Are you sure Alex will be okay with us invading his place?" she asked. "I know how he likes his peace and quiet. We're anything but." She made a gesture that included her three daughters and herself.

"I just texted him." Jax waved the cell in his hand. "He can't wait to see everyone. So, what do you say?" His smile made her heart turn over.

"Sure." Mia was certain she had a silly grin plastered across her face. "Dinner together sounds like fun. What night are you thinking?"

"Whatever works for you," he said.

"How about tomorrow at five? The girls are with me, and for once we don't have any activities on the calendar."

"Tomorrow it is. I'll let Pops know." Jax started typing on his phone.

"Are you a good cook?" Aurora asked Jax. "Mommy said you burned the baked mac and cheese she made for Pops."

Mia was pretty sure her cheeks were flaming. "She asked me why I was making another pan for Pops when I'd just made one."

"If you can't cook, what are we gonna eat for dinner?" Kiera's little face scrunched up as if she were trying to work out the puzzle and couldn't.

"I, ah…" Jax stammered.

"How about I bring a lasagna and some garlic bread?" Mia suggested. "It's no trouble." She had one in the freezer. She could take it out when they got home this evening and let it defrost in the fridge overnight.

A look of relief crossed Jax's face. "That sounds great. I'll make a salad to go with what you bring."

"Are you sure?" she asked. "I don't mind throwing one together."

"Positive." Jax's lips quirked up. "I don't have to heat anything, so I think I can manage."

"All righty. Now that we've settled what we're having for dinner tomorrow night, what do you say we figure out what's on the menu for this evening?" Mia turned her attention to her daughters. "Pepperoni and cheese for you, ladies?"

A round of yesses ensued.

"How about you, Jax?" she asked.

"That works for me, too." He grinned.

Aurora looked at Jax. Anticipation glowed in her eyes. "I can't wait for tomorrow. I'm so excited to show you my pictures."

"I'm excited to see them." Sincerity lit his gaze. "Bring your camera, too, so you can practice some of the techniques I'm going to show you." He turned his attention to Brooke and Kiera. "And you two make sure to wear your soccer cleats and shin guards. We're going to learn some new skills."

Mia's heart beat in double-time. His genuine interest in helping her daughters floored her. Mia had always known Jax was a nice guy, but this was something different. Something more.

His willingness to spend time with her girls, teach them... Nurture them. It was a side of him she'd never seen before. And one she liked—a lot.

"Mommy. What are you going to do with all of this stuff?" Brooke yawned as they exited the home and garden center.

Mia glanced at her watch. *Damn. Eight twenty already.* She needed to get home quickly. Their bedtime was in ten minutes, and they needed their sleep. "I'm going to prepare a presentation board after you and your sisters go to sleep and show it to Mr. Papadopoulos tomorrow," she answered.

"Pops is thinking about having your mother redesign some of the rooms in his house," Jax added.

"Like in our house?" Aurora asked.

Mia nodded. "Exactly."

"Why don't you just show him our house?" Kiera asked.

Jax turned his attention to Mia. "I agree with Kiera's suggestion. I caught a glimpse of your living room when we went upstairs earlier. It's stunning. I love how you removed the wall between the living room and kitchen to make it one big open space. There's so much light in there, especially with the colors you used—something like that might be good for him.

Pops's house is like the Before on one of those fixer-upper TV shows, and yours is the impressive After. I think you should show him. He'll see firsthand how talented you really are."

"Thanks." Outside she looked calm and composed—at least, she hoped she did—because on the inside, she was jumping and screaming at the top of her lungs and doing a mean rendition of her happy dance, which was similar to an orangutan doing the hokeypokey (or so her brother had once told her), jerky movements and all. So yeah, she prayed she was cool and collected. Otherwise, Jax was going to think she was crazy.

"You're welcome." The warmth and sincerity in his voice made her feel as if she were walking on air.

"Maybe I can bring him over tomorrow morning, if he's feeling up to it?" he added.

What was it about his smile that made her go all soft and mushy inside?

"Sure. That sounds good." Yep. That goofy grin was back and plastered across her face. She was sure of it.

"We'll come over at nine," Jax said.

"That works. I'll just stay at my house instead of coming over."

Jax grinned. "We've got ourselves a plan."

Mia grabbed the key fob that was clipped to her purse and pressed the button to unlock the doors. "Hop in, everyone."

Aurora, Brooke and Kiera slid into the back seat while Mia popped open the trunk.

"Let me help you load all of this." Jax pointed to the contents of her cart.

"You don't have to do that." His nearness sent a wave of pleasant tingles zinging through her. "It's only a few floor samples and some eight-ounce paint cans."

"They still need unloading." Jax reached for a ceramic tile at the same time she did.

His hand brushed against hers, and her pulse soared. Now she was wishing his hands would touch other parts of her body.

Heat pooled low in her belly. Her body hummed and zipped, anticipation coursing through her like a raging river.

She was going to have to take a cold shower when she got home. *It's either that or buy a vibrator.* And where was she going to get one of those? Certainly not here in New Suffolk, that was for sure.

Her gaze lowered to a certain part of his anatomy. *Nope.* The vibrator wouldn't feel as good as the real thing.

Great. Now she wanted him to press her back against the car and take her right here.

No.

What was wrong with her tonight? Mia clenched her hand around the vinyl flooring sample. Snatching it up, she practically threw it into the back of her SUV.

It was being near him, that's what. A low, heady heat had thrummed through her from the moment she'd seen him on her doorstep, the smoldering embers just waiting to be ignited to a fiery inferno only he could extinguish.

This was why having dinner with him was such a bad idea. What was she going to do if something like this happened tomorrow night? At least the darkness outside hid her aroused body—Mia angled away from him just to make sure Jax couldn't see the thrust of her nipples as they strained against her bra and T-shirt. She wouldn't have that luxury sitting around Pops's dinner table.

Where was this sound reasoning when Jax had issued the invitation? *Shoulda thought about it then.* It was too late now. She'd already committed. She'd blasted him for not making promises he couldn't keep. She needed to do the same.

"Mia?" His voice snapped her back to the present. "Are you okay?"

Her gaze collided with his. "Yes. Sorry." She flashed a nervous smile.

"You spaced out there for a minute," he said.

"I was just thinking…whether I had everything," she lied. "Don't want to make two trips." *Stop babbling, for crying out loud.* She reached into the cart, but it was empty. Jax had loaded everything into her car.

"Thanks." Mia gestured to her neatly stacked purchases.

"You're welcome." His smile sent her heart racing.

"I'll put the cart back." Her words came out in a rush. "Be right back."

Mia strode toward the cart return at top speed. She needed to put some much-needed distance between her and Jax as quickly as possible.

What was up with her tonight? She'd never experienced this…breathlessness, this giddiness before over a guy. Not even when she was a teenager. Certainly not with Kyle.

She'd found Kyle attractive enough, but—

Mia frowned. The truth was, he'd pursued her after they'd met, not the other way around. And their love life…she'd believed it was great, but knowing what she did now, it had been satisfactory at best.

Mia wanted spectacular, *orgasmic.* She laughed as she walked back to her SUV. One night with Jax, and nothing less would do.

Lord, why was she thinking about sex with Jax—again?

Be honest. You haven't stopped thinking about it since you heard he was back in town.

Mia tugged her fingers through her hair. What was she going to do about him?

She hadn't missed the heads that had turned her way when she and the girls had walked into the pizzeria with him earlier. Her shoulders sagged. It was probably going to be all over town by tomorrow.

News of her split with Kyle had spread faster than a wild-fire fueled by high winds when he'd walked out on her a year and a half ago.

She shuddered. She wasn't prepared to go through that again.

"Hurry up, Mommy." Kiera's voice pulled her from her musings.

"Coming." She shoved the cart into the designated area and made her way back to her vehicle. When she returned, the trunk was closed, and Jax was sitting in the passenger seat. Mia slid behind the wheel and started the car. "Everyone buckled up?"

A round of yesses ensued.

Mia exited the parking lot and drove along Main Street towards her home. The back seat chatter slowly drifted to silence. She looked in the rearview mirror. Eyes closed, Brooke and Kiera sat slumped in their seats. Aurora had turned her head and was staring out the window.

She turned her vehicle onto her street a few minutes later.

Mia couldn't help noticing how Jax stiffened as they passed by his parents' house. "Is everything okay?" she asked.

"Yes. Whose car is that?" Jax pointed to the Audi Q7 parked in her driveway.

"Daddy's here," Aurora screeched. "Brooke, Kiera, wake up."

Mia sucked in a deep breath and blew it out slowly. Why had he come over at this hour?

A thousand watts of bright light flooded the driveway as she pulled in and brought the SUV to a stop beside the Audi Q7.

Kyle slid out of his car. Hands shoved in his trouser pockets, he strode over to her vehicle.

"Daddy!" her girls cried in unison. The three of them scrambled from the car, squealing with delight.

Mia opened her door. She jumped out and joined her daughters.

Jax appeared by her side a moment later.

He extended his hand to Kyle. "Jax Rawlings."

"The photographer." Kyle's gaze narrowed. "I remember you from Piper's gallery opening last February."

"Right." Jax nodded. "It's nice to see you again."

Kyle shook Jax's hand, but looked anything but pleased.

"What are you doing here, Daddy?" Kiera asked.

"Yes." Mia straightened her shoulders and held her head high. "I'd like to know that, too."

"Go inside, girls," Kyle demanded. "I need to talk to your mother."

"But, Daddy," Brooke protested. "You just got here."

"No. I've been waiting for you to come home for almost an hour now." Kyle glared at Mia.

Mia frowned. "Why didn't you call and tell me you were coming?" He hadn't mentioned anything when he'd called and canceled earlier.

Kyle arched a brow and cast an I'm-not-a-complete-moron glance at her. "I did. You didn't answer."

She grabbed her cell from her pocket. It wasn't on. *Crap.* "Sorry. My phone died."

"How unfortunate for me," Kyle said.

Kiera scrunched up her nose, and said, "Poor Daddy."

"It's all right," Kyle said in a calm, soothing voice. "I'm sure your mother didn't keep me waiting on purpose."

Mia frowned. "Of course I didn't. I didn't know you were coming." She would have thought that much was clear when she'd asked him what he was doing here.

He draped his arms around Aurora, Brooke and Kiera. "It *is* my night with my daughters."

Her brows drew into a deep V. "Yes, but you called and canceled your visit earlier." Why was he being so obtuse?

"Actually—" Kyle began.

Was he going to contradict her? Make her look like the bad guy in front of their daughters?

Mia recalled the last time he'd picked up the girls for dinner. He'd invited her to join them and she'd declined. He'd tried on that occasion to make her look bad in front of their girls.

Aurora interrupted him before he finished his sentence. "Yeah, Daddy. You told me you had to work very late tonight because you needed to finish up a presentation for an important client you're meeting with tomorrow."

"Ah… Right," Color invaded Kyle's cheeks.

Mia drew in a quick breath. He had been trying to paint her as the bad guy. Why was she surprised? She shouldn't be.

He really was a jerk.

"I finished early, and I wanted to say good-night to the three of you," Kyle said. "I missed seeing you tonight." He pulled Aurora into his arms and kissed her cheek.

"I want a hug, too," Kiera and Brooke said at the same time.

"Of course." He hugged all three girls, then straightened. "Now… You need to get to bed. You've got school tomorrow. Don't worry. I'll see you again soon."

"Go ahead in, girls." She opened the car door and pressed the button to lift the garage door. "I'll come up and say good-night in a few minutes."

"Bye, Daddy," her daughters chorused as they ran inside.

"I'll see you later," Mia said.

"Yes, good night, Rawlins." Kyle shot Jax an expectant look.

Mia placed a hand on Jax's arm to stop him from leaving, but never removed her gaze from Kyle. "I was talking to you, not Jax."

Kyle arched a brow. "There's something I need to discuss with you. In private." He glared at Jax. *Oh for crying out loud.* "Can't it wait?"

Kyle's expression turned serious. "No. It's important."

"Fine. Give me a minute." She grabbed Jax's hand and pulled him behind her car. "I'm so sorry."

"Don't worry about it." He shook his head. "Want me to stick around, just in case you need some backup?"

Mia smiled. "No. That won't be necessary."

"You sure? I'm here if you need me." Jax's expression turned serious.

Could the man be any sweeter?

Her lips quirked up into a smile. "Good to know, Rawlins. I appreciate that." *More than you know.*

"Anytime." He lowered his head to hers.

He was going to kiss her. Her heart beat a rapid tattoo. Because she remembered what his mouth could do to her. The way he tasted her, teased... She trembled.

Jax pressed the tenderest kiss she'd ever received against her cheek. Just the lightest press of his lips on her heated skin. Mia melted.

It wasn't what she'd expected, but oh... How could such a simple gesture make her feel all fluttery inside?

A smile played on her lips. "See you tomorrow." Was that breathless voice hers?

"Count on it." He started down the driveway and stopped halfway. Turning, he faced her. "Thanks for letting me tag along tonight."

"You're welcome."

He came back to where she stood and clasped her hand in his. Mia marveled at the gentle touch. "I had fun with you and your daughters."

"Me, too." Mia was pretty sure a goofy grin was plastered on her face, but she didn't care.

"I know Pops is going to love everything you selected." He released her hand.

Fingers crossed. "I hope so." She waved as he backed away.

Kyle strode over to where she stood after Jax had disappeared across the street. "What was that all about?"

Talk about a buzzkill. Mia shook her head. "What do you want, Kyle?"

"You've kept our daughters out way past their bedtime. What were you thinking? They have to go to school tomorrow."

"What's the big deal?" Mia glanced at her watch. "It's not that late. The girls will be fine. Now, what did you want to discuss with me?"

"You know how Aurora gets when she doesn't get enough sleep. She has a math test tomorrow."

"I understand that." She kept her voice calm. No way would she allow him to goad her into losing her temper. "I told you when you called earlier, *and canceled*, that I had errands to run tonight. I was planning to go when they were at dinner with you, but since *you canceled*, I needed to change my plans. I got home as quickly as possible."

"Help me understand, Mia. What could be more important than the welfare of our children?"

She shook her head. "It's not that late. The girls will be fine."

She was done explaining. Why had she even bothered in the first place? "I think we're done here."

Kyle made no move to leave. Instead, he peered through the rear window of her SUV. He popped open the trunk and grabbed one of her bags before she could stop him.

"Hey," she protested. She tried to snatch the bag, but he dodged her. "Give it back."

He reached inside and pulled out a handful of various samples. "What are these for?" His brows drew together in a deep V. "They look like floor and paint samples. Why do you need these? Are you planning to redo the house?"

"It's none of your business. Now give me the bag."

His gaze widened. "You're looking at starting your own interior design business again, aren't you?"

It wasn't an accusation. Still, his voice held a note of...
not disapproval, exactly. More like apprehension, or concern.

Mia sighed. He'd been against her starting her own business
from the start. "What if I am?" She straightened her shoulders
and held her head high.

"We've talked about this." He spoke with a quiet voice. "I
did the math. It will take *years* for you to be able to make a
living doing this. How are you going to support yourself and
our daughters in the meantime? And then there's the issue of
who will stay with the children. That's why teaching is perfect for you. You're on the same schedule."

"Like I said, it's none of your business anymore." Mia gritted her teeth. "Give me the bag."

"You're right," he said. "But you're going to have to dedi-
cate a lot of time to get your business off the ground. Have you
considered how that will impact our girls? They need you."

Mia gawked at him. Was he kidding? He acted as if she
were abandoning their children.

"You're going to have to put the girls in daycare." Kyle's
gaze held a note of concern and disappointment when it connected with hers. "Neither of us wanted that."

"Circumstances have changed. I don't have the luxury of
staying home anymore."

Kyle held his hands up as if he were surrendering. "I'm
just worried about our daughters. It's another change they'll
have to deal with. That's why teaching is the best solution."

Except teaching didn't make her happy. There were aspects
she liked, but she wasn't passionate about it.

She'd chosen the career because...

Kyle's subtle comments had made it seem that if she chose
otherwise, she wouldn't be doing what was best for their children.

He'd manipulated her into doing what he wanted. Not just
tonight. He'd been doing it for years.

And she'd allowed him to do it. What was wrong with her? Talk about a bad example to set for your daughters.

Mia shook her head. Why had she been so blind to the truth until now?

I wasn't. The realization jarred her.

She'd ignored the signs from the beginning, and they'd been there.

The truth was, she'd been in a bad place when they'd first met. Her mother had sunk into a deep depression after her father's death. The whole family had struggled during that time; grieved.

She'd been lost and alone, at least it had felt that way. Kyle came along, and for the first time, in a long, long time, she'd experienced joy, happiness.

At least in the beginning.

Somehow, she'd convinced herself that if she ended things with Kyle, she'd plunge back into hopelessness and despair.

Mia couldn't go back there. Not ever.

She'd been wrong about what would happen if things ended. Sure, the last year and a half had been tough, but she hadn't sunken back into the abyss, as she'd once feared. No, with the help of her friends and family, she was thriving. Life was good, and there were endless opportunities to make it better. She could see that now.

"Mia." Kyle shook her gently. "Did you hear what I said?"

She stared at him. She couldn't allow him to manipulate her anymore.

She looked Kyle in the eyes. "Teaching is not what's best for me. It's not what I want to do for the rest of my life."

She wanted to do home design.

Designing a room…filled an empty place inside her. It gave her a keen sense of satisfaction to see her designs come to life, and yes, she couldn't deny the thrill she received when someone looked at one of her spaces and smiled. *That* made her happy.

"Mia—" Kyle began.

Nope. It was time to end this conversation. She cut him off before he could get started again. "Relax. I'm not giving up my teaching job, yet." She wasn't a complete idiot, contrary to what Kyle believed. She would do what was best for her and her daughters. "I'm helping Alex Papadopoulos redesign his first floor to accommodate a master suite."

"Oh. Why didn't you just say that?"

Mia shook her head again. "Please just give me the bag."

He did, and she turned toward the house. "Good night." She'd had enough.

"Hold on. We still haven't talked about what I had wanted to discuss."

Not happening. She continued toward the front door. "I'll call you in the morning."

Kyle appeared in front of her and blocked her path. "About Jax," he started.

Mia prayed for patience. "Jax is none of your business."

"Think about our daughters' welfare, Mia. You're exposing them to a complete stranger."

Mia's jaw dropped. "Oh, that's rich coming from you. You practically moved in with Oriana—while we were still married, I might add. You certainly weren't worried about any adverse effects that might have, were you?"

"That's totally different." Kyle's voice thundered. "And you know it. I was—"

Jax's voice cut off whatever else Kyle planned to say. "Everything all right over there?"

He appeared at the foot of her driveway a moment later. Silhouetted in the moonlight, he looked like some kind of an avenging angel.

Her pulse kicked up a notch.

He stopped when he reached her and stood by her side. "I thought I heard yelling."

Mia should have been mad, or at least annoyed. She'd told him to go. He'd left, but he'd watched over her nonetheless. Truth be told, she was grateful. Not because she needed protection, but because Jax had meant what he said. He'd come to stand beside her at the first sign of possible trouble.

"Everything is fine," she replied. "Kyle was just leaving." She gave him a pointed look.

He hesitated for a moment, then turned on his heel and strode to his car.

Kyle backed his car down the driveway and disappeared down the street a moment later.

Mia breathed out a sigh of relief.

"So." Jax gave her a look that made her heart slam against her rib cage. "I guess I should apologize for interfering like I did, but I won't." He stood tall and proud. "I wouldn't mean it, and I'm not going to lie to you.

"I get that you're a grown woman and you can take care of yourself, but your ex was gunning for a fight from the moment you jumped out of your SUV. Kudos to you, by the way, for not letting him provoke you, because he was trying like hell to do just that. I couldn't hear what you two said to each other—but when he raised his voice to you, no way was I going to allow anything to happen."

He'd done more than have her back. He'd protected her. She liked that. She liked that a lot.

Chapter Eight

"Ready, Pops?" Jax walked into the den.

"Just a minute. I'm still looking over the proposal Mia sent me last night. I have to say, I'm impressed with the level of detail she included. There's a base cost for the work. I know that will change depending on what finishes I choose, but I'm liking what I see so far."

"That's good. We should go over to her place now so you can see what she's done firsthand."

"All right. All right." Pops set his laptop aside. "I'm ready now." He glanced at Jax. "Unless you think I'm a little under-dressed for the occasion."

Jax peered at Pops's gray sweat suit and matching slippers. "You're fine."

"All righty then. Let's go." Pops pushed the button on the side of his new recliner. The seat moved and helped him stand. "I like this contraption. Makes standing up a lot easier."

Jax grinned and handed him his crutch. "I thought it would."

"Turns out you were right," Pops grumbled. "I'm glad you suggested I buy it."

"I wanted to treat you," Jax said.

"No way. I got plenty of money saved. I can, and will, pay my own way. That includes the cost of Bill and Mia, and the daytime caregiver when he or she becomes available."

Jax held up his hands as if he were surrendering. "I'm

not arguing with you." It was a matter of pride for Pops. He wouldn't take that away from him. He tapped a hand on the wheelchair. "Let's get over to Mia's. You're going to be impressed." He certainly was. The woman had a wealth of talent. She could rival the top New York City interior designers. He ought to know. He'd hired the best to decorate his loft. She'd come highly recommended from a long list of A-list clients. Too bad he'd hated the final product. The chrome and white on white might be modern, but it lacked any real warmth.

Mia… Her house felt like home.

"My, my, my, aren't you in a hurry," Pops said. "I thought we weren't supposed to go over until nine?" He glanced at his watch. "It's only a quarter till now. Doesn't take fifteen minutes to cross the street."

He lifted one shoulder in a casual shrug. "Just making sure you get moving. We don't want to be late."

"Of course not," Pops agreed. He eyed Jax up and down and let out a low whistle. He tapped Jax's cheeks with the palms of his hands. "Nice jeans. Nice shirt." He gave an exaggerated sniff. "Cologne, too. Oh my." He sent him a speculative glance as he lowered himself into the wheelchair.

"What's that supposed to mean?" Jax shot him a wary glance as he extended the foot plate for Pops to rest his non-injured foot on.

"Touchy, too." A smug grin crossed Pops's face. "That's curious."

Crap. Leave it to Pops to notice he'd stepped up his game this morning. "I don't know what you're talking about, old man."

"I'll bet you don't." Pops let loose a low chuckle. "I do find it interesting, though, that this is the second time within the last twenty-four hours that you've gone out of your way to wear nice threads."

Jax burst out laughing. He couldn't help it. "You're a little out of date with the expressions, Pops. By like a few decades."

"Don't sass me, boy. You know damned well what I mean. You're dressed to impress."

"Hey, I always look good." Jax grinned.

"You're arrogant, too." Pops scowled. "Women don't like that in a man."

Jax pushed the wheelchair toward the front door. "Who says I'm trying to impress a woman?"

"Don't be daft. We both know you've got a thing for Mia." Pops pointed across the street at Mia's house. "You gonna deny it?"

"Mia and I are just friends," he insisted. Maybe if he said it enough, he'd believe it.

"Right. That's why you invited her and her daughters to have dinner here tonight. Cuz you're *friends*."

Okay, yes. He liked Mia. More than he'd anticipated. More than was smart. That didn't mean he was going to do anything about it.

He wasn't.

Jax shook his head. "You can think what you want, but it doesn't change the facts." She was off-limits.

He opened the front door. Turning around, he backed through the opening and lowered the chair the half step down to the front porch.

Pops muttered something Jax couldn't make out.

Jax pushed the chair across the street and up to Mia's front door. She opened it before he could ring the bell.

"Here, let me help you." She stepped outside and held the screen door open for him.

Jax maneuvered the chair inside, and Mia followed.

"Thanks for coming," Mia said.

"Thanks for inviting us over." He kissed her cheek. Something he'd done all his life—well, at least from the time he was a teenager. It shouldn't affect him. So why did he want to linger just a little longer and feel her soft, smooth skin beneath his lips? Press her close against him and breathe in her heady scent. Run his fingers through the silky strands of her hair.

Jax stepped away.

"Let me show you around," she said.

Focus on the reason you're here. "The place looks great." Jax smiled as he gazed around the space. Sun spilled in through the large picture window in the front and the two narrower windows that flanked it. Light also shone through the sliding door that led out to a back deck.

Decorative pillows sat on the couch. Flowers filled decorative vases, brightening the room. Mia had even placed a blanket over the fabric chair by the fireplace.

The space looked like a page out of *Better Homes & Gardens*. She really was amazing.

"Whoa." Pops darted his gaze around the room. "It's all open down here. I wouldn't have believed you could do that."

"Yes." She moved into the center of the large room. "The wall between the kitchen and dining room was non–load-bearing, so I could remove it without complication, but I did need to add an engineered beam in the ceiling when I removed the wall between the kitchen and living room, to hold up the upstairs."

"This is really nice." Pops's awed expression made Jax smile. She'd wowed him, all right. "It's bright and airy, and with no walls, the space looks huge."

"And you've still got three distinct spaces. Living room." Mia gestured to the room they stood in. "Dining room." She pointed to her left. "And kitchen." She pointed behind her.

"Where are the stove and the fridge?" Pops frowned and peered around. "I assume they used to be on the wall that divided the two spaces. Like my kitchen."

"The way all the Cape-Cod-style homes in the neighborhood are configured." She motioned for them to follow her and stepped into the kitchen. "Come see for yourself."

Jax grabbed the wheelchair handles and followed her. "Ah, the stove is in the island. I didn't notice that from the other room."

"It matches the island countertop, and it's flush-mounted. Take a look at this." She reached a hand under the edge of the countertop, beside the stove. A rectangle-shaped vent descended from the ceiling.

Jax grinned. "Now that's cool."

"Yeah," Pops agreed. "Wish I had something like that at my place. It would have come in handy when you burned the mac and cheese the other night."

To her credit, Mia said nothing. But she couldn't hide her smile. "The fridge is here." She gestured to her right.

"You closed off the opening that leads into the hall and stuck it there." Pops's expression was filled with admiration. "That's smart. You don't need it because you can still access that area from the living room."

"Exactly." Mia moved to the island and tapped the white quartz surface. "This is custom-designed, with cabinets on both sides for extra storage, and a wine cooler on the end cap. You might like this as well." She pulled open a large drawer next to the refrigerator.

"It's an extra cooler for beer and soda," she said. "You can't even tell it's here. The panel on the front makes it look just like another storage drawer."

"That's pretty cool," Pops said. "The whole space looks sleek and fresh."

"Thanks." Mia grinned. "That's what I was going for when I designed it. What do you think of the space as a whole?"

Pops looked Mia in the eye. "You did all of this?"

She assumed he wanted to be sure, even though she'd already indicated as much earlier. "I did." She stood tall and proud. "I've been working on it since the day we moved in. I still have more I'd like to do. Sandstone on the fireplace from floor to ceiling to make it a feature when you walk in. Contemporary furniture in the living room. Some updated artwork."

"Maybe Jax can help you with that." Pops nudged him, his elbow hitting Jax's thigh. "He is a photographer, you know."

Her gaze flickered to his. "If you ever decide to do nature photos, let me know. I'll need something to hang over the fireplace once it's done."

He shot her a curious glance. "What do you mean by nature?" Lots of different settings came to mind for him, including the images he currently captured.

"Waterfalls, wooded areas, the beach." She made a little gesture with her hand. "You know. Nature."

"Maybe you should show him," Pops said. "Spend some time together. Take him to some of your favorite spots around town."

Jax blew out a breath. The man was relentless. "Don't listen to him." He waved off Pops's suggestion.

"Really," Pops persisted. "Didn't you tell me the other night that you're looking for some new things to photograph?"

He should have kept his mouth shut on that subject, but as a kid, Jax had always talked his problems through with Pops.

And he'd always given good advice.

"This could be it," Pops finished. Directing his attention to Mia, he added, "Do you think you might have some time to help Jax out?"

Jax shot Pops a warning glance. "She's going to be too busy when she starts renovating your place."

Pops scowled at him.

"I'm sure I can find some time," Mia said.

Pops flashed him a gloating grin.

He shook his head. "Maybe we can get back to what we came here for?"

"Right." Pops nodded. Turning to Mia, he asked, "Who did the construction work for you?"

"I removed the walls myself, but I had TK Construction do the beam work. I'd like to use them for your project, since I know they do quality work."

"They have a good reputation," Pops agreed. "When can you start?"

A mile-wide grin spread across Mia's face, and Jax's heart turned over.

Jax walked into Pops's spare bedroom that he'd turned into an office an hour later. He pulled out his laptop from his backpack and set it on the makeshift desk he'd crafted out of a piece of plywood he'd found in the garage and two sawhorses from Pops's workshop in the basement.

Once the computer was up and running, he started surfing through his archives. Mia's comment earlier about nature shots flitted through his brain as he flicked through his folders.

He wasn't sure how long he'd been at it when his phone started to ring.

Jax stiffened. The ringtone he'd assigned to his mother blared over the low sound of music playing in the background. He grabbed the cell from the tabletop.

Sure enough, his mother's number flashed across the screen. *Damn.*

Jax had seen her car in the driveway last night when Mia had driven by the house after their shopping trip. For the first time in days, the lights had been on, which meant she was home. Probably his father too.

It was only a matter of time before they figured out he was here, if they hadn't already.

He let the call go to voice mail and shoved the phone in his pocket.

He returned his attention to the laptop and opened another

folder. He'd taken these shots on a trip to Zambia a few years ago. Most of them had been published. Jax clicked on the next image.

He smiled. "But not this one."

At the time, it hadn't fit in with his brand. Given his brand needed to change…yes, it might work.

"Knock, knock." Mia opened the bedroom door a few minutes later and poked her head inside. "Do you want to join us for lunch?"

His stomach rumbled. "Yes. That sounds great. Is it ready now?"

"Uh-huh." She nodded. "See you downstairs."

"Wait. Do you have a minute?" he asked. "I'd like to show you something." He valued her opinion.

She shot him a curious glance. "Yes, of course. What have you got?" Mia entered the room and came over to where he sat.

She'd changed from the skirt and top she'd worn earlier in the day to a pair of navy shorts and a slate-blue cotton T-shirt. Fitting, given the temperature would soar into the eighties by late afternoon.

He couldn't help but notice her long, shapely legs and her bare feet with her unpolished toenails. Her riotous curls were pulled back into a ponytail. She really was quite pretty in that girl next door kind of way. All fresh-faced, with a smile that made you feel happy inside when she turned it your way.

He liked it. He liked it a lot.

"What was it you wanted me to see?" she asked.

Hints of the fragrance she wore tickled his nostrils as she stood beside him. He drew in a deep breath and savored the sweet scent.

"Jax?" She turned an uncertain expression at him.

"Yes?" He blinked.

"You wanted to show me something?"

Right. Focus, man. Jax gave himself a mental shake. "What

do you think of this? It reminded me of what you said this morning about nature shots."

"Oh my God." Mia's jaw dropped. A look of awe and wonder spread over her features. "This is amazing, Jax. When I said waterfalls, I was thinking of the one at Long Pond right here in town, not this. But this…it's spectacular. Where was this picture taken?"

"It's Victoria Falls in Zambia."

Her eyes rounded. "As in southern Africa?"

"Yes." Jax chuckled. "I was shooting in the area a few years ago. I photographed this on a weekend excursion at the end of the shoot." Words couldn't describe the thrill he'd received experiencing such majestic beauty.

"Wow. Just wow. I can almost hear the roar of the water as it thunders over the edge. Do you have other images like this one?"

"I have lots." He'd captured at least a couple hundred images that day. Jax called up three more. "Take a look."

"This one." She pointed to the second image. Excitement laced her voice when she spoke. "The double rainbow is totally awesome, and the sun glittering off the water as it thunders over the edge…" She sucked in a deep breath. "It's gorgeous, and powerful, and awe-inspiring all at the same time." Mia ran her palms up and down her arms. "I can almost feel the mist on my skin as it rises from the rocks below."

"I take it you like it." Jax grinned.

"Of course I do. It's incredible. You really are quite talented."

His chest filled to bursting. "Thanks." He was pretty sure his goofy grin had returned. "Maybe you can take a look at the rest of them when you have some time? I'd love your opinion on some of the others."

She smiled, and his heart skipped a beat. "Sure, I'm happy to."

"Perfect." He flashed an answering grin.

"If you two don't come down now, I'm eating without you." Pops's voice boomed from downstairs.

Mia laughed. "We should head down."

"We're coming now, Pops," he called.

The doorbell chimed when they were seated at the table.

"Are you expecting anyone?" he asked.

"No," Pops responded. "It's probably that guy from the solar company again."

"Right." Mia nodded. "He stopped by yesterday. Wanted to speak to the homeowner. You were resting, Pops, and I told him you weren't available. He said he was going to stop by another time."

"I already know I'm not a good candidate. Can you get rid of him for me?" Pops asked.

"Sure thing." Jax rose from the table. He strode toward the door and opened it. "Shane." His brows knit together. "What's up, man? What are you doing here?" Not wanting to disturb Pops's and Mia's lunch, he stepped outside and closed the door.

The sun, which had been out in full force earlier, was hidden behind an ominous black cloud.

"Hey," Shane said. "I wanted to talk to you about something."

"Sure. What is it?"

"It's about Mia. Rumor has it you had dinner with her last night." Shane's voice was calm, but tension radiated from him in waves.

Shit. He'd forgotten how fast the rumor mill worked in this town. "Yes." What else could he say? He wouldn't lie. Not again.

Okay, he hadn't lied before either. Not technically.

Shane had never asked Jax if anything had gone on between him and Mia when he'd visited New Suffolk last winter. Why would he? He'd left Donahue's just as Mia had walked in. He never knew they'd spent that night talking to each other while the others in their little group had watched the football game on the big screens, or how Mia had challenged him to a game of pool, and after a few beers, the talking had turned to flirting.

Shane hadn't known that Mia had followed him out to the parking lot and that somehow their flirting had escalated to not-so-innocent touching, or how they were in his rental car and driving to his hotel in Boston before either of them could come to their senses.

Shane shoved his hands in his pockets. "Was that really a good idea? We both know your time in New Suffolk is temporary."

"The dinner is not what you're thinking." He held up his hands. "We grabbed a bite to eat on the way to the home and garden store. We weren't even supposed to go to the pizzeria, but Mia's ex canceled his dinner plans with her daughters at the last minute, and she needed to feed them."

His answer seemed to throw Shane. "Why were you going to the home and garden store?"

"Oh yeah." Jax grinned. "That's right, you don't know. Pops hired Mia to redesign a couple of rooms downstairs so he can have a master suite on the first floor." He gestured to the house behind him. "It takes the stairs, and another possible fall, out of the equation. Which is fantastic, as far as I'm concerned. We went to the home and garden store to pick up floor and paint samples. Mia even snapped a few photos of bathroom vanities to show him."

"My sister wants to do this?" Shane's bewildered expression shocked him. He appeared to have no idea she was interested in doing such a thing.

"Yes. It was her idea. She laid out a floor plan with one of those interior design programs on her tablet. She showed Pops and me everything she's done to her place this morning. Both Pops and I agree. Mia is quite talented."

Shane nodded, but he still looked confused. "Okay. I won't hold you up." He turned and headed back to his truck. "You want to get together tonight and shoot some pool at Donahue's?"

"Can't." Jax sucked in a deep breath. He could leave it at that, but he wouldn't. He wanted—no, *needed*—to be up front with his friend. Shane deserved that from him.

Jax walked over to where Shane stood. "Your sister and her girls are coming here for dinner tonight. I invited them."

Shane stiffened. "I'm sorry. Could you repeat that? I don't think I heard you correctly."

Jax sighed. "Yeah, you did. I like your sister. She's smart and caring, and I enjoy spending time with her." He hadn't planned on saying that, but he couldn't deny the truth any longer. What that would mean going forward, he couldn't say yet.

All Jax knew for sure was that he wanted to get to know her better. To do that, they needed to spend time together, and Shane needed to know that he planned on doing that.

"No way." Shane shook his head. "I won't see her hurt again."

"I know what you're thinking," Jax said. Shane knew he didn't have the best track record when it came to relationships. Jax wouldn't deny it. He didn't want to see Mia hurt either. "I'm not—"

Shane cut in before he could finish what he'd intended to say. "It's *not* happening."

"Yes, it is." Mia appeared by Jax's side.

He hadn't heard her come outside, but he was glad she was here. She needed to have a say in this as much as he did.

"Why are you making such a big deal about us spending time together?" Mia pointed to him and back to herself. "Jax is a good guy."

"Yeah?" He glanced at Mia, and she smiled.

"Yeah." A hint of pink stained her cheeks, and he grinned. Shane glared at him.

Mia turned her attention to her brother. "So, what's your problem?"

Shane straightened. "You're my sister, and—"

"And what?" She cut Shane off before he could finish his sentence. "You think that gives you the right to dictate my life?"

"Whoa." Shane stepped back. "That's not what I'm doing."

"Really? Because it seems that way to me. I love you, and I appreciate you wanting to protect me, but I am sick and tired of other people making decisions for me and not bothering to ask what I want."

"But—" Shane began. He stopped and started again. "Okay. You want to have dinner with Jax. Fine."

"Ah... Now it's okay because *you* decided that." Mia folded her arms over her chest and glared at Shane. "What part of *I'm a grown woman and I can take care of myself* do you not understand?"

"I know you are." Shane's eyes rounded. "I don't deny that. It's just—"

Mia straightened up to her full height and held her head high. She looked like a goddess. "Let. Me. Make. Myself. Perfectly. Clear. I will do what I want with whomever I want. *I* make the decisions." She pointed a thumb at herself. "Not you and not anyone else. Got it?"

"I, ah... Yeah," Shane stammered. "You make your own decisions."

Mia blew out a breath. "Good. I'm glad we've cleared that up." She gave Shane a peck on his cheek. "Now I'm going back inside to see how Alex is doing. Be nice." She gave her brother a pointed look and marched inside.

Shane stared at him. He looked as if someone had knocked him upside the head with a baseball bat. He opened his mouth and closed it without saying anything. He opened the truck door, pausing before getting in. "Don't hurt her. Or you know what will happen."

Jax nodded. Shane would kick his ass, and he'd deserve it. "Got it. So…" Jax looked his friend in the eye. "Are we good?"

Shane rolled his gaze skyward. "You having dinner with my sister tomorrow night, too?"

He shook his head. "Nope." At least he hadn't planned on it. "Why?"

"Donahue's. Eight thirty. Game on." Shane hopped into his truck.

Jax grinned. Yeah, they were good. "See you there."

He went inside and found Mia sitting with Pops at the table.

"Everything okay?" Pops asked. "Took you long enough to get rid of the guy."

Mia turned a worried expression his way.

He answered Pops's question, but he didn't take his gaze off Mia. "Everything's fine. There's nothing to worry about."

A slow smile crossed her face, and everything seemed right with his world.

Chapter Nine

Mia sat at Alex's dining room table, inputting the rest of his order for the bedroom makeover and bathroom conversion.

She glanced out the glass doors that led to a brick patio and the backyard. Jax was showing all three of her girls some basic soccer skills.

Having finished the task, Mia rose. Walking over, she slid the door open. She stepped outside and sat on one of the wrought iron chairs.

Despite the ominous clouds earlier in the day, the sun shone bright in the early evening sky. The light breeze took the edge off the hotter-than-usual temperature.

She watched as he showed them how to perform a stop-and-go move with the inside foot. Brooke and Aurora picked up the skill fast, but Kiera struggled. It was probably a little advanced for a six-year-old who was just learning how to play the game, but Kiera insisted she was as good as her older sisters.

Mia marveled at the patience and encouragement Jax showed her youngest daughter as she tried over and over to get it right. Finally, after several minutes, Kiera was able to master the move.

"You did it." Jax pumped his fist in the air. "Way to stick with it."

"Good job, Kiera," Brooke said.

"Yeah. That was great," Aurora enthused.

Kiera smiled a mile-wide grin and performed the move again.

"Oh, yeah. You've got it now." Jax gave her a high-five.

He was really good with them, and that surprised her. Not because he wasn't a nice guy, but because children weren't a part of his life. He rubbed elbows with New York's rich and elite art crowd. He didn't play soccer with kids in a backyard in small-town suburbia.

"Did you see that, Mommy?" Kiera waved. "I did it. Just like Brooke and Aurora."

Jax turned and gazed at her, a huge smile on his face.

Mia smiled back. "I did, sweetheart. Great job." She gave her a thumbs-up.

"Is dinner ready?" Aurora asked. "I'm hungry."

"Me too," Brooke said.

"I'm extra hungry, cuz I worked really hard." Kiera rubbed a hand over her belly.

"Not quite yet." Mia glanced at her watch. "The lasagna needs to cool for about fifteen more minutes."

"Who wants to help me make a salad and set the table?" Jax gazed at her three daughters.

"I do," they chorused together.

"All right. Let's clean up and head inside." Jax pointed to the borrowed balls and cones that he'd placed in a straight line a few feet away.

The girls scattered to do his bidding. Soon all the items had been gathered and returned to the nylon mesh bag she'd given him when they'd first come over.

The four of them marched to the patio, with Aurora leading the squad.

"We're going to teach Jax how to cook salad," Kiera announced as she walked by.

"Yep," Brooke agreed.

Mia burst out laughing as Jax approached her.

He grinned. "I'll leave this here for now. I'll remember to grab it when I walk you home later." Setting the bag down near the door, he walked into the house.

Would they share a good-night kiss when they arrived at her door? Mia smiled at the thought. "Wash your hands," she called as she joined them inside. "All of you."

Kiera, Brooke and Aurora raced to the kitchen sink.

Jax paused by her side. "We didn't get much of a chance to talk after your brother left." His soft breath tickled her ear.

She shook her head. "No, we didn't."

Alex had wanted to get back to finalizing his selections for his new bathroom as soon as they'd finished lunch. They'd worked on that until it was time for her to pick up her girls from school.

She'd hoped to catch him when they returned for dinner, but he'd wanted to spend time with Aurora to look at some of the photos she'd taken.

Mia and Alex had played card games with Brooke and Kiera to keep them entertained while Jax and Aurora huddled over the small portfolio Piper had helped Aurora put together.

She couldn't hear what they'd talked about, but her daughter was all smiles, and that was what had mattered to her.

"Maybe we can talk later?" He flashed a hopeful smile.

It was a good thing she'd rushed outside before Shane could get carried away.

She'd probably overreacted a smidge, but after her run-in with Kyle the night before, Shane's high-handedness today had really gotten under her skin.

No, dammit. She hadn't overreacted in the least. She was sick and tired of doing what everyone else wanted her to do. For too long she'd gone along with what Kyle had wanted, to keep the peace.

Look where that got you.

Nowhere good. That's for sure.

Well, no more. She was done placating others and denying her own wants and needs.

So what if she had dinner with Jax? Screw the gossipmongers and anyone else who thought they could influence her life. What she did was no one's business but hers.

And if she wanted to have more dinners with Jax…

That's my decision.

So what did she want?

The truth was, she wasn't sure. She liked spending time with him. Moreover, she liked the man he was turning out to be. Caring, compassionate, supportive. He even seemed to like her kids.

But he was only in town for a short time. He'd go back to his real life as soon as Pops was able to fend for himself. Maybe even sooner, if he hired a daytime caregiver.

Where would that leave her?

"Mia?" Hand on her hip, he kissed her cheek.

She sucked in a deep, steadying breath. Heaven help her, she loved when he touched her. "Yes. Let's talk later."

"Ahem." Leaning on his crutch, Pops stood at the entrance to the dining room. He coughed and gave them a pointed look. "Something in the kitchen smells like it's starting to burn."

"Oh crap. The garlic bread! I put it in the oven before I stepped outside to watch Jax and the girls play." She hurried around the half wall that separated the kitchen and dining room. "I need to take it out before it burns."

"Pops, why don't you sit here while we get the rest of the meal ready." Jax pulled a chair away from the table. Once Alex sat, Jax turned his attention to her girls. "All right, ladies. Let's cook a salad."

Mia watched as her daughters issued instructions and Jax executed them perfectly. Fifteen minutes later, after a boatload of giggles and laughter from all, Jax set a large glass bowl filled with lettuce, tomatoes, cucumbers, diced onions and shredded carrot in the center of the table.

They added plates, glasses, silverware and napkins, and everyone sat.

As they ate, the conversation and laughter reminded her of dinners she'd shared with her family growing up. It was something she hadn't experienced in a long, long time. Even when she was married to Kyle.

Even when they'd sat down as a family, meals were… They weren't quiet, not with three kids, but she'd never experienced this easiness and sense of togetherness.

Mia liked it.

The sound of a phone ringing pierced the air.

Jax pulled his cell from his pocket. "Sorry." He rose from his chair. "I need to take this. I'll be right back." He strode from the room. A moment later she heard his footsteps on the stairs.

"Well." Alex set his fork and knife atop his empty plate. "That was delicious."

"Yeah, Mom," Aurora said. "You're a good cook."

"But not as good as us." Brooke pointed to the empty salad bowl. "Jax says we have mad skills."

Mia chuckled. "Yes, you do."

"So…" Alex turned a curious expression on them. "Who wants dessert? I have fudge pops in the freezer." He rubbed his hands together.

"I do!" Kiera raced to the fridge and jumped up to reach the freezer handle. She tried several times but couldn't grasp it.

"I'll get them." Mia rose and walked over to where Kiera stood. She opened the freezer and handed a Fudgsicle to each of her daughters and Alex.

"Aren't you going to have one?" Alex asked.

"No." She shook her head. "I'm way too full from dinner. Thanks anyway." She was about to sit down when the doorbell rang.

Alex frowned. "I wonder who that could be. I'm not ex-pecting any visitors."

"I'll go check." Mia walked to the front door and opened it. Jax's parents stood on the front porch. "Francine. Gary. It's nice to see you." She wasn't sure what else to say. Alex wasn't expecting them, and Jax hadn't mentioned anything about it either. "Can I help you?" she asked when they just stared at her.

"I'm looking for Jax. Is he here?" Francine smiled.

Jax chose that moment to walk down the stairs and into the living room.

"He's right here," Mia said.

"Sweetheart." Francine brushed past Mia and strode into Alex's living room with her arms held open. Gary followed.

Mia cringed when the color drained from Jax's face.

"Mom. Dad. What are you doing here?" he asked.

"See." Gary gave a pointed look to his wife. "I told you we shouldn't just come over. But no. You never listen."

"Why should I when I know you're wrong?" Jax's mother retorted. "My Jackie is happy to see me. Right?"

"His name is Jax," Gary said. "How many times does he need to tell you, he doesn't like being called Jackie."

Mia's jaw dropped. What was going on?

"Would you two just stop it, please?" Jax looked like he was developing a migraine.

His parents continued bickering as if Jax hadn't spoken.

She shouldn't be here for this. She needed to give them their privacy. "I'll let you three talk." Mia returned to the dining room and found it empty. She walked through the kitchen to the small hall that led to Alex's den. Opening the door, she found her three girls seated on the couch, watching a Disney cartoon.

Alex, who was seated in his recliner, motioned for her to come over.

Mia moved inside and shut the door.

In a low voice, Alex said, "When I realized who was here, I thought it was best to move us as far away as possible."

Mia nodded. Jax obviously had issues with his parents. Given that she'd never seen him in the neighborhood once, in all the years she'd lived here, it made sense. What was the problem?

None of my business. She wouldn't pry. If Jax wanted to tell her at some point, he would.

"We're watching a movie," Kiera said.

"Pops likes this one as much as we do," Brooke added.

"Why don't you join us?" Pops gestured to the couch and gave her a pointed look.

She sat, waiting to see what would happen next.

There was a soft knock on the den door a few minutes later. It opened and Bill walked in. "Hey, everyone."

"Evening, Bill. When did you get here?" Pops asked.

"I just arrived. Jax said you were probably in here. Told me to come on through."

He must still be dealing with his parents, she thought. Otherwise, he would have joined Bill.

Attention trained on Bill, Pops nodded. "Jax was right. You know Mia." He pointed to where she sat. "These are her daughters." Pops introduced Aurora, Brooke and Kiera. "Have a seat. We're watching a movie."

"Actually," Mia started, "I think it's time for us to go. The girls have school tomorrow." Turning to her daughters, she said, "Come on, kiddos. It's time to head home."

A round of "but Mom!" and "Can't we stay just a little longer?" ensued.

"Not tonight," she responded. "What do you say?" She gave a discreet nod of her head toward Alex.

"Thanks, Pops." Kiera marched over and planted a kiss on Alex's cheek. "I had lots of fun."

"Me, too, munchkin." Alex grinned. "Me, too."

"Thank you for having us over tonight, Pops." Brooke tried to hug Alex as best she could.

Aurora copied her sister.

"Thanks again, Alex." Mia kissed his cheek. "I can't remember the last time I had so much fun."

"Why don't you call me Pops?" he said. "Everyone else does." He gestured to her three girls.

A rush of warmth filled her chest. "I'd love to." She leaned down and kissed his cheek again. "Good night, Pops."

Mia found the living room empty when she walked in a moment later.

"Where's Jax?" Aurora asked. "I want to say good-night to him, too, and thank him again for helping me."

"He's not here right now," Mia said. "You can thank him the next time you see him."

"But where'd he go?" Brooke asked.

"Yeah, Mommy. He just disappeared." Kiera peered around the room.

"I'm not sure." Mia wasn't lying. She had no idea where he'd gone off to. "Let's go home now." She herded her daughters to the door.

"I hope he's okay," Kiera said.

Me, too.

Chapter Ten

Jax left his hotel just before eight-thirty the next morning. He drove through town and turned onto Pops's street a few minutes later.

He slowed as he passed his parents' house. He still couldn't believe they'd just shown up at Pops's place last night with no warning.

Actually, that wasn't true. It was what he'd feared might happen if they found out he was here. *This is why you don't live in New Suffolk anymore.* Hell, it was why he spent most of his time traveling to other parts of the world. *Far, far away.* They couldn't drop by if he wasn't around.

He pulled into Pops's driveway a moment later and hopped out of the car.

He hadn't handled things well last night. It had been bad enough that Pops had overheard their behavior. Then again, he'd seen it before, but Mia...

Perspiration covered his skin just thinking about the horrified expression on her face when she'd seen them in action.

Jax opened the door and stepped inside. "Morning," he called.

Bill walked into the living room a moment later. "Hey, Jax. I'm going to head out now. Alex is in the den, watching TV. He's eaten his breakfast. Said he didn't need a pain pill yet."

"Okay, thanks. Any issues last night?" he asked.

"None at all. I'll see you later." Bill strode to the front door.

"Bye," Jax called as Bill stepped outside and closed the door.

Jax walked into the den and sat on the couch. "Hey, Pops." He picked up the paper and began reading the front page.

"Is that all I get? Aren't you gonna tell me what happened with your parents?"

Jax sighed. "Yes. I was going to explain. I was just working my way up to it."

"Well?" Pops gave him a pointed look.

"Not much to tell." Jax shrugged. "I told them that it wasn't a good time, and I asked them to leave."

"You left, too."

"Yeah. As soon as Bill arrived." He hadn't even said good-bye to Mia and the girls. The sudden jolt of seeing his parents standing there, in front of him, had set off the fight-or-flight response inside him. All of a sudden, he was a kid again, and he'd bolted as fast as he could.

Idiot, idiot, idiot.

He wasn't a kid anymore. He was a grown man. He needed to act like one.

"Probably not the best course of action," Pops said.

"Nope." Jax dragged a hand through his hair. "Definitely could have handled things better." Especially with Mia. He wouldn't blame her if she was pissed as hell at him. He deserved it for the way he'd acted.

The doorbell chimed. A moment later, a feminine voice called out, "Good morning."

"That'll be Mia." Pops gave Jax a pointed look. "I'll stay in here and give you two some privacy."

"Thanks." Jax set down the morning paper and rose. He needed to try to explain.

Jax exited the den and closed the door. He walked down the short hall and into the living room.

"Hi, Jax." Mia shot him a curious look.

"Hey." He walked over to where she stood and grasped her hands in his. "I'm so sorry, Mia. I wanted to call you last night, but it was after midnight before I got back to my hotel." He'd walked around downtown for hours after he'd left Pops's place. "I didn't think you'd appreciate me waking you up."

She gave a soft chuckle, and he started to relax. "You're right, I wouldn't have." Her expression turned serious. "Are you okay?"

Was he? He wasn't sure. *Isn't that just pathetic?*

Why did he keep letting his parents get to him?

Jax dropped down on the living room couch and scrubbed his hands over his face. "I'm sorry you had to see…" *A glimpse of what my family is really like.* His stomach churned.

"We don't have to talk about what happened if you don't want to." Mia sat beside him and kissed his cheek.

Jax rarely talked about his parents with anyone. Why would he want people to know just how dysfunctional his family was?

He didn't. That was why he presented his happy-go-lucky image to the world. The enigmatic, easygoing artist who didn't have a care in the world.

The thing was, he wanted to talk about them with *her*. Jax wanted Mia to know the real him.

He blew out a breath. Lord, he couldn't even think about what that meant now.

"I'd like to tell you." He paused for a moment, to steady himself, and began. "As you've probably figured out, my parents don't exactly have the best marriage. The truth is, I'm not even sure why they're still together."

"Do they fight all the time?" Mia's quiet voice was filled with compassion.

Jax sucked in a deep breath and released it. "I wouldn't call it fighting. They bicker. Over anything and everything. The shortest distance into town, which car gets the best gas mileage." He shook his head. "It doesn't make any sense. They have the same make and model, just different colors."

Mia smiled and he did, too.

"Anyway, they've been that way for as long as I can remember. It may not sound like such a big deal. Lots of couples quarrel now and again, but they do it all the time. It wears on you after a while. You get to the point where you'll do anything to avoid being around it."

Mia squeezed his hands, but said nothing.

"It's like they're in competition with each other, with me stuck in the middle." Agitated, he released her hands. Jax stood and started pacing back and forth across the living room. "You saw that last night. My father insisting he was right and my mother doing the same. They turn to me to decide the winner."

"I can't imagine what that must have been like for you."

Most people probably couldn't. As far as he was concerned, it wasn't normal to make your child choose one parent over the other. "It's a no-win situation, that's for sure. The only way I can deal with it is to spend as much time away as I can. When I was younger, I used to hang out at Pops's. Your house, too."

"That's why you left town the minute you graduated from high school, isn't it?"

"I needed to be away."

Mia stood and came over to him. "I understand."

"You're probably wondering why I don't just cut ties and be done with them."

She shook her head. "Family dynamics are never that easy."

"No," he agreed. "You know what the kicker is?" He didn't wait for her to answer. "There have been times, over the years, when I would interact with each of them one-on-one, and I'd think, man, this is great. This is how it's supposed to be. It didn't happen frequently but—"

"It gave you hope," Mia said.

He nodded. What a fool he'd been to have that. "Last year,

my dad had a heart attack. I remember standing in the hospital thinking, I can't lose him. Despite everything, I loved him."

"Jax." Care and compassion filled her gaze. "There's no shame in that."

"To my amazement, the bickering and competitiveness stopped." Jax let loose a mirthless laugh. "It was like they'd morphed into different people overnight. We were like a real family, rallying around each other during a tough time. It was how I'd always dreamed it would be. I remember thinking that as bad as Dad's heart attack was, at least one good thing had come of it."

"The peace didn't last," Mia said.

"Nope." He'd been a fool to believe it would. "They started in on each other before Dad was released from the hospital— right back to their old ways as if nothing had happened."

"Oh, Jax. I'm so sorry." Mia hugged him.

Jax clamped his arms around her and held on as if his life depended on it. Maybe it did.

Oh, man, he needed to get a grip. Fast.

He released his hold but didn't move away. "So…now you know the truth."

"I do." Mia locked her gaze with his. "It doesn't change anything, as far as I'm concerned."

"Are you sure about that?" Wasn't she worried that maybe, just maybe, he was just like his parents? He sure as hell was. It was his worst fear. It was why he'd left New Suffolk all those years ago. It was why he stayed away.

It was why he avoided real relationships.

He couldn't be like them.

"One hundred percent," she said.

Jax shuddered. "How do you know?"

"Because I know you. You have a huge heart." Mia's smile lit up the dark places inside him.

No one had ever said such a thing about him before. Ever.

"I see it in the way you helped a little girl you don't even know all that well learn how to master a skill. Instead of belittling or embarrassing her, because she couldn't get it on the first try, you encouraged her and cheered her on.

"I see it in the way you care for Pops, and in the way you've inspired Aurora." Mia let loose a soft chuckle. "She wants to go on a photoshoot around town and practice some of the things you taught her.

"Then there's the way you've encouraged me to pursue my dream of home design. And let's not forget how you came over because you thought I was in trouble the other night."

Jax didn't like Mia's ex, and he wasn't about to let him push her around, if he had anything to say about it.

"So yes, trust me when I say you're one of the good guys, Jax. And don't you forget it." She grinned again. "Now, where's Pops? I need to update him on the status of his remodel."

Jax blew out a breath, happy with the subject change. "In the den watching TV." He jumped up and stood beside her.

Mia crossed the living room and started down the short hallway. "I talked to my mother last night."

"How is Jane doing?" She'd always been good to him growing up. "I haven't seen her in a while."

"She's good. Busy with work. She says that they have someone at TK Construction who can start immediately."

"Who?" he asked.

"Nick Turner."

"How's he doing these days?" Jax shot her a quizzical glance. "Last time I saw him, he was supposed to be getting married."

"Isabelle broke things off about a month ago. Nick has been in a major slump ever since."

"Oh man. That sucks. Maybe we can go for a beer while I'm in town."

Mia smiled a mile-wide grin. "See? One of the good guys."

Jax chuckled. "You are so good for my ego," he said, only

half joking. The truth was, she had a way of making him see himself in a new light.

He felt...different with her. Freer, or maybe more content with himself. Which meant what?

He wasn't sure, and that made him a little nervous. A lot nervous, if he was being honest.

"Ha ha. I just call it like I see it," she quipped. Opening the door, she walked into the den. "Good morning." Mia greeted Pops with a peck on his cheek. "How are you doing today?"

"Feeling fine." Pops shot him an is-everything-all-right look. Jax nodded, and Pops smiled.

"Good." Mia sat on the end of the couch closest to Pops. "I've got an idea." Her eyes twinkled with delight.

His heart beat a rapid tattoo. She really was quite beautiful, especially when she smiled.

"Oh yeah?" Pops sent her a quizzical glance. "What's that?"

"How about we go for a little field trip today?" she suggested. "The weather is perfect this morning for a walk on the pier. I can load your wheelchair into the back of my SUV. The fresh air will be great for you."

"That sounds great," Jax said. "Mind if I tag along?" Because, yeah, he wanted to spend more time with her.

"I thought your agent was coming up here today to check on you?" Pops grumbled.

"She's not checking up on me," he protested. Although Pops was probably right, despite what Cate had told him when she'd called first thing this morning. He couldn't blame her. He was slacking off when he should be focusing on saving his career. While it was still one of his top priorities, he could no longer say it was the most important or the only thing he cared about.

He hadn't realized it before, but he was burned out. He'd been pushing himself for more than ten years now. Show after show. Shoot after shoot. Yes, he'd become successful and quite wealthy, but he wanted—no, *needed*—more.

What that meant going forward, he couldn't say. But Cate was right about one thing. He needed to make some changes.

"Cate was supposed to come today, but she postponed until next week. She's taking a last-minute trip to Iceland with friends."

She'd tried to convince him to come with her. *Just think about the topography. All that lava, and those glaciers. Talk about raw and edgy. It could be the new thing you're looking for.*

He'd declined. Of course he had. He couldn't leave now. Not until he could hire a daytime caregiver to help Pops while he recovered.

Cate wasn't pleased. She was pissed as hell.

Yes, she was planning to come up in person to check up on him, all right. Jax wouldn't think about it now. "That leaves me free to join you."

Mia grinned from ear to ear, and his heartbeat kicked up a notch.

What am I going to do about you, Mia?

"Perfect," she said. "We'd love for you to come along, right, Pops?"

"Sure. Why not." He flashed a smug little smile at Jax.

Jax laughed. He couldn't help it. The matchmaker was gloating.

"Give me a minute to grab my camera." Maybe he'd find some inspiration while they walked. It couldn't hurt, that's for sure.

"Sounds like a plan," Mia said.

Twenty minutes later, Mia pulled her SUV into the parking lot at the town beach. It was still early enough in the season to find a parking spot near the fence that divided the dunes from the hardtop.

A light breeze blew as he hopped out of her vehicle. Jax lifted his head and let the sun shine down on his face.

"Happy?" Mia came up beside him.

He nodded. "I love the beach. There's something about the water that soothes my soul."

"Me, too. I remember coming here with my dad when I was little. We used to grab cookies at the Coffee Palace. That was back when Abby's mom owned the place.

"We'd walk along the boardwalk and talk." A sad smile crossed her face. "I'd tell him all my secret hopes and dreams."

"Including wanting to be a home designer some day?"

She nodded. "We were going to be a team."

"So what happened?" he asked. "Why give up that dream?"

"It was hard to think about pursuing those dreams when Dad couldn't be a part of them anymore."

"It hurt too much." Jax remembered the impact Victor's death had had on him. It would have been so much worse for Mia and her family.

"Especially in the beginning." A shudder ran through her.

Jax put a arm around her and gave her a quick hug.

She flashed a small smile. "And then I got married. The kids came along." Mia shrugged. "And... Life happened."

"Yes. It tends to do that." He gave a soft chuckle. The wind blew, and a curl fell in her face. Jax brushed it away, luxuriating in the feel of her soft, smooth skin beneath his palm. "Don't give up on your dreams. It would be a shame to waste your talent."

Mia headed toward the back of her SUV. "When was the last time you went to the beach? Was it in some exotic location, like Africa or any of the other interesting places you've traveled to since you left?"

Jax peered around. "I can't even remember the last time I went to the shore." He thought about it for a minute. "Anywhere. I probably haven't been to the beach since I left New Suffolk last."

"I come as often as possible. It reminds me of fun times.

Life is short, and you need to enjoy as many of the special moments as possible."

Jax grinned. "Amen to that."

She shot him a quizzical glance. "Do you ever miss it? New Suffolk, I mean?"

Jax shrugged. "I never really had time to think about it. I was always off somewhere on a photo shoot somewhere." The truth was he never *wanted* to think about his life here. It was easier that way. "I've missed Pops. I wish I could spend more time with him."

"I know he loves having you here." Mia opened the trunk.

What about you? he wanted to ask, but couldn't. He'd promised Shane he wouldn't hurt her, and he wouldn't. "I like being here, with him too," he said instead. "Let me get that." He reached for the wheelchair at the same time Mia did.

Their hands touched, and a hundred-gigawatt jolt of want shot through him. Could Mia feel it too?

Her gaze flew to his. She couldn't hide the need in her eyes.

Mia moved her hand away. Too soon for his liking.

"Thanks," she said.

"Will you two stop jabbering and get me out of here?" Pops turned his body toward him and Mia and glared. "You promised me some fresh air today. Near as I can tell, I'm not gonna get that sitting in here."

"Relax." Jax chuckled and set the chair on the pavement. "Do you want Mia to think you're a grumpy old man?"

"I'm not old," Pops retorted.

Mia laughed. She grabbed the chair handles and wheeled it around to the passenger side of the car. "All right. Let's get you out of there."

Pops twisted and lowered his good foot toward the ground, inching forward until it was firmly planted on the pavement.

"Lean on me," Jax encouraged, wrapping an arm around Pops's waist.

Pops placed a hand on Jax's shoulder.

Mia brought the chair up next to him, and Pops sat. With a push of a button, she locked and closed the door. "Okay, Mother Nature. Bring on the fresh air." She pushed the chair toward the pier.

"Are we going to walk to the lighthouse at the end?" Pops asked.

"Yes." Mia nodded. "It's not too far. About a half mile round trip. We can try the boardwalk after, if you're feeling up to it. It's concrete, so it shouldn't be any trouble."

"That sounds good," Pops said.

Mia looked at him. "With any luck, we'll see some seals today. It's still early enough in the season that they should be here."

Pops turned his attention to Jax. "I used to take you here to see them when you were a little kid."

"I remember." He'd loved to see them frolic and play.

Mia maneuvered the chair from the asphalt onto the concrete pier. As they walked, a light wind blew.

"It really is a perfect day to be outside," he said. "Not too hot and not too cold."

They walked in silence for a few minutes, enjoying the mist from the waves crashing against the quay and the sounds of seagulls squawking.

"Oh look." Mia's voice was laced with excitement. "On the rocks." She pointed off to the right.

Jax smiled. "The seals." He lifted his camera and started shooting.

Pops let out a loud hoot when one of the bigger seals pushed a smaller one off the rock so he could sun himself. The smaller guy went skidding down the slight hill and landed with a thud in the cold water.

"Oh, that poor little guy," Mia said.

Jax turned to her, and the breath whooshed out of him.

With the breeze gently blowing her curls and a huge smile on her face, she looked absolutely stunning. Jax snapped a few frames, wanting to capture the moment.

Slight color tinged her cheeks when she realized he was photographing her. "We should continue walking."

"Absolutely," Pops agreed.

"I'm going to grab some images of the tide coming in," he said. "I'll meet up with you when you come back this way."

"Okay," Mia and Pops said in unison.

"Good luck," Pops said as he turned to leave.

"Thanks." He was going to need it. An idea was forming in his head. Thanks to Mia, he might have found his new direction.

Chapter Eleven

Mia's front doorbell chimed later that evening. She placed the last dirty plate in the dishwasher and dried her hands on a paper towel.

Then she walked to the front door and opened it.

Piper and Layla stood on the front porch with big grins on their faces.

Mia's brows drew together in a deep V. "What are you two doing here? Did I forget we were supposed to be getting together tonight?"

"No," Piper said. "We want the scoop on you and Jax."

"Yes," Layla agreed.

Piper crossed her arms over her chest. "I can't believe you had dinner with the man. *Twice.* And never told me about it. I had to hear it from Layla. Who had to hear it from *Shane.*" She shot Mia a curious glance. "Speaking of our brother, was he as bad with Jax as he was with Cooper?"

Mia laughed. She remembered Piper telling her how their brother had caught her and Cooper Turner in a not-even-close-to-being-innocent embrace when they'd first started dating. "I'd say he reacted about the same." She stepped aside and motioned the two women to come in.

"Where are my nieces?" Piper asked. "I expected one of them to answer the door instead of you."

"With their father. He picked them up after school today

for the Memorial Day weekend. He's got them until Monday night."

"You okay?" Piper walked over and wrapped an arm around her shoulder. "This is probably the first time you've been without the girls for more than a day since Aurora was born."

"I know. I'm more concerned about them than me." She wiped at a tear that had formed in the corner of her eye. "Aurora called earlier. She said that Kiera was crying because she wanted to come home."

"Ah, hell." Piper squeezed her tight.

"I talked to her, and she did calm down but…" Mia shook her head. "I can't change this. We're all going to have to get used to how it is now."

"You'll get through this." Layla squeezed her hand.

"I hope so." Mia gave her a watery smile.

"You will," Piper asserted. "And the girls will be fine. You know how I know?"

Mia shook her head.

Piper smiled. "Because you're a great mom and love them with all your heart."

"She's one hundred percent right." Layla grinned.

"You guys are the best." She threw her arms around both women. "What would I do without you?"

"Lucky for you, you don't have to worry about that," Piper said. "Oh, and look who else just arrived." She pointed to the car pulling into Mia's driveway.

Mia laughed as Abby and Elle stepped out of Abby's car and walked toward the front door.

"What have you got there?" Piper pointed to the large box Elle was carrying as she stepped inside.

"Just a few treats from the Coffee Palace." Abby hugged each of the women.

"I made some carrot cake muffins with cream cheese frosting," Elle said.

"But that's not all." Abby wiggled her brows. "She also made some kind of chocolate concoction that is to die for."

"That's why they call it Death by Chocolate." Elle grinned. "I just gave it a new twist. Instead of a parfait, I added the filling to a chocolate shell."

"It sounds delicious. Is this a coffee night, or should I break open a bottle of dessert wine?" Mia asked.

"No need to break into your stash." Layla reached inside the bag she was carrying and handed Mia a bottle. "Piper and I stopped at the store on the way over."

"Well then." Mia gestured for everyone to grab a seat. "Let me take this into the kitchen and open it."

"I'll grab some plates." Piper followed her to the kitchen.

"Wait, we're coming with." Abby rushed to join them. "We all want to hear what's going on with Jax and Mia."

"That's right," Elle said. She and Layla followed.

Mia grabbed a corkscrew from the drawer. "Sorry to disappoint. There's nothing to tell." She uncorked the bottle and set it back on the counter.

"But you had dinner together." Layla handed her five wineglasses.

"Twice," Piper said again.

"Come on. Dish." Elle placed the pastries on a plate she found in one of Mia's cupboards. "Inquiring minds want to know."

Mia shook her head. "There's nothing to tell. Really. We went to the pizzeria the night before last because Kyle canceled at the last minute, and I needed to feed the girls."

"I can see that. It's your go-to place when you're in a hurry." Piper grabbed a stack of paper plates and napkins from Mia's pantry. "But why was Jax with you?"

Mia sighed. None of them were going to leave this alone until they got every last detail. "We were supposed to go to the home and garden store. I'm doing a little work over at Alex

Papadopoulos's house." She gestured to Pops's house across the street. "Jax was going to help me pick out some color and floor samples for Pops to choose from."

"Shane mentioned you were doing that," Layla said as they all walked back into the living room. "He seemed really surprised you wanted to do something like that."

"What's she talking about?" Piper asked.

Mia understood why Piper was staring at her as if she'd grown another head. She used to talk about going into business with her father a lot when she was younger, but she'd lost interest after he passed.

Mia told them about her dream of opening her own home design firm someday.

"How long have you wanted to do this?" Elle asked.

"A long time now," Mia admitted.

"So you're opening your own business." Abby gave her an approving nod.

"It's about time." Piper wrapped an arm around her shoulders and grinned. "I'm so proud of you."

Mia held up a hand to stop whatever was about to come next. She needed to clarify. "Not quite yet." All of her old reasons for waiting were still valid. The biggest was that she wasn't in a position to quit her teaching job yet. "But this project over at Alex's house is the perfect opportunity for me to dip my toes in the water and see what I can do."

Abby peered around the room. "I think your designs are great. I might even have a job for you, if you're interested. After you're done with your current project, that is."

"What are you looking to do?" Mia couldn't hide her excitement.

"I've wanted to make some changes to the Coffee Palace for a while now."

"I remember you saying that when Cooper and I were renovating the space above Layla's restaurant for my art gallery," Piper said.

"That's right." Mia grinned. "Let's talk when you have some time."

Abby nodded. "I'll call you later in the week."

"All right. Now that we've got that settled, let's get back to you and Jax." Elle grinned and rubbed her hands together. "We want all the juicy details."

"I told you, I don't have any juicy details." So far, nothing had happened between them. Not since that first night. Was it really four months ago?

The truth was, she'd felt different since then. Sure, the sex had been fantastic. *Phenomenal.* But something had changed that evening. She'd finally realized she deserved better.

Jax was better. More than that. He was someone she could be herself with. Something she'd never been able to do with Kyle.

"But you want there to be juicy details." Her sister grinned.

"Yes." Mia groaned, but she was smiling.

"Where are you off to?" Pops gave Jax a speculative glance.

"Meeting Shane at Donahue's for a game of pool."

Two full days had passed since Shane had showed up here and had confronted him about Mia, and he and Mia hadn't talked yet. Which meant what? Was she having second thoughts?

No. He wouldn't consider the possibility.

"Have fun," Pops said.

That wouldn't be hard. As much as he wanted to see Mia tonight and figure out where they stood, he wanted to hang with his friend. He enjoyed the comradery they'd shared since the first day they met, back in kindergarten. Twenty-five years of true friendship. Even when they'd gone their separate ways after high school, they'd get together and pick up right where they'd left off. It was still like that to this day.

How lucky was he to have a friend like that?

Lucky indeed. He was going to miss Shane when he went back to the city.

"I will. See you tomorrow." Jax hugged the older man. "Don't give Bill a hard time."

"Don't worry. He won't." Bill walked into the den with two glasses of water in his hands.

Pops muttered something under his breath that Jax couldn't make out, and he chuckled.

Jax slid behind the wheel of his Porsche and drove the short distance into town.

He pulled his car into a spot in the rear parking lot at Donahue's, away from everyone else. No use taking a chance someone might hit his vehicle. Exiting his car, he texted Shane.

Here.

The last of the sunlight faded away as he made his way to the back entrance to the bar.

He walked inside and headed left.

Jax peered around the establishment and spotted Shane at the far pool table. He strode over.

"Rawlins," Nick Turner said as Jax approached the table.

Nick's brothers, Levi and Cooper, appeared by Nick's side.

Jax's brows drew together. "Hey, guys." He acknowledged the three men with a nod of his head. "Didn't know you'd be joining Shane and me tonight."

"We've got a few questions for you," Levi said.

He shot a curious expression at them. "Okay." Shoving his hands in the front pockets of his jeans, Jax adopted a casual stance. "What's up?"

"We just want to make sure we're all on the same page when it comes to you and Mia," Levi said.

Shit. Jax shot a questioning glance at Shane who stood across from him, on the other side of the table.

Shane lifted a brow and lifted one shoulder as if to say, can you blame them?

No. He couldn't. The Turner men might not be Mia's biological brothers, but that didn't matter. The two families had a long history together. Their fathers had been best friends since childhood. They'd started TK Construction more than thirty-five years ago. The Turner and Kavanaugh kids had grown up with each other. That made for one hell of a strong bond.

Resigned to the inquisition, Jax sighed. "News sure does travel fast in a small town."

Cooper nodded. "It sure does. So, what's going on with you and Mia?"

At this point, Jax wasn't sure what to say. Technically, nothing had happened between them.

"We don't want to see Mia hurt." Nick shot an accusing glare at him. "Not again. She's been through enough the last year and a half."

"I know that," he said.

Nick got up in his face. "The last thing she needs is someone toying with her emotions."

"Whoa," Cooper said.

"Take it down a notch, brother." Levi clamped a hand on Nick's shoulder and jerked him away from Jax.

Jax let the aggression slide this one time. He had a funny feeling Nick was reacting more to what his ex-fiancée had done to him than anything related to the current situation.

"Guys," he pulled his hands from his pockets and lifted them in a placating gesture. "I know that you're trying to protect Mia." Jax couldn't be mad at them for it. As a matter of fact, he respected the heck out of the three brothers for having Mia's best interests at heart. "I appreciate you've got her back, but there's nothing going on between Mia and me. We had a couple of dinners together."

Shane walked over to stand beside Nick, Levi and Cooper. He clapped Jax on the shoulder. "You said you liked her."

"I do." A lot, but he wasn't going to say that out loud. Not to these guys. Especially when he wasn't sure how Mia felt, and he didn't want to guess. "I'd like to spend some time getting to know her better."

"What does that mean to you?" Nick asked, "Because Mia isn't a fling kind of girl, and you're not sticking around New Suffolk for any length of time."

He wasn't saying anything Jax didn't already know. The truth was, he wasn't sure how to address either of those issues at this point in time. "I want to go on a few dates with her and see where it goes."

Levi opened his mouth to speak, but Jax lifted a hand to stop him. He straightened his shoulders and held his head high. "Look, guys. I don't have a crystal ball. I don't know where Mia and I go from here, but I *can* tell you this. I care about Mia. What's more, I respect her. I won't lie to her and I won't play games." He paused for a moment and added, "And I won't make promises I can't keep."

"That's good to hear, Rawlins." Levi nodded. "Cause you know what will happen if she sheds even one tear over you."

"Exactly," Nick practically growled.

"Lay off, you guys." Cooper rolled his gaze skyward. "There's no need to threaten the man. I think we've made our position clear."

Jax nodded. "I'm glad Mia has so many people who care about her."

Cooper clapped him on the shoulder. "Now let's have a drink and play some pool."

"I'm in." Levi flashed a cocky grin. "Especially since Rawlins is buying tonight."

"That's mighty friendly of you," Cooper said.

Jax laughed. "Sure. Why not."

"Okay for me to join in now?" A gruff voice said behind him.

"Hey, Duncan," Levi greeted. "Yep. We're done now."

Jax walked over to where Duncan stood. "Glad you could make it."

"Me, too," Duncan said.

"Enough chit chattin'," Shane said. "Let's play."

Jax caught a glimpse of Nick heading toward the door. He hurried to catch him. "Leaving already?"

Nick's expression turned wary. "You might have already noticed I'm not good company these days."

Yet another reason he had avoided a serious relationship like the plague. It wreaked havoc on you when things ended. "Come on. A night out with the guys will do you good," he said.

Nick nodded and walked back to the table beside him. He shot a sidelong glance at Jax. "You're okay in my book."

A rush of warmth flooded his chest. "Thanks, man." He grinned.

Chapter Twelve

Jax pulled his Porsche into the empty parking lot at the public beach at five the next morning. Technically, the beach was still closed. It wouldn't open until sunrise, twenty minutes from now. Still, he couldn't pass up the opportunity to capture some images as the darkness faded and golden rays touched a cloudless blue sky.

He looped the camera strap around his neck. Snagging the cup of coffee he'd grabbed from the hotel, he exited the car and locked the door.

Jax sipped the aromatic brew as he walked to the path that led from the parking lot to the beach. He listened to the ebb and flow of the waves crashing on shore.

The black sky had faded to gray by the time he reached the sand. Jax sucked in a lungful of sea air and gloried in the magnificent beauty surrounding him.

He headed toward the water and started walking along the shore, snapping images as he made his way.

Jax stopped short when he spotted the huge, partially washed away sandcastle in front of him.

He smiled. How many times had he and Pops built whole sand cities here when he was younger?

Too many times to count, that's for sure.

He peered around. The beach might be empty now, but it

wouldn't be for long. Once school let out for the year, the sand would be filled with umbrellas, blankets, and towels.

He'd had some good times here, especially when he was a teenager. He and Shane and their friends would hit the beach every day during the summer. Boogie boards and games of volleyball by day, hanging on the boardwalk at night. Not to mention their favorite activity—bikini watching.

He let loose a soft chuckle. Yeah, they'd done a lot of that.

Mia and her friends were here, too.

He used to watch her, covertly of course. He hadn't wanted Shane to know he was… curious, yes that was the right word, about his sister. There had always been something about her that had tugged at his senses.

Jax started walking again. A sand crab scurried across his path. He lifted his camera to grab a shot, just like he'd done all those years ago after Pops had given him the camera.

He grinned, remembering how he'd entered that photo in the school's art show that year. It had earned second prize.

Jax thought for a moment, it was also the first picture he'd ever taken of wild life in its natural habitat.

The start of my illustrious career.

He turned and made his way back the way he'd come. He looked around again. Not another soul dotted the landscape. Yes, he was alone, like most of his photo shoots, but this morning he was filled with a sense of peace and contentment.

He marveled at the concept. Never in his wildest imagination would he have guessed he'd experience such a thing. Here, in New Suffolk, of all places. Sure, the run-in with his parents had…sucked. There was no other word for it. Talking to Mia had lightened the burden in a way that talking to Pops couldn't.

Another novelty he'd never experienced before.

The first hints of dawn glimmered in the sky.

Jax gulped the last of the coffee. He tossed the empty cup

in the trash can by the changing cabana, and started snapping more images of the sea and sky.

A few minutes later, hues of blue and yellow streaked the heavens.

He lowered the camera, taking a minute to review the shots he'd taken. A smile crossed his face. Yes. These would do nicely.

Maybe, just maybe, he'd found his new groove.

Jax pulled his Porsche into Pops's driveway an hour later. He popped the rest of the breakfast sandwich he'd purchased at the Coffee Palace into his mouth and hopped out of the car. After grabbing his camera, he slung it around his neck. He'd edit the photos this morning and, with any luck, convince Mia and Pops to go on another walk around lunchtime.

He walked the short distance to the front door and stepped inside. *What the—*

Stacks of boxes littered the living room floor. They hadn't been there last night, when he'd left to meet Shane at Donahue's.

Bill walked in carrying another box. "Morning, Jax. You're here early."

He nodded. "What's going on? Where'd all the boxes come from?"

"The den." Mia appeared and set yet another box down on the living room floor.

He stared at her. "What are you doing here? It's only—" He glanced at his watch. "Six thirty."

"I've been packing up all of Pops's things."

"He's in there now. *Supervising.*" Bill let out a chuckle. He set the box he'd been carrying on the floor. "I'm going to get his breakfast started and head out as soon as he's done eating."

"Thanks, Bill," Jax said.

"You're welcome. Just doing my job." Bill grinned and disappeared into the kitchen.

"I'm going to grab another box." Mia turned to leave.

"Wait." Jax walked over to where she stood and placed a hand on her arm. The sensation of smooth skin mixed with a hint of fresh-cut flowers flooded his senses. "You don't need to do this."

She smiled. "Yes, I do. Nick will start work on Tuesday, and the room needs to be completely empty by then."

"Where are your girls?" he asked.

"They're with their father."

"Still, I should be doing this. Last I checked, you're the home designer. You're not responsible for clearing a client's space."

"No, but I don't mind helping. Besides, don't you have photos to take?" She pointed to the camera in his hand.

"I was going to edit the images I captured this morning, but that can wait."

"Lucky for you, it doesn't have to." Mia waved her hand around the room. "As you can see, we're pretty much done. Go do what you have to do with your photographs. I've got this."

"Okay, okay. I'll go." Jax lingered a moment longer. Heaven help him, he liked being next to her.

He sucked in a deep breath and blew it out slowly. "Thanks." He pressed his lips to her cheek.

"You're welcome," she said.

How was it that a smile from her could make everything better, even when things weren't bad?

Jax knew he should leave, but a team of wild horses couldn't have dragged him away.

Mia must have been suffering from the same affliction, because she didn't move either.

Lord, he wanted to kiss her. Feel the press of her lips beneath his. Tangle his tongue with hers. So much so, he ached with the need.

Did she want that too? He needed to find out. Sure, this

wasn't the best time or place to have a private discussion, but if he waited for that, he'd grow old and gray.

"Mia." Jax trained his gaze on her. "I—"

"Hey, are you guys hungry?" Bill walked into the living room. "I don't mind making extra eggs and toast."

"No, thanks." Mia let loose a nervous chuckle.

"Mia, can you come help me with this?" Pops called from the other room.

Jax sighed. Just his lousy luck. "Nothing for me either, Bill, but thanks for the offer."

"I should go and see what Pops wants," Mia said.

He nodded. "See you later."

"I'm counting on it." Mia grinned. Turning, she walked toward the den.

His pulse soared.

Jax leaned back in the chair and rubbed the back of his neck with his hand.

He clicked through photos he'd been editing from the shoot this morning at the beach.

They were different, all right. Not just the composition, but the feeling it conveyed.

The waves seemed to ebb and flow in a peaceful easy way. The complete opposite of what he remembered; the angsty tumultuous, churn of his youth.

The calm after the storm?

The truth was, the water wasn't any different today than it had been all those years ago.

It was all about perspective.

Maybe his was changing?

Jax's stomach gave a loud rumble. He glanced at his watch. Two o'clock. Mia had come up earlier to see if he wanted to join her and Pops for lunch, but he'd declined. He'd wanted to finish editing the pictures he'd taken this morning.

He stood and stretched. Pops's house seemed quieter than normal. Frowning, he walked downstairs and peered around.

The sound of the television drew him to the den. Pops sat in his recliner with a light blanket over him. A soft snore indicated he was asleep.

Where was Mia?

The bedroom door was cracked open, and he looked inside. She stood in the far corner of the room, rolling paint on the walls and dancing to music he couldn't hear.

He walked over and tapped her on the shoulder. "Hey, Mia."

A small scream came from her. Paint roller in hand, she whirled around to face him, a startled expression on her face.

"Oh my gosh. You startled me." She pulled an ear bud from her ear. "What's up?" Her smile turned to a cringe when she noticed the paint she'd flung on his face and T-shirt. "I'm so sorry."

Jax blinked a couple of times. "Don't worry about it." He grabbed the hem of his shirt and wiped his face. "Those were some epic dance moves you had going there."

"You saw that?" Mia's face turned fire-engine red.

"Yes, I did." He waggled his brows. "What were you listening to?"

"Taylor Swift."

"You're a Swiftie?" he asked. "Me too."

She grinned. "So are Aurora, Brooke and Kiera. We have dance parties together when I'm cooking dinner."

Jax chuckled. "If I'd known that, we could have had a dance party the other night."

"There's always next time."

He liked that she wanted a next time.

"You know, the paint is supposed to go on the walls, not on you." He wiped at the light gray streak on her left cheekbone.

"I was hurrying. I want to get as much done as I can before Pops wakes up. I need to get this room done before work starts on converting the den to a bathroom." Her eyes widened. "Yikes. I really got you good, didn't I?"

"My fault. I shouldn't have startled you." He grinned.

"Indeed." She grinned back. "Take off your shirt before the paint dries."

Heat pooled low in his belly. "That sounds promising." He winked at her.

Her cheeks flamed even brighter. "I meant so I could toss it in the laundry. If I wash it while the paint is still wet, it might come out."

"I'm not arguing." He pulled the shirt over his head and dangled it on his finger in front of her. "Here you go."

She made no move to take it from him. She just stared, wide-eyed, with her lips slightly parted, and yeah, he heard the quick, tiny inhale of breath.

Jax mustered his best innocent expression. It wasn't like he was going to start anything with Pops snoozing in the next room. He wasn't about to tempt fate again.

Still...he loved the way she was looking at him right now. There was so much want in her glittering gaze.

He swallowed hard. "I thought you wanted to throw this in the wash." Was that gruff voice his?

One little kiss couldn't hurt, could it?

He wouldn't be able to stop at one. No. When he and Mia got together again, and they would if he had anything to say about it, he wouldn't allow anything to interrupt them.

"Umm...right." Her gaze snapped into focus. She grabbed the shirt and turned away. "Be right back," she called over her shoulder.

Jax chuckled. He couldn't help it.

Crap, crap, crap. Mia practically raced from the bedroom. But, oh my. The man was built like a Greek god.

She opened the basement door and headed down the steps and over to the washing machine.

That was no reason to stand there gawking like some hormonal teenager.

But gawk she had, and there might have been a little drooling going on, too, while her brain conjured up all kinds of erotic fantasies that she very much wanted to make real.

She might have if the reasoning part of her mind hadn't kicked in when it had.

Thank God for small mercies.

If she and Jax got together…

When, the naughty part of her brain screamed.

Mia nodded. *When* she and Jax got together, she didn't want the possibility of Pops or anyone else walking in on them.

Given how Pops had mastered getting around the house with his crutch over the last few days, that could have been a real possibility.

She lifted Jax's shirt to toss it in the washer. His signature scent hit her as she dropped it in the tub.

Heaven help her, she wanted him with an intensity she'd never experienced before.

Enough waiting. Tonight was the night.

Her cell buzzed.

Mia grabbed it from her back pocket, sighing when she saw the number on the screen. She connected the call. "Hello, Kyle."

"Hey, do you have any plans for tonight?"

Oh, hell. "Actually, yes. Sorry."

"Any chance you can change them?" Kyle sounded…concerned, overwhelmed.

"Why?" she asked.

"It's Kiera. She's having a really hard time being away from you. I thought…if there's any chance…it might make things easier for her if you could come to dinner tonight. Actually, I think all three of the girls would like that. That way they could see you.

"Being away from home is much harder on them than I had anticipated. You tried to tell me that when we discussed visitation, and I didn't want to listen. I was wrong, and I'm sorry."

Mia lowered the phone from her ear and stared at it. *Who are you and what have you done with my ex-husband?*

Kyle started talking again, and she raised the phone to her ear.

"I just want to do what's best for our daughters," he said.

Her gaze narrowed. Was he trying to manipulate her again? She wouldn't put it past him.

"Please, Mia," he said. "They really miss you."

She remembered the call from Aurora, and how Kiera had sobbed into the phone. She couldn't stand the thought of that happening again. It was traumatic enough hearing her cry last night.

"All right. I'll come. For dinner only." Like it or not, the girls would have to get used to being away from her.

She needed to come to terms with that scenario, too, but not tonight.

"Great. Aurora, Brooke and especially Kiera will be super excited." Kyle sounded relieved. "I'll pick you up at six."

"No. I'll meet you." She didn't want to give her daughters the wrong impression. Everything was already confusing enough for them.

"What restaurant did you have in mind?" she asked.

"How about the new Mexican place that opened on Main Street?"

"Perfect. I'll see you at six."

"Thank you, Mia." Kyle sounded sincere. "I really do appreciate this. You're a good mom."

Mia's eyes widened. He'd never said anything of the sort when they were married. "Umm, thanks."

"You're welcome. See you at six." He was business as usual again.

"Yes. Bye." Mia ended the call.

She started the wash and headed back upstairs.

"Hey," Jax said when she stepped into the kitchen. "Pops is awake He's not interested in taking a walk, so I'm going to head out on my own and shoot some photos."

"Okay." Mia smiled.

Jax started to leave, then turned to face her. "Do you want to have dinner with me tonight?"

Mia's shoulders sank. He'd finally asked her out and she couldn't go.

The problem was, she wanted to. More than anything else in the world.

Chapter Thirteen

Mia parked her SUV in the rear parking lot of the new Mexican bistro at 6:00 p.m. sharp. She exited the car and walked around to the Main Street entrance. A light breeze blew, a welcome relief to the stifling heat earlier in the day.

Her stomach jumped and jittered. It wasn't nausea swirling around her belly, and it wasn't dread, either, but something had her nerves on edge.

This was wild. It was just dinner. Lots of divorced couples had a meal together with their kids.

It wasn't like she didn't get along with Kyle. At least she tried to. For her daughters' sakes.

Mia pulled the door open and stepped inside. The aroma of chili and fresh cilantro filled the place. Her stomach rumbled. Although she'd cooked a grilled ham and cheese sandwich for Pops around noon, she hadn't eaten much of the one she'd made for herself. He'd drifted off to sleep and she'd rushed to get as much of his new bedroom painted as possible.

An image of Jax standing in front of her, bare-chested, floated into her mind. Her naughty brain picked up where it had left off earlier today with the erotic fantasies.

So not the time.

Mia repeated the mantra and hoped her heated body would get the message.

Looking for a distraction, she peered around at the decor.

The space surprised her. She had expected a traditional Mexican restaurant complete with vibrant Southwest colors and decorative tiles. This place was the complete opposite. A subdued cream color covered the walls. Trendy pendant lights hung from ceiling and white linen tablecloths covered dark wood tables.

"May I help you?" A middle-aged man dressed in a tailored black suit, white dress shirt and matching bow tie approached her.

Mia's brows drew together in a deep V. He seemed a bit overdressed for a family restaurant to her. She peered around. The servers wore similar upscale attire, and the other patrons…weren't dressed in a pair of dressy shorts and a T-shirt.

Mia gritted her teeth. Why hadn't Kyle told her this was an upscale restaurant? She stuck out like a sore thumb. "Um…"

She caught a glimpse of Kyle sitting in a booth on the other side of the restaurant. He gave a discreet wave of his hand.

Turning her attention to the man in front of her, she said, "I'm meeting the people sitting over there."

"This way, please." The maître d' escorted her across the room. To his credit, he didn't comment on her lack of appropriate clothing.

"Thank you." She smiled when they reached the table.

"Mia." Kyle stood. Dressed in a light-colored blazer, a dress shirt and a pair of khaki trousers, he looked…good, she supposed.

Funny, she used to find him quite attractive, and she guessed he still was, if the not-so-discreet gazes from the two women sitting at the table next to them were anything to go by, but…

An image of Jax formed in her mind.

Kyle held no appeal anymore.

"You look…nice." His gaze traveled up and down her body. Disapproval flickered across his features before he could hide it with an affable smile.

Mia winced and wished the earth would open up and swallow her whole. *Way to make me feel even more self-conscious.*

She sucked in a deep, fortifying breath and released it. There was nothing she could do now. She straightened her shoulders and lifted her head high. "Thank you. This place is nothing like I expected. I'm surprised you wanted to bring the girls—"

Her brows drew together in a deep V as she stared at the empty bench seat opposite her ex. "Where are our daughters?"

Kyle returned to his seat and gestured for her to do the same. "They'll be here any minute."

"What do you mean?" A note of panic filled her voice. Why weren't they here with him?

"They're fine, Mia. They're with my mother. She's baking cookies with them. It took a little longer than expected."

"Oh." Relief flooded through her.

"Would you just sit down?" He gave her a knowing look. "People are staring at you," he added in a low voice.

She peered around, and yes, several pairs of eyes were trained on her.

Heat crept up her neck and flooded her cheeks. She'd overreacted. It was just that she'd expected them to be sitting with him, and they weren't.

A server appeared and placed a bottle of her favorite red wine on the table. Mia cocked her head to the side. "What's this for?"

"I thought we could have a drink while we wait." Kyle nodded, and the woman uncorked the bottle.

The server poured a small amount in the glass in front of Kyle.

As he swirled it around the glass and sipped, Mia couldn't help but wonder why he'd picked this restaurant to have a family dinner. With three young children, the pizzeria or the diner would have been a much better choice. Not that their daughters were wild or rambunctious. They were just…kids. Sometimes they were loud. That wouldn't go over well in this place.

"Cheers." Kyle lifted his glass.

Mia glanced down. She hadn't noticed the server pouring wine in her glass.

"You're supposed to touch your glass to mine," he said.

"Forgive me, but I find this all a little…" Mia gestured around the fancy dining room. "A little over the top. What are we doing here? This place is not suited for young children."

"It's fine, Mia. Don't worry," he said. "Drink your wine. Relax. Let's enjoy the few minutes we have together."

Mia's gaze narrowed. He was acting as if this were a date. *Not!*

She glanced at her watch. They'd been sitting here almost ten minutes now. "Where are the kids?"

"I'm sure they'll be here in a few minutes. In the meantime, why don't we order an appetizer while we wait?" He signaled the server.

Mia shook her head. "No. Call your mother, please. Tell her to bring the girls now. That's why I'm here. To have dinner with them. Not to sit around sipping wine with you."

"All right." Kyle held up his hands as if he were surrendering. "I'm texting her right now." He pulled out his phone and started typing. "Don't be surprised if the girls are upset when they arrive. They were having a great time with my mother."

"Then why didn't you call me and postpone dinner by thirty minutes or so?"

He set down the phone and looked her in the eyes. "I was hoping we could use the time to talk about what I wanted to discuss with you the other night. It's important."

Here we go again. Mia's hands curled into tight fists. "This is why you wanted me to come tonight. It had nothing to do with our daughters' well-being."

He opened his mouth as if to argue, then closed it. "I'm

sorry. I should have been up-front with you when I called earlier. It's just… Things have been a little crazy lately. I've been stressed out with work and—"

Mia held up her hand to stop him from saying anything more. "I don't want to hear your excuses."

"Please, Mia. I really need to talk to you. I've been trying for days now."

"Are the girls even coming?" she asked. Mia wouldn't put it past him to say they were when they weren't. "Because I'm out of here if they're not."

"Of course they are." Kyle showed her the answering text from his mother, indicating she was on her way. "I wasn't lying when I told you how upset Kiera was. I just wanted a few minutes alone with you to talk. I swear."

Mia gritted her teeth. "You have two minutes."

She wasn't prepared for what came next.

Kyle smiled and grasped her hands in his. "Our divorce. It was a huge mistake. I can see that now."

She jerked her hands away. "Huh?" Her brain couldn't form more elaborate words.

"I think we should get back together. It's the best thing for the kids. You do want what's best for them, don't you?"

She only stared at him. This time her mind couldn't form any words.

"What do you think of the idea?" He gave her a hopeful grin.

The sun sat low in the sky as Jax exited the diner with a Reuben sandwich and fries.

After shooting pictures around town for a few hours, he'd headed back to Pops and done some editing. He was quite pleased with how the images had turned out.

He'd missed Mia. She'd left at five to go home and wash the paint out of her hair. At least, that's what Pops had told him.

After bidding Pops good-night, he'd headed to the diner

for something to eat. It was too nice an evening to sit inside, hence the to-go order. He'd drive back to the hotel and eat on the patio by the pool.

He'd call Mia once he finished his sandwich. He didn't want to interrupt her evening with her daughters.

As he walked to his car, he couldn't help noticing the influx of people in town compared to last week.

This holiday weekend marked the unofficial start of summer, which meant longer lines at restaurants and fewer parking spots along Main Street. Hence the need to walk a couple of blocks to his car.

A horn blared behind him. *Not to mention the increase in traffic.*

He noticed Mia sitting on a park bench as he passed the town green. Her hunched shoulders were visible even from this distance. What was wrong with her? Wasn't she supposed to be having dinner with her daughters? Had something happened?

Jax crossed the street and hurried toward her, remembering another occasion when he'd found her seated in that exact spot...

"Look at that dork, Wilson, dressed in that monkey suit," Smitty smirked. *"I mean, who wears a tux to the diner?"*

Jax chuckled. *"A junior with a date to the senior prom, that's who."*

"Yeah, man." Shane pointed to the petite blonde seated *across from their classmate. "Check out the girl he's with. She's smokin' in that minidress."*

Shane wasn't wrong. She was pretty hot.

"I could have had a date to the senior prom if I'd wanted," Smitty insisted.

"Yeah, right." He and Shane burst out laughing.

"You two need to get over yourselves. It's not that funny," Smitty insisted.

"Yeah, it is," Jax said.

"Diner closes in fifteen minutes." Their server approached the table. "I need you to settle the bills now." She placed three checks in front of them and moved to her next customer.

"Damn. I gotta go." Shane pulled out his wallet and dropped a few bills on the table. "As fun as it's been hangin' out with you dorks tonight, it's almost midnight."

"Aww..." Smitty laughed. "Little boy has a curfew, does he?"

"Shut up, idiot." Jax mock punched Smitty's arm. "You're in the same boat as Kavanaugh. We all are."

Smitty grumbled something under his breath Jax couldn't make out, then tossed a few bills on the table.

"I'm parked out back." Shane headed toward the rear exit.

"Me too." Smitty followed.

"See you guys later." Jax laid a ten and a five next to the rest of the money and strode to the front exit.

Outside he walked the short distance to where he'd parked his car. He noticed Mia Kavanaugh sitting on a park bench on the town green.

What was she doing there alone at this time of night?

Jax crossed the street and hurried to where she sat. Why was her head down? And her shoulders were all hunched up. "Hey there." He folded his large frame down on the bench next to her. "What's going on?"

"Nothing." She didn't lift her head and look at him.

He peered around. No one else was in sight. "Why are you sitting here all alone?"

"I, ah..." Mia sniffled.

Was she crying? Shit. He hated when girls cried. He never knew what to do.

"Knock, knock," he said.

After a moment of silence Mia said, "Who's there?"

"Banana," he replied.

"Banana who?"

"Knock, knock." He went through the whole thing again.

Mia snorted. "Knock, knock." She looked up at him, and there was a hint of a smile on her face.

She was intentionally taking over the joke. Jax grinned. "Who's there?"

"Orange," she said.

He'd play along. "Orange who?"

"Orange you glad I didn't say banana?" Her grin sent a flood of warmth rushing through him.

"I see you've heard that joke before."

Mia nodded. "I've heard a knock-knock joke or two in my life."

He nodded. Her father used to tell them all the time. Jax wouldn't say that, though. He didn't want to make her start crying again.

"Why are you sitting here all alone?" He eyed her up and down. Dressed in a long, figure-hugging, lilac strapless dress, he guessed she'd been at the senior prom earlier. It must have ended, otherwise Wilson and his date wouldn't have been at the diner. "I would have thought you'd be with your prom date."

"Um..." She looked away.

Jax heard another sniffle. He wrapped his arm around her. "Seriously, what's wrong? Where's your date?" Or maybe she didn't have one? He shook his head. Who wouldn't want to go with her?

Jax eyed her up and down again. His heart slammed against his chest. Yeah, any red-blooded straight guy in his right mind would want her.

Not that he was interested. She was Shane's sister, and that made her off-limits. At least for him.

No biggie, he told himself. There were plenty of fish in the sea.

"My date is...not here." She hiccupped. "He left."

"Someone just left you here?" Jax shook his head. What idiot would do that? "Why?"

"He wanted me to... A bunch of people were going to Long Pond."

New Suffolk's version of Make Out Point. At least, that's what they called it in those old movies Pops always liked to watch on Friday nights.

Jax smiled. He'd been to Long Pond a time or two, and had some very pleasurable experiences.

"You didn't want to go?" He couldn't hide the curiosity in his voice.

"No, I didn't." Mia jerked her gaze to his. "Not with Bruce. He's...and I haven't... No. Not with him."

What was she talking— Jax's eyes bugged out. Was she saying what he thought she was? She'd never done...it before?

"Mia." He drew in a deep shuddering breath.

"Yeah?" Glittering sapphire eyes gazed at him.

Jax swallowed hard and stared at those lush pink lips. What would they taste like if he pressed his mouth to hers?

He wanted to kiss her. Needed to, like he needed air to breathe.

Dammit.

He was in deep trouble.

Jax blew out a breath. Maybe it was a good thing Mia had other plans for dinner this evening. He'd asked her because they still hadn't talked about where things stood between them since she'd chased Shane from Pops's house two days ago.

Maybe he already had his answer— Mia wasn't interested.

No that wasn't true. The attraction was mutual. He was sure about that. It was what she wanted to do about that attraction he was unclear about.

Hell, he was unsure, too. As much as he wanted something with her, he didn't want to hurt her.

The guys were right about him not sticking around New

Suffolk for any length of time. How could he? Sooner rather than later he needed to get back to his real life.

The one night with her all those months ago had been…

Electrifying, satisfying, and not just in the best-sex-ever kind of way, although that was definitely true.

Being with Mia had been like satiating a need deep inside him he hadn't known existed. Like coming home.

He rolled his gaze skyward. *Wow, that's really deep for a guy who can't fathom the idea of commitment.*

He needed to stop thinking about it.

Sound advice. Too bad his brain wouldn't get the message.

Jax dropped down next to her on the bench. "Hey, there."

"Hi." Mia stared straight ahead.

"Everything okay?" he asked. "You look a little upset."

She looked at him. A hint of a smile formed on her face. "Aren't you going to tell me a knock-knock joke?"

"You remember that night?" He couldn't hide the surprise in his voice.

"I was so miserable and feeling like a complete idiot, and this sweet boy came along and made me laugh with a stupid joke. Kind of like now."

"Knock, knock," he began.

She laughed and slid closer to him. "I'm kidding. We don't need to go through it again. Once was enough, believe me."

"Don't mock the knock-knock joke."

Her laughter was sweet music to his ears.

"Okay, so what's bothering you? Did something happen at dinner with Aurora, Brooke and Kiera? Where are they?"

She told him everything that had happened.

"Kyle wants to get back together?" He hoped his voice sounded calm, cool and collected, because he felt anything but.

"Can you believe it?"

He couldn't tell if she was stunned happy or stunned mad that Kyle would suggest such a thing. Jax hoped and prayed it was the latter. The thought of Mia with…anyone else but him, ripped his insides to shreds.

He wasn't even going to consider what that meant.

"Is that what you want?" He held his breath and waited for her to answer.

She looked at him. "You know, there was a time not so long ago when I would have given everything for that outcome, but now, no. I don't want that. I don't want *him*."

Relief flooded through him like a wave crashing on shore.

"I couldn't see it before, but I realize now that Kyle did me a huge favor by leaving."

"How?" he asked. He couldn't deny he was curious as to what her answer would be.

"I don't love him anymore. To be honest, I'm not sure I ever did."

"Hey, we all make mistakes."

Mia laughed. "That was a pretty big one." Mia's expression turned thoughtful, and the hint of a smile crossed her face.

"What are you thinking about?" he asked.

"When I was younger, I used to fantasize about finding this grand, epic love—like my parents had." She snorted. "Kyle definitely wasn't that."

"I wouldn't know anything about that kind of love." He sounded wistful. What was that all about? He wasn't interested in anything of the sort—right?

Right.

"You've met my parents," he said.

She laughed again and laid her head on his shoulder. "We're quite a pair, aren't we?"

Jax liked the feel of her head resting on him. "Actually, I'd like to find out *what* we are." The words spilled from his mouth, because yeah, despite what he'd been thinking earlier, he needed to know.

The truth was, he'd always been drawn to her, an irresistible tug he couldn't ignore.

So yeah, he needed to figure this out. Ignoring whatever was between them wasn't going to work.

She lifted her head and faced him. "I guess we never did talk about that, did we?"

Jax shook his head. "I haven't been able to get you alone."

"It has been a bit of a challenge," she agreed.

"So…what do you want?" Jax held his breath and waited for her response.

Chapter Fourteen

My decision. Mia smiled. It was an easy choice. "We're two adults who have a mutual attraction for each other. I say we spend some time together and see where that leads."

His smile made her insides go all soft and mushy.

"Sounds like a plan," he said.

Mia moved a little closer to Jax. She flashed her best sexy smile. "Should we seal our deal with a kiss?"

The look in his eyes sent a jolt of electricity sizzling through her. "I can do that." He closed the distance between them and lowered his mouth to hers.

Anticipation hummed and buzzed inside her. Lord, what was wrong with her? It was just a kiss. It wasn't like they hadn't already done that. A number of times.

This was different. Four months ago…while they might not have been strangers, she didn't know this handsome, compassionate man who sat beside her. Now she did. And she liked him. A lot.

The last time they were together had been about proving something to herself, but this time…

She wasn't sure, but she couldn't wait to find out.

The gentle press of his lips on her cheek made her pulse quicken. "You're teasing me."

"No," he denied. "I want to take my time." He grasped her head with his hands and caressed his thumbs over her cheekbones. "Your skin is so soft."

He kissed her eyelids, the tip of her nose. "I want to savor every touch."

Mia pressed her hand against his chest. She luxuriated in the flex of his hard muscles beneath the smooth skin of her palm.

"Yes," she murmured. "Oh." She exhaled a breathy sigh as he dotted butterfly kisses along her jaw and down to the throbbing pulse in the crook of her neck. Mia swallowed hard. "You're really good at this kissing thing." She couldn't hide the effect he was having on her. Hell, she didn't want to. She just wanted to enjoy this moment.

"I'm just getting started." His lips finally pressed against hers, and she moaned with sheer pleasure.

"Really, really good at the kissing, in case I haven't mentioned it before," she said as he nuzzled the hollow behind her ear.

Jax rested his head against hers. "If I don't stop, I'm going to embarrass both of us in front of the whole town."

"You do make a good point." She smiled and kissed the corner of his mouth. "Let's get out of here." She jumped up and tugged him to his feet.

"Where do you want to go?" he asked.

"Well, we can either go for a walk while we share your now-cold sandwich from the diner…" She pointed to the bag with the diner logo sitting on the bench.

"Or?" he arched a brow.

"We can go down to the boardwalk and grab some fried whole belly clams or burgers, if you're in the mood for one, but I'd recommend Layla's place if you want a burger. She makes the best in the state. Even won an award for them."

"Fried clams sound great. And maybe some ice cream after?" He looked like a little boy hoping for a sweet treat.

"Sounds perfect," she said. "Are you up for a walk? We can come back for our cars later."

"A walk sounds great, but I do want to stop and grab my camera, if that's okay." He fastened his palm to hers.

She liked the way his hand gripped hers. Gentle, secure. *Right.* "That's a great idea. The boardwalk should be hopping."

They crossed Main Street and walked the short distance to where Jax had parked earlier.

She noticed the For Sale sign wedged into the ground in the small front yard of the old Victorian farmhouse that sat between the former library and the bank. The black paint on the wood sign over the front entrance was a little faded, but you could still make out the words, The Toybox.

"Oh, no. The girls are going to be so disappointed."

"About what?" Jax peered at her over the Porsche's open trunk.

She pointed to the real estate sign. "Loni must have decided to close her toy store. The girls loved coming here."

Jax smiled. "I remember that place. Pops used to bring me for my birthday when I was a kid. He let me pick out any toy I wanted. Loni seemed old to me then. She must be well into her seventies by now."

"Yes. She did talk about retiring the last time I saw her. I just didn't think she'd actually do it."

"Real estate prices are insane right now. It's a good time to cash out."

"I know. The property probably won't be on the market for long," she said.

"Probably not." Jax grabbed a thick, padded nylon bag and unzipped it. Removing the camera, he looped the strap over his neck. He set the bag back in the trunk and closed it.

"I'm set." He smiled. "Let's go."

"So, how is the picture-taking going?" she asked as they strolled along. Darkness filled the sky, but the streetlamps provided plenty of light.

Jax dragged a hand through his hair and blew out an audible breath. "I'm happy with what I've captured so far."

Mia arched a brow. "I'm sensing a but coming."

Jax chuffed out a laugh. "It's a new direction for me. Don't get me wrong, I need a change. I've been stuck in a rut for a long time." He shook his head. "I didn't even realize it. Or maybe it's more accurate to say I didn't want to acknowledge that fact."

Who could understand that better than her? Hadn't she recently admitted some hard-to-face facts about herself and her relationship with Kyle?

She sent him a quizzical gaze. "Sometimes it can feel like there's no other way to approach something, so you go through life status quo until something forces us to change."

Jax smiled. "You might be right about that."

"I am." She shot him an I'm-an-expert-on-that-these-days expression. "Let's face it, change is hard. It leaves us uncomfortable until we find our footing."

"You seem to have done that," he said.

Mia grinned. "Yes." Thanks to him and the support of her family and friends. "I've come a long way in the past year and a half." And she was damned proud of herself. "You'll figure out what's best for you."

"I hope so," he said.

They walked in companionable silence. After a while, Jax said, "I'd love to show them to you. My pictures," he added. "You can tell me what you think?"

Mia smiled. That he valued her opinion meant the world to her. "I'd love to see your work. I plan to be at Pops's tomorrow. Maybe you can show me then."

"Tomorrow is supposed to be your day off. You don't work weekends, remember? Besides, it's a holiday weekend. You should enjoy yourself. You deserve a break," Jax said.

"That's sweet, but I want to get the wood strips installed on the feature wall in the primary bedroom while I've got nothing else going on. It'll be more difficult to do the installation if I have to stop every time Pops needs something. He's decided on a more complex pattern than I originally proposed. I need to concentrate to make sure I get it right."

"Okay. I'll make sure he doesn't disturb you. In fact, I'll even get him out of the house so he's not tempted to sit and watch you."

Mia grinned. "I appreciate that. He can be…"

"Bossy?" Jax wiggled his brows. "Or perhaps a little grouchy if you're not doing things right? And by *right*, I mean not doing things his way."

Mia laughed. "He does like to be in charge."

Jax shot her a look. "I know he appreciates everything you do for him. And I'm not just talking about the last week. He told me you've been stopping by on a regular basis since you first moved in to check up on him. Dropping off Christmas cookies, inviting him over for summer barbecues. You always make sure he's got somewhere to go for all the holidays."

"No one should be alone," Mia said. "I'm so glad Pops has you. And you have him."

"There's that big, caring heart again. You always want to make sure others are all right. Who does that for you?"

"I have people who care about me." *You cared enough to have my back the other night when Kyle was acting like a complete ass in my driveway.*

Which meant what, exactly?

Don't overthink it. This thing between them wouldn't last. She knew that going into it, and that was okay. She wasn't going to ruin whatever this was by wishing for more.

No. She didn't want more…right?

Right. She wanted to enjoy this time with him.

"My mom. Piper. Shane." Mia grinned. "That is, when he's not being an overprotective grizzly."

"He loves you, Mia. He doesn't want to see you get hurt. That's all."

"Is that why he went after you? He thinks you're going to hurt me?" The words came out before her brain could engage. So much for just enjoying the time they had.

"Don't answer that." She didn't want to think about it right now.

"No. You need to know who it is you're getting involved with," Jax said. He wouldn't lead her on. As much as he wanted to spend time with her, he wouldn't if she was expecting more than he could give. "I care about you, Mia, but let's face it. I'm not good at relationships. Your brother knows that. That's why he went after me." Like it or not, it was the truth. Look at his record so far. Was it any wonder Shane wanted him nowhere near his sister?

No.

"I know who you are, Jax. You're a kind, loving person. I see it in your compassion for Pops. In the kindness and patience you show my girls. In how you always have my back." Her smile lit up places inside him he didn't even realize were dark. "Don't you dare sell yourself short."

Did she know how amazing she was? Lord, she made him feel like a king among men.

"Trust me," she said. "I get how hard it is to put yourself out there. I'm terrified. What if I screw up yet another relationship? What will it do to my kids? To me?"

They shared similar fears, yet Mia was brave enough to face them. What did that say about him?

"I'm not asking you for forever, Jax. Heck, I've been divorced less than six months. After nine years of marriage, I'm still processing what all of it means for me and my daughters. I care about you too, but I need to rediscover who I am again."

He liked that she wanted to do that with him. He couldn't

deny that it made him feel…special. No one had ever made him feel that way before.

Not true. Pops had always made him feel… loved, wanted. His parents… not so much.

The rational part of his brain insisted he cut ties with them, but his heart, it wanted, longed for more. Everything he had with Pops, but not with them.

Family dynamics are never easy. Mia had been right about that.

"I like the person I am when I'm with you. I'm not afraid to stand up for myself. I'm not afraid to go after my dreams. I like spending time with you. You're fun to be with."

"I feel the same way when I'm with you." It's why he'd pushed back with Shane. Why he wanted to spend time with her. He liked the man he was when he was with her—content, at peace.

The real me. No false facades.

"I can be myself around you," she said.

Jax frowned. "Have you been pretending to be someone else all this time?"

"Honestly, yes. I tried to be the perfect wife. The perfect mother. The perfect daughter and sibling, but I'm none of those things. That night you walked into Donahue's pub four months ago…" Mia shook her head.

"Why me?" He needed to know. "You mentioned that night that your divorce had just become final. I assumed it was some kind of revenge sex thing."

She looked at him, and he wondered if she was going to answer his question. Finally, she spoke.

"I was in a really bad place that night." She told him about Oriana and how Kyle had told her he planned to propose.

"I'm so sorry you had to go through that." He pulled her into his arms and held her tight. Her ex was a complete asshole as far as Jax was concerned. "You didn't deserve that."

He couldn't believe someone could be so insensitive. It was like rubbing salt in an open wound. "I've never met Oriana, but I don't need to, to know you've got her beat, hands down."

Mia rested her head on his shoulder, and he liked how her soft curves pressed against him. "Now I'm actually starting to believe that, but that night, my confidence and self-esteem were at an all-time low.

"The way you looked at me..." Mia lifted her head. She looked him in the eyes and smiled. "I thought that if a guy like you was interested in me, then maybe things weren't as bad as I thought."

"A guy like me?" Jax arched a brow. "What is that supposed to mean?"

"Gorgeous, and sexy, and caring," she said.

"Caring." He still marveled that she saw that in him. Most women believed the opposite. One or two had even claimed he was a robot who showed no emotion at all.

"Yes," she nodded. "You've always been that way. Why else would you have stopped when you found me sitting alone on a park bench, and made sure I was okay all those years ago?"

She was right. He hadn't gone over to her out of any sort of obligation. He'd done it because the thought of her alone and upset had torn at his heart. He'd needed to make sure she was all right.

He'd wanted to be the person who could make her smile again.

Her smile... Jax grinned to himself. Just thinking about it made him feel happy inside.

Sappy much?

She eased away from him, and they resumed walking.

He held her hand again. "I have a confession to make."

She peered up at him, a curious expression on her beautiful face. "Oh yeah, what is it?"

"I wanted to kiss you that night."

"You know what?" She flashed a mischievous grin. "I wanted that too."

He jerked his gaze to hers. "You did?" She couldn't have surprised him more.

"Oh, come on. Don't look so surprised. Just about every girl in high school had a thing for you at one point in time."

Yes, but the beautiful woman standing in front of him right now wasn't everyone. She was adorable and wonderful. She made him feel as if anything was possible when she was with him.

"You really had no idea?" Disbelief flickered in her gaze.

"No. I didn't." Jax shook his head. "Why didn't you say anything?"

"I was all hormones and awkwardness back then. Looking back on it now, I was a mess. I was still grieving my father's passing. My mom had pretty much checked out for the same reason."

Jax nodded. "And it became your job to hold your family together. Make sure they were all right, or as all right as they could be." He hadn't realized things were such a mess for her and her siblings at the time. Shane had never said anything. Not that he'd expected him to. He'd never told Shane about his home life either.

"I guess that is what happened, although I don't think I realized it at the time. I was just trying to get through each day."

He wrapped an arm around her shoulders and pulled her close as they kept walking. "That was a lot to ask of a person who was so young."

"No one asked. I just did what needed to be done," she said as if it were no big deal. She didn't even realize that others in her situation might not have stepped up to the challenge.

Her expression turned thoughtful. "You know, I don't think I've ever fully acknowledged how much my father's death affected me. The choices I made..." Her expression turned serious. "I can't help but wonder what my life would be like if he'd lived."

He wondered the same thing about his parents. What if they'd been different? More caring, loving, nurturing... "What-ifs can drive you crazy." They could hurt, too.

She let loose a soft chuckle. "Amen to that. Our experiences make us what we are. We can't change the past, but we don't have to allow it to affect us for the rest of our lives. We can choose a different outcome."

Easier said than done. Some wounds ran deep and never quite healed. A heavy weight settled in his chest, making it hard to breathe.

He didn't want to think about the past.

Mia stopped walking and turned to him. "Want to know something else?" Her sultry smile sent a jolt of want sizzling through him.

"What?" His voice came out rough and gravelly.

"I'm hoping for a repeat of our night together."

Jax swallowed hard. He wanted that, too. More than he could say. If he were being honest, he'd wanted a repeat of that night with her from the moment they'd parted ways the next morning. "How tied are you to the idea of going to the boardwalk tonight?" he asked in as casual a voice as he could muster.

"Do you have a different suggestion?" She gave him a knowing look.

"I was thinking we could go someplace a little more... private."

"Sounds perfect." Mia's expression turned serious. "I want to enjoy whatever time we have together. Whether that's days, weeks, or just tonight."

Jax nodded. "I want that, too."

Chapter Fifteen

Mia sucked in a deep breath as they exited the elevator on the fourth floor of the New Suffolk Inn and headed toward Jax's room.

Her heart was hammering so loud the people on the ground floor could probably hear it beating. Why was she so damned nervous?

Because despite everything that she'd told him earlier, she was worried. Not because he might hurt her. She wouldn't allow that to happen.

Things were different between them now. She'd gotten to know the man the sweet boy of her youth had become, and she liked him. A lot. More than she should. More than was smart.

Jax opened the door, and they walked inside.

Mia peered around the space. "Wow. This is really nice for a hotel room, even for an upscale place like the Inn." The subtle gray walls, light wood flooring and white linens gave the room a zen, beachy feel.

He came over to where she stood. He tucked an errant curl behind her ear. The soft touch of his fingers on her face was like heaven on earth.

"We don't have to do this, you know." He grasped her hands with his.

He'd sensed her unease and was willing to change the plan, if that's what she wanted.

Mia smiled. "I haven't changed my mind. I want to be with you."

"But you're nervous, and that's okay. I'd be lying if I said I wasn't."

She stared at him. His words couldn't have surprised her more. "Why?"

Dropping her hands, he looped his arms around her neck and held her in a loose embrace. "I think we both know that things have changed between us. Last time, we each had our own agenda, and this time it's a mutual decision."

"You never did tell me why you agreed to be with me that night," Mia said. "You know why I asked. Will you tell me why you accepted?"

Jax gazed into her eyes. "How could I say no? You're gorgeous and sexy."

No man had ever used those words to describe her. That this man would was like a balm to her soul.

His gaze glittered, and a lick of heat rushed through her. "Did you really not have any idea how much I wanted you that night?" He dipped his head and stroked his tongue over her lips. "I was afraid to stand up for fear of embarrassing myself." He gave her a wry smile. "That's why I walked out of the bar and into subzero weather carrying my coat instead of wearing it."

He slid his palms over her shoulders and down her arms. "The truth is, I hoped you'd follow me out that night. I wasn't on a call when you found me standing against my car in the parking lot. I was waiting for you. I didn't want that night to end."

His confession made her heart turn over.

"You sweet, sweet man." Mia rose up on her tiptoes and covered his mouth with hers.

He moaned and tangled his tongue with hers. Jax pressed her against him.

His arousal sent a rush of want jolting through her. She'd never experienced anything like it with any other man.

"I need you inside me." Mia stepped back. She pulled her T-shirt and sports bra off, tossing both on the floor beside them.

Jax's gaze went soft and unfocused. He cupped her breasts with his palms, stroking his thumbs over the already distended tips.

"Oh." A languid heat filled her.

His gaze traveled over her taking in her body. "You are exquisite."

Not compared to the women he was probably used to. "I don't know about that." She gave a nervous laugh. "I'm a little worse for wear after giving birth to three kids."

"No." His hand glided down over her soft belly and back up again. "You're beautiful because of those experiences."

"Jax." She touched his face with her fingertips. His words… she couldn't articulate what they meant to her. Mia pulled his head down to hers and kissed him, giving the flood of emotions swirling around inside her free rein.

Jax dragged his mouth from her. "Mia." He gasped her name as if she was the answer to all his prayers.

He lowered his head and captured the tip of one breast with his mouth.

Mia groaned. She'd died and gone to heaven.

"I love how you respond to my touch." His gruff voice swept over her in the most delectable way.

"I love it when you touch me." Heart racing, she grabbed the hem of his shirt and pushed it up over his head. "I want to touch you, too." She laid her hands on his bare chest, luxuriating in the flexing muscles beneath her palms. "Oh yes. I remember this." She ran a hand down his pecs and over his washboard abs, stopping when she hit the waistband of his shorts and boxers. "These need to go." With a quick tug, the material pooled on the floor.

She couldn't help admiring his naked form.

He stopped her when she reached for his erection.

"Sweetheart. You touch me now and this will be over before we even get started." He flashed a wolfish grin. "Neither of us wants that."

"I certainly don't." She grinned and dropped a quick kiss on his lips.

"You find this situation funny?" His tone came out serious, but his eyes danced with delight.

She laughed, and it felt so good. "Maybe just a little."

"This is no little matter." He gestured to the lower part of his anatomy with a tilt of his head.

"No. It's not." She agreed. "It's a rather…" Mia cleared her throat. "Large matter."

"That it is." His sexy smile sent another rush of heat through her.

"I love this." Mia looped her arm around his neck. "We're all passionate need one minute, and lighthearted fun the next."

"I aim to please." His eyes went dark and smoky.

Shivers skated down her spine at the thought of what his hands and mouth could do to her. Mia swallowed hard. "Maybe you should show me."

"I plan to. As soon as I take care of one more thing." He lifted her in his arms and strode with purpose to the bed.

He yanked back the plush white comforter and laid her down on the cool sheets with a gentle tenderness that almost brought tears to her eyes.

"Aren't you going to join me?" she asked when he didn't move.

"You have too many clothes on." He winked and gave her a sexy grin. "I need to remedy that first."

There was that frivolity she absolutely adored. Funny, sweet, caring and handsome, all rolled into one sexy-as-all-get-out package. And he was here with *her*. Not out of obligation, but because he wanted to be.

How lucky was she?

Lucky indeed.

"That's much better." He lay down beside her, letting his palm slide over her shoulder, down her rib cage, and over the soft curve of her belly.

Mia closed her eyes and luxuriated in the sensations he evoked in her. Need, yes. But it was more. It was as if she'd been living in black and white, with a cold, bleak outlook for the future. Now her world was filled with bright color, warmth, and hope.

How was that even possible?

"I love it when you touch me," she confessed.

"Good." His mouth captured hers in a slow, drugging kiss. "I don't plan to stop. I can't stop. I think I'm addicted to touching you."

Mia dragged her palms over the broad expanse of his shoulders, the hard planes of his chest, and the lean line of his hips and thighs. "I suffer from the same affliction." She nipped at the corner of his lips, his jaw, his neck, until she reached the pulse beating at the base of his throat.

He trembled when she licked the throbbing spot.

"I especially like this." She repeated the action, and he trembled again. "I want to explore every inch of you."

"Next time." Jax hopped off the bed.

"Where are you going?" Her gaze went wide.

He gave her a sexy smile. "I need to get something from the bathroom."

He disappeared and returned a moment later with a strip of foil packets.

"That's a lot of condoms." Heat pooled low in her belly just thinking about using each and every one of them tonight.

He grinned again. He tore off a packet and dropped the rest on the bedside table. "Now, where were we?"

The mattress dipped when he returned to her side.

Mia grabbed the packet from him and tore it open. "Right about here." She rolled the condom over his hard shaft.

"I want to be inside you." Jax covered her body with his. "I can't wait any longer."

His face was filled with such passion. Such need. The depth of his desire, *for her*, blew her mind.

Kyle had never looked at her the way that Jax was now. Not even when she'd believed they'd loved each other.

"Yes, please. I don't want to wait, either," she said.

He sank into her in one swift movement, filling her completely. Mia moaned. She couldn't help it. "So damned good."

"It's always good with you." His dark eyes seemed to look into her soul. "Always."

They moved together. Slowly at first, touching, savoring, exploring.

Jax's movements quickened, and the pleasure inside her increased to a fever pitch. With a guttural groan, he plunged inside her one last time.

Mia went over the edge, and Jax followed a beat later.

As she lay in his arms, sweaty and sated, everything seemed right with her world.

A girl could get used to this, she thought.

I could get used to this.

Jax wasn't sure how long they'd been lying together before he heard Mia's rhythmic breathing. She'd fallen asleep.

He gently extracted himself without waking her and rolled to his side. A soft, satisfied smile played across her peaceful face. He wished he could capture the image with his camera, to show the world just how beautiful she was. He wouldn't, couldn't. Not without her permission.

Sighing, he rose from the bed and strode to the bathroom. Disposing of the condom, he turned on the shower and stepped beneath the steamy spray.

Lathering the soap, he scrubbed his hands over his face.

He thought about what had just happened with Mia and… holy shit. He'd never experienced anything like it in his life. Sure, the sex was great, but there was so much more.

He'd connected with her on more than just a physical level.

Lord, that sounded insane to his ears, but it was true nonetheless.

The way she'd touched him, like he was her most precious treasure…

It was a heady feeling, all right.

Heaven help him, he wanted more. He wanted everything she could give.

Which meant what? He dragged the soap over his chest and legs. He wasn't a relationship guy. He wouldn't end up like his parents.

The curtain moved, and Mia stepped inside. "Hey there. I woke up and you were gone."

"I was just getting cleaned up."

"Why?" She flashed a wicked grin and looped her arms around his neck. "We're just going to get dirty again."

Jax's brows rose. "Oh really?"

Mia nodded. "I've had this longtime fantasy of having sex in the shower." She stood up on her tiptoes and covered his mouth with hers.

"Didn't we do that the last time we got together?" He couldn't hide his smile. The teasing banter they'd developed in and out of the bedroom was fun and actually enhanced the experience of coming together. He would never have thought that possible.

The truth was, he'd never experienced anything like what he and Mia shared. Not with any other woman.

It wasn't just the physical act of having sex. It was fantastic for sure, but there was more to it. The way she touched him, like he was her everything. The way she gave herself completely. The way she liked him, for him, and not because of his bank account or what he could do for her.

"Once is not enough. Not when it's with you," she said.

Lord, she made him feel incredible. Like everything was possible.

She removed an arm from his neck and waved a foil packet in front of him. "What do you say?"

He pressed his body against her. She felt so good in his arms. He enjoyed the sense of peace and tranquility that filled him when she was near.

How could just holding someone like this bring such satisfaction, such contentment?

It was like coming home after a long absence.

Jax blinked. What was wrong with him tonight? Home was in New York City. His posh, comfortable Manhattan place.

New Suffolk was *not* home. Not by any stretch of the imagination. He wouldn't be here now if it wasn't for Pops. Every time he'd come back, it was for Pops.

New Suffolk is not home. He repeated the mantra and prayed his brain would get the message.

"I'm thinking it's yes, based on the evidence I feel." Mia's chuckle drew him from his musings.

He smiled into her hair. "I think that's a pretty good assumption."

She gazed up at him, her blue eyes a deep shade of sapphire, and her body turned languid in his arms. "I don't want to think. I just want to feel you inside me again."

Grabbing the packet from her, he took care of business and lifted her in his arms.

Mia wrapped her legs around him. "I want you now."

He wanted the same. He leaned her back against the shower wall and plunged into her. "So damned good," he moaned.

"Yes." The wild look on her face sent a jolt of electricity sizzling through him.

Mia panted. "You've really taken this 'aim to please' pledge to heart."

He chuckled and pushed into her again. He couldn't get enough of this woman.

Her cry, as she reached her climax a moment later, was music to his ears.

Jax drove into her one last time and tumbled over the edge.

"Wow." She lifted her head from where she'd rested it on his shoulder. "That was pretty amazing."

He grinned. "Yes, it was." Each time with her got better and better.

Jax locked his gaze with hers. The look on her face, like he was everything she'd ever need, sent a flood of warmth rushing through him.

How was he going to walk away from this? From her?

Chapter Sixteen

Mia woke the next morning to a complete darkness that disoriented her, and it took her a minute to realize where she was.

Jax's hotel room.

A hint of light shone through the blackout curtains that covered the windows. She lay there for a few minutes, reveling in the silent stillness.

The rhythmic rise and fall of Jax's chest indicated he was still asleep. His heart beat out a strong, steady rhythm beneath her palm.

Mia marveled at the sense of well-being that filled her. How could lying here, nestled in the crook of Jax's arm with their legs tangled together, fill her with such peacefulness, such tranquility?

The way he held her, pressed against him with gentle, tender strength. The perfect fit of their bodies together. She sighed.

This closeness was new to her. Kyle hadn't been a cuddler. He'd never been interested in just lying together and enjoying the connection.

Jax had scooped her into his arms and held her close all night long. She liked it. It was almost as intimate as having sex. Maybe more so.

"Good morning, beautiful." His husky voice washed over her in a delightful way.

It took her breath away every time he used that word to describe her. She wasn't under any illusion she was a drop-dead gorgeous, sophisticated diva. She was more of the pretty girl next door type, but that was clearly okay with him.

There were no subtle innuendos about how makeup would cover "those pesky freckles" on her nose, or how a sleek, more stylish hairdo would suit her better.

She was enough for him. As-is. He didn't want to change her. Didn't need to. He let her be her.

That was appealing, and sexy as all get-out.

"Morning." Mia smiled and snuggled in closer.

"What are you smiling about?" He pulled her on top of him so she covered his body.

She folded her arms and laid them on his chest. "I'm just thinking about how great I feel."

"Oh yeah?" He wrapped his arms around her. "Want to feel even better?" He flashed a wolfish smile.

Mia caught a glimpse of the bedside clock and gasped. "That's going to have to wait until tonight." She scrambled off him. "It's seven forty-five. You have to relieve Bill at eight."

"Crap." Jax jumped out of bed.

"Good thing we showered…after we showered." Mia let out a soft chuckle. They'd spent quite some time last night getting clean, followed by extremely satisfying and enjoyable bouts of getting dirty.

"Yeah. Not much time for showering this morning." He grinned as he yanked on a clean pair of boxers and his jeans.

Mia sucked in a deep breath. He was one fine specimen of a man. And he was all hers.

For however long this thing between them lasted, she reminded herself.

He grabbed a shirt and pulled it over his head as he strode to the bathroom.

Mia took the opportunity to dress. She needed a fresh set of clothes and a toothbrush, fast.

Jax appeared a moment later. "I really need to run."

"I'm ready," she said.

He pulled her against him so that every inch of her came into contact with every inch of him, and kissed her.

"What was that for?" she asked when he let her up for air.

"It's a prelude to what I'm going to do later tonight." The look in his eyes sent a rush of need coursing through her.

Mia sucked in a deep breath. "I can't wait."

They exited the hotel a few minutes later and hurried to their cars.

The sun painted streaks of blue and gold in the clear sky. Seagulls squawked in the distance.

Jax pulled out a key fob and unlocked his car door as they approached. "See you soon." He gave her a quick kiss and slid behind the wheel of his Porsche.

She waved as he backed out and exited the parking lot. Mia rubbed her palms over her arms as she walked the short distance to her car. It was too cold for shorts at this time of the morning, but it would warm up soon enough.

She opened the door of her SUV and hopped inside.

Mia couldn't stifle a wide yawn as she made her way back to her house. They hadn't slept much. Maybe two or three hours in total. She'd need caffeine to get her through the day, for sure.

The Coffee Palace came into view, and Mia made a spur-of-the-moment decision to make a quick stop for some sustenance.

She pulled into the parking lot. The line for the drive-through window wrapped around the lot. It would be faster to go inside.

Parking her car, she hopped out and headed to the entrance.

Mia walked inside as her sister, Piper, and Piper's fiancé, Cooper, were leaving.

"Hey. Fancy meeting you here." Piper gave her a big hug. "What's up?"

Mia shrugged. "Same old, same old." She wasn't about to tell her sister about last night with Cooper Turner hanging around. That was the last thing Jax needed. Cooper, Levi and Nick Turner were as overprotective of her as her brother.

She smiled. She might have one biological sister and brother, but the Turner men were part of her chosen family. Her father and Ron Turner had been best friends, and the families were still close.

"It was nice to see you, Mia." Cooper gave her a kiss on the cheek. "But we need to run. I've got some paperwork I need to catch up on this morning. I'm in the middle of a construction project, so today is the only time I'm free to do it. Since I'll be at work, Piper is going to do a few things at the gallery. I need to drop her on my way."

"My car is in the shop," she told Mia. "Honey." Piper turned her attention back to her fiancé. "I want to catch up with Mia." She gave him a quick kiss. "You go ahead. I can walk to the gallery from here. It's a beautiful morning."

"Oh, but I was just going to grab takeout and head out," Mia protested.

"Can't you spare a few minutes? I'd really like to catch up with you."

"She wants to know what happened with you and Jax last night." Cooper kissed Piper. "By the way, we read him the riot act the other night."

Mia groaned. "All three of you?"

"Yep." Cooper grinned.

"Shane was there, too," Piper added.

"We just explained a few things to him. To make sure we're all on the same page. Bye now." He gave a little wave and walked away.

Piper linked her arm with Mia's. "Okay, spill. I want to know every juicy detail." She grinned like a Cheshire cat.

"What makes you think anything happened?" Her voice came out calm and steady, which was the complete opposite of how she felt right now.

They walked up to the counter and waited in the short line.

Piper leaned in close and whispered, "Because you're wearing the same clothes you had on yesterday."

Mia's jaw nearly hit the ground. "You saw me yesterday?"

Piper nodded. "You and Jax were walking past the gallery just as I was getting into Cooper's car. We waved when he pulled out of the parking lot, but you were too busy kissing a certain someone to see."

"Too busy kissing who?" Elle interrupted.

"Jax." Piper grinned.

Elle turned to the teen who stood a few feet away from her. "I'm going to take a break, Tommy. You've got the front for the next ten minutes." To Mia, she said, "The usual?"

Mia nodded. "And two of whatever the pastry of the day is, too." She was hungry. They never did get dinner last night. And now that she was dining in, she wouldn't have time for breakfast once she got home.

"Oh, my." Elle rubbed her hands together. "I can't wait to hear this." Elle stepped away to fill Mia's order.

"Hey, guys." Abby smiled as she walked in from the kitchen. "What's up?"

"Mia was just going to tell us." Elle handed Mia her order. She motioned to Abby. "Let's all go to the private patio out back."

Abby grinned. "Well, all right. I'll just grab a coffee first and meet you there in a minute."

"Grab me one, too, please." Elle stepped out from behind the counter and strode toward the back of the restaurant.

Mia and Piper followed.

Elle stopped at a table in the rear where two women sat. "Come on." She motioned for Layla, and her sister, Zara, to follow them.

"What's going on?" Zara asked.

Elle winked. "Mia's got some news she wants to share."

She shook her head. "No, I don't."

"Okay, but you know we're going to keep pestering you until you fess up." Elle dropped a friendly arm around her shoulder. "Come on. Be a sport. Some of us are living vicariously through those of you who actually have a man in your life."

"That's your choice." Abby joined them and handed Elle a to-go cup.

"She's right," Piper agreed. "You swore off men."

"I did." Elle sighed. "Maybe I need to rethink that."

"I told you her man moratorium wouldn't last long." Abby flashed a satisfied grin.

They all burst out laughing.

"Let's head out," Elle said.

"That's a good idea." Abby gestured to some of the people who were now staring at them. "Besides, it's the perfect opportunity for me to discuss with Mia what I want to do back there when I remodel."

"Now, that I can agree with." Mia smiled.

Abby walked the short distance to the back exit and opened the door. The rest of them followed. "So when did you get in?" Mia asked Zara as they made their way. Zara might not live local, but she was still a part of her group of friends. Mia liked to spend time with her when she was in town.

"Late last night. Traffic was horrible leaving Manhattan. It took me almost six hours to get here."

"Bummer," Piper said.

Zara shrugged. "That's the way it is sometimes. You just learn to live with it."

Outside, a small area paved with bricks sat beneath a pop-up tent. Planters filled with an explosion of colors and textures outlined the area. A few bistro tables and several chairs sat in the center.

"This is really cute," Mia said.

"I know," Piper agreed. "Elle and I used to hang out here when I lived in one of the apartments upstairs."

"I want to turn this into a tea room," Abby said. "Expand the footprint. Enclose the space. We're going to start serving afternoon teas, and I want to go all out."

"Oh." Elle ran over and threw her arms around Abby. "You liked my idea."

"I *love* your idea," Abby countered. "I've been racking my brain trying to come up with some way I can expand, and I think serving a full English tea is the perfect way."

"Fantastic," Piper agreed.

"I want you to design it, Mia," Abby said. "You'd be working with Elle on this. It's her baby, and I want her to run with it."

"Yay." Elle clapped her hands together. "I've got loads of ideas."

Mia gawked at her. She couldn't believe her luck. "Are you sure? I would understand if you want to go with someone more experienced."

"I'm positive." Abby nodded. "I love what you've done with your home. I think you're the perfect person for the job."

"Thank you." Mia grinned. "Give me a couple of weeks to get things under control at Alex Papadopoulos's house, and we can meet and discuss concepts. Does that work?"

"You betcha." Elle's smile was a mile wide.

"Well, now that we've got that settled…" Abby grabbed one of the seats and motioned for the rest of them to join her. "You need to dish." She pointed to Mia.

Mia laughed and sat in one of the vacant chairs. "I'm not

going to kiss and tell." She made a motion of locking her lips and tossing the key away.

"We don't need you to tell us about the kiss." Piper sat beside her. "I witnessed that firsthand last night. So did half the town." She turned to the others, who were now seated. "Let me tell you, it was pretty steamy."

"It was not." Heat flooded her cheeks. Not because she was embarrassed, but because Piper was right. "And I don't care who saw. I'm through caring about what others think. Jax and I weren't doing anything wrong or inappropriate in public."

"Ooh, you go, girl." Elle pumped her fist in the air.

"Seriously, what's the big deal anyway? I like Jax. He likes me. We're both adults," she said.

"You're right," Piper agreed. "It's nobody's business. So you like him?" She nudged Mia with her elbow.

Mia grinned. She couldn't help it. "Yeah. He's a nice guy."

"You more than like him." Elle flashed an I-told-you-so expression to everyone. "I can tell by the look on your face."

Mia shook her head. "What look? We're just enjoying each other's company while he's in town. That's all."

"You can deny it all you want." Elle lifted one shoulder. "I can tell. You have the same look that Layla did when she fell head over heels for Shane, and that Piper did when she finally admitted she was in love with Cooper. I'm telling you."

Piper scrutinized Mia's face. "You do have a certain…glow about you."

Elle nodded. "And not just the I-had-the-best-sex-of-my-life glow."

"All right, fine." Mia admitted the truth. "I like him a lot." *A lot*, a lot. If she wasn't careful, he could break her heart, a lot.

No. She wouldn't allow that to happen.

"It doesn't change anything," she continued. "He's going to leave. His career, his life, is in New York. Mine is here. There's no way it could work." Mia shook her head. "I'm not ready for a serious relationship. I just got divorced a few months ago." All her reasons for not getting involved were still valid as far as she was concerned.

"Don't let these romantics force you into doing something you don't want," Zara said.

"Oh, come on." Layla groaned. "You had one bad relationship. You can't give up on love for the rest of your life."

Zara ignored her sister. Turning to Mia, she said, "You do what's right for you."

"Don't worry, that's another thing I'm done with. Succumbing to peer pressure." She chuckled.

Another round of laughter ensued.

A cell phone warbled.

Piper grabbed her phone. "It's Mom." She smacked a hand to her head. "I totally forgot I'm supposed to get together with her and Cooper's mother to talk about more wedding stuff this morning. They're probably waiting for me." Piper stepped away and connected the call.

"I need to leave too." Mia stood. "I need to be at Alex's house at nine."

Everyone stood.

"Hey, tell Jax to give me a call if he wants to do another show." Evidently done with her call, Piper walked back to where Mia stood. "I know I'm small potatoes compared to the galleries he's used to, but I'd love to have him. Besides…" She nudged Mia again. "It would give him an excuse to stay in town a little longer."

Mia let out a loud snort. "If you want him so bad, why don't you call him?"

"Maybe I will," Piper said.

"I'll see you ladies later." Mia gave a little wave. To Elle, she added, "I'll set up a time for us to talk."

"I can't wait," Elle said.

Neither could she.

Mia walked into her house a few minutes later. She had just enough time to grab a quick shower and head over to Pops's.

The quiet surprised her as she walked inside. The house was always filled with noise. Laughter, joyful screaming, and yes, a few tears now and then. Or maybe it was the fact that no shoes or backpacks were littering the front entry. No clothes dotting the furniture where Kiera had been sitting and changed while watching television. No books Aurora was reading and no crumbs on the floor from the snack Brooke ate.

No sign my girls live here.

Okay, yes, her last thought had been a little overdramatic. Obviously, her kids still lived here. It was just…

"Things are different now. This is how it's going to be moving forward," she said aloud in the silent space. Aurora, Brooke and Kiera would be with her some of the time and with their father the remainder. It's what happened. She might not like it, but that didn't change things.

She dismissed the melancholy and hurried upstairs.

After a quick shower, Mia donned a clean pair of shorts and a matching tee. She rushed downstairs and out the door, locking up the house before she strode across the street to Pops's place.

Mia gave a brief knock to let Pops know she'd arrived and strode inside. Her phone dinged before she could call out her morning greeting.

Mia pulled her cell from her back pocket and looked at the text. Aurora had sent a picture of Kiera eating an ice cream cone with a big grin on her face.

She read the text.

Dad took us for ice cream last night on the boardwalk.

Mia blinked back the sudden moisture in her eyes. She was glad her girls were happy and having fun.

"Hey." Jax walked into Pops's living room, a look of concern on his handsome face. "What's this all about?" He brushed away the single tear on her cheek.

"It's nothing." She smiled.

"You're upset. That's not nothing." His voice was filled with compassion. "It's okay. You can tell me."

"Just missing the girls, that's all. Sorry. I don't mean to be a crybaby about it."

"You can be a crybaby if you want. I know this is a big deal for you." Jax brushed a curl from her face and tucked it behind her ear. "No judgment here."

"I know." That fact made her like him all the more. "I just feel really silly getting all emotional over the whole thing."

"You shouldn't." He dropped a tender kiss on her lips.

Mia blinked back more moisture. Lord, what was wrong with her?

"Okay. You leave me no choice. Knock, knock…"

Her heart turned over. He knew exactly what to do to cheer her up. "You sweet, sweet man." She kissed him back, because she wanted to feel their connection for as long as possible. "I just need to keep busy. I'll check in on Pops and get back to work on the renovations on his primary bedroom."

Her phone dinged again. Jax's too. Mia reached for it and looked at the incoming message from Layla.

With all the gossip—she inserted two smiley face emojis—and talk about the new tea room, I forgot to mention we've got a few bands playing on the patio at The Sea Shack today to kick off the season. Fun starts at noon. Hope you can make it.

"Or…" Jax cocked his head as if he were considering an idea. "We could take Pops out for the day and have a little fun. Shane just texted me."

Mia grinned. "Live music at Layla's place. I know. She just sent out a group text to the Sisterhood."

"Who is the Sisterhood?" Jax asked, a look of confusion on his face.

Mia chuckled. "Me, Abby, Elle, Piper, Layla. Oh, and Layla's sister, Zara. The best friends a girl can have."

"I see." Jax smiled. "So, what do you say? Can you take the day off from working on Pops's room and have a little fun with me?"

She twined her arms around her neck. "Oh yes."

Jax's hands clamped around her hips, and he hauled her up against him. "Good." His mouth crushed hers.

"Hey, what's going on out there?" Pops called from the den. "You think you two can stop your canoodling long enough for one of you to get me a glass of water?"

Mia stiffened. "He knows?" she whispered.

Jax nodded. "Is that a problem?"

"No." She shook her head. "I'm just surprised, that's all."

Jax chuckled. "The man doesn't miss anything. He says there's been sparks flying between us since the first day you came to visit."

"He's not lying," she agreed.

Jax released her. "Coming right up, Pops." To Mia he said, "I'll grab the water."

Mia smiled. "I'll tell Pops about our plans for this afternoon and make sure he's on board."

"I'm sure he will be. He asked earlier if we could go for another walk today. He's going a little stir-crazy. I think that means he's feeling better."

"I think you're right." Mia started toward the den.

Jax grasped her arm and pulled her back to him. "One more kiss for the road." He pressed his lips to hers.

"A guy could die of thirst here," Pops barked.

"We should go," Mia said with a reluctant sigh.

"I'd rather stay here and kiss you. It's much more fun."

Mia laughed. Lord, she adored this wonderful, sweet, funny

man who told her knock-knock jokes to make her smile, who always had her back, who liked her as-is and didn't want to change her.

What was she going to do when he left?

Because he would.

By his own admission, he wasn't a relationship kind of guy.

The problem was, with him, she just might be a relationship kind of girl.

Chapter Seventeen

The doorbell chimed an hour later.

"I'll get it," Jax called. Coffee mug in hand, he strode out of Pops's kitchen. He opened the front door. Shane, Nick, Levi, Cooper and Duncan stood on the front porch. "What are you guys doing here?" he asked.

Nick gestured inside the house. "Heard you might need help moving some furniture."

Jax's brows knitted together in a deep V. "What are you talking about?"

"You need to clear out all of the furniture in the den, remember?" Nick asked.

Right. The room needed to be empty by Tuesday morning so Nick and his crew could start the renovation. Mia might have boxed up the books, knickknacks and pictures already, but she wanted to wait as long as possible to move the furniture so that Pops could be comfortable.

He nodded. "Yeah. I almost forgot about that."

"Well, today's your lucky day. We're here to help," Levi said.

A warm pressure filled his chest. "I'll say." A few days ago, he'd been wondering how he was going to move everything out by himself. He certainly wasn't going to make Mia help him. Not that she wasn't capable—she certainly was—but moving furniture wasn't part of her home designer, or caregiver job description.

His brow furrowed. Maybe she'd mentioned something to her brother, and they'd come to help her?

"So, you gonna stand there with a confused look on your face all day, or let us in?" Cooper smirked.

"Yeah," Duncan said. "That furniture isn't going to move itself."

"No. Of course not." Jax stepped aside to make room for them to enter. "Please, come on in. And thanks for the assistance. I can really use it."

"It's no problem," Shane said.

"Friends help friends," Cooper said.

"It's what we do," Levi added.

Truth be told, he was surprised Nick, Levi, Cooper, and Duncan would volunteer to help him. Shane, yes. They'd been friends since kindergarten. They had history, but the others...

They might shoot a few games of pool, or have a beer when he was in town, but those instances were few and far between. They barely knew each other anymore. Yet here they were, ready to help him.

None of his acquaintances in Manhattan would do something like this for him. *That's for sure.*

"Can I get you guys anything before we start? Something to drink, maybe?" The one thing his parents had done right was teach him to be polite.

"No thanks, buddy." Nick clapped him on the shoulder. "I think we're good."

Buddy? Jax grinned. He couldn't deny the delight it brought hearing him use that word in reference to him.

"What's going on?" Mia walked into the living room with a paint roller in her hand. She seemed as surprised to see the guys as he was.

So they're not here because she'd asked them to come. His smile broadened.

Shane dropped a quick kiss on his sister's cheek. "Figured we'd stop by and give Jax a hand moving the stuff in the den."

"That's great," she said. "We really appreciate it."

Jax smiled. He liked the sound of "we." "Yes." He draped an arm around Mia's shoulders. "We do."

Five sets of eyes stared at them, but no one said a word.

He dropped his arm from Mia's shoulders. "Den's this way." He gestured for the guys to follow him.

"What's all this?" Pops asked when the six of them walked into the room.

"These guys are going to help me empty the room so that Nick can start framing out your new bathroom on Tuesday," Jax said. "You know Shane." Jax pointed to the man on Shane's left. "And Duncan was the other emergency medical services person that came to the house after your fall."

Pops extended a hand to Duncan. "I can't thank you enough for all your help."

"You're welcome." Duncan smiled.

"This is Nick, Levi and Cooper Turner." Jax pointed to the three men to Shane's right.

Pops nodded. "Nice to meet you. Thank you all for coming."

"It's no problem," Levi said.

"All right." Nick gestured around the room. "Where are we moving this stuff to?"

Mia appeared in the open doorway without the paint roller this time. "Everything but the chair Pops is sitting in, the TV stand and the television go into the garage. The recliner, TV and stand go into the living room." She handed Pops his crutch. "We can show you where." Mia pointed to her and Pops.

Levi slanted a look in his direction. "She's bossy, isn't she?"

"You got a problem with that?" Mia arched a brow.

"Nope." Levi shook his head.

Jax chuckled. "Me either."

He thought about last night and what she'd done to him. Jax grinned. No, he didn't have a problem with her being bossy.

He rather liked it.

"That's the last of it," Shane said an hour and a half later as he walked into the now-empty den. "I'm going to take off. I'm heading over to The Sea Shack to see if Layla needs anything."

"Me too," Nick said.

Mia sucked down a swig of water from the bottle she held in her hand and brushed the hair back from her face. "Are you and your band playing at Layla's place today? She just said live music."

"Yes." Nick nodded. "In fact, Big Brother goes on first, so I need to head over there too. I'm meeting the rest of my band there. We've got a sound check in fifteen. You guys coming?"

"Absolutely." Mia wrapped her arm around Jax's waist and grinned. "I love hearing you guys play."

"I'll be there too," Levi, Cooper and Duncan said in unison. Laughter ensued.

"First round of beer is on me," Jax said. "It's the least I can do for you guys."

"Hey, thanks, man." Levi clapped him on the shoulder. "I've got to get going too." He started toward the door.

"He's my ride." Cooper shook Jax's hand. "That means I'm outta here too." He turned to Mia and gave her a brotherly hug. "Piper says to save us some seats. We'll do the same if we arrive first. Take care." He followed his brothers and Shane.

"I'll see you guys there." Duncan gave a little wave and left.

Jax peered around the room. The guys had even disposed of the wall-to-wall Berber carpeting. How lucky was he to have such good friends?

He pulled Mia in closer, loving the way she fit perfectly in the crook of his arm. Lifting her chin, he brushed his lips over hers, savoring the sweetness.

"What was that for?" she asked.

"No reason. I just like kissing you." He liked having her near him. Was filled with contentment when she was around.

Mia pressed herself against him so that every inch of her touched every part of him. "I like that too. A lot."

Jax sighed as she brushed a tender kiss on his cheek.

Heaven help him, he adored this woman. He *might* even love her.

Noooo. Not a snowball's chance in hell.

He didn't do the love thing.

He must be off his rocker for even thinking along those lines.

Sure, Mia was great.

He liked her.

A lot.

He'd just gotten carried away in the moment.

That's all.

He was one hundred percent *not* in love with Mia, that was for sure.

It would be a major disaster if he was.

Mia looked into Jax's eyes and the tenderness, the adoration she saw in his gaze, was almost her undoing. No man, not even Kyle—*especially* not Kyle—had looked at her as if she was everything he could want.

No, dammit. That's what she *wanted* to see. Which was totally insane. That's not what this affair was about.

All of her reasons for not getting emotionally involved were still valid. *Newly divorced. Single mother of three young children who relied on her to be there for them. Still trying to figure it all out.*

Not to mention that Jax specifically told her he wasn't a relationship guy.

Mia was all right with that. At least, she had been just a few short days ago.

And now…

She wanted more.

Oh yeah. She must have a screw loose or something. The idea of her and Jax…

No. She wasn't going to go there.

She couldn't.

He could leave at any time.

"You have some paint on your face." He touched his lips to her jawline.

Mia melted. She couldn't help it. She loved when he touched her. When he held her in his arms, like he was doing now.

"Oh no. You've got a smidge of paint on your sleeve," Jax said. "And right here." He pressed his lips on her right collarbone.

The simple caress filled her with such contentment. Mia smiled.

She could stay here like this with him forever.

Mia stiffened. Dear God. *She was in love with him.* Helplessly, hopelessly head over heels for the man.

How had this happened? They'd been together such a short time.

"I need to go home to shower and change." She flashed a nervous smile. The truth was, she needed some space right now. Being this close to him was scrambling her brain. "I don't want to go to The Sea Shack with paint on me."

"Sure." Jax dropped another kiss on her lips and released her. "It's no trouble."

"I won't be long. We should probably leave when I return."

"Good idea. I'll make sure Pops is ready to go."

Mia nodded and fled from the house as fast as she could without raising suspicion that something was wrong.

Once outside, she sucked in a lungful of much-needed air, and repeated the action several more times.

She was back in control by the time she reached her driveway.

She wasn't in love with Jax. Couldn't be. It was impossible to fall for someone that fast.

She was infatuated with him. Yes, of course. Like she'd been in high school.

And just like all those years ago, she'd get over her crush. It hadn't lasted long back then. She wouldn't expect anything different now.

All that phenomenal sex was going straight to her head.

Yes. That had to be it.

She'd gotten carried away in the moment. That's all.

Mia entered her house, glancing at her reflection in the mirror at the foot of the stairs.

See—there's a perfectly reasonable explanation for all of this.

"There is," she said to the woman who stared back at her, not at all convinced.

Mia climbed the stairs to her bedroom. She hopped in the shower, scrubbing her body so that no paint remained.

Mia donned the lacy bra and panty set Piper had given her for her birthday last month. At the time she couldn't imagine having an occasion to wear anything this sensual, but now… She grinned. Jax was going to love it.

Striding to her closet, Mia grabbed her flirty red sundress with the small floral print. She dressed quickly and slipped her feet into a pair of matching sandals.

Sitting at the antique makeup vanity her parents had given her for her fourteenth birthday, she applied mascara and a touch of lip gloss.

Perfect for a day, *and night*, of fun.

Fun was what this relationship was all about.

"Jax and I are not a forever couple," she told her reflection. "We're not." She said it again to make sure her reflection got the message.

Too bad her heart didn't seem to be listening.

Chapter Eighteen

"You okay?" Jax asked Mia as she pulled her SUV into the parking lot at The Sea Shack a short time later.

He wasn't. As much as he'd tried to deny it earlier, he might just be in love with this beautiful, sexy, funny woman sitting next to him. How could he know for sure? It's not like he had a lot of experience with the emotion.

Nada, zero, zilch, to be clear.

What was he supposed to say to her? How would this even work?

His life. His career. Everything that mattered was in the city. Her family, her daughters were here. It's not like she could uproot them and move to New York City. He doubted her ex would allow that, especially now that he wanted Mia back.

So, what was he supposed to do? A long-distance relationship? He could come here more often, and maybe she could visit him?

Who was he kidding? With her busy life here and his travel assignments for work, they'd never see each other. Wasn't that part of the problem she'd had with her ex? He was never around?

She'd resent him if he did the same.

His heart gave a painful squeeze. Jax couldn't bear the thought of that.

"Of course I'm okay. Why do you ask?" She smiled, but it didn't reach her eyes.

There was something off. She wasn't her bright, bubbly self. More like a muted version. "Are you sure?" he persisted. Something had happened to upset her between the time she'd left Pops's house to go home and change and the time she'd returned.

Only *upset* wasn't the right word. She seemed disappointed. No. That wasn't right either. He'd noticed a hint of sadness in her gaze when she'd returned. Yes. That was it. Why?

Had she picked up on his vibes? Could she tell everything he was feeling by just looking at him? Lord, he hoped not.

"I'm positive." She gave a little chuckle. "I'm fine."

Was he imagining things that weren't there? Was he projecting all of this confusion and uncertainty swirling around inside him to her?

"If you're talking about when I got back to Pops, I was just a little stressed because I wanted to make sure we got here early. I knew the place would be packed, and I wanted to make sure we'd find a parking spot," she added.

Jax heaved a sigh of relief as he peered around. Mia was right. The lot was nearly full, and they'd arrived thirty minutes before the event started.

Boy, this might-be-love thing could really mess up a guy.

Enough contemplation.

Forget about it and enjoy the day.

Yeah, he could do that.

"I'm really looking forward to hearing Nick play," she continued. "You're going to love his band."

"Oh yeah?" Jax grinned. The old Mia was back, and he was happy about it. "Why is that?"

"They've got a great sound, and the music is fun to dance to."

Dancing meant he'd get to hold Mia in his arms again. This day was getting better and better. "I love them already." He flashed a wolfish grin.

"Your friend couldn't have picked a better day for this, especially since the weather is supposed to turn lousy later." Pops said from the back seat.

"Right?" Mia grinned. "It's absolutely gorgeous out today. Look at that sunshine." She opened the car window. "Feel that ocean breeze. I love it."

"You're right. It's ideal. I just hope we can still get a table on the patio. With all of these people, I'm not sure we'll be able to."

"Don't worry." Mia waved off his concern as she turned down the next row, searching for an empty parking space. "Layla said she'd reserve one table, but we're going to have to share it with everyone. That'll be twelve of us if everyone shows up at the same time."

"Twelve?" Pops asked. "That's a lot of people."

"Yes, it is. Do you mind hanging out with some of our friends?" she asked.

Our friends. Jax liked the sound of that.

"Nope. Sounds like fun. I hope they don't mind hanging out with an old curmudgeon like me," Pops said.

"You're not old," Mia protested.

"I noticed you're not disputing the fact that I'm a curmudgeon, though," Pops grumbled.

"You wouldn't want her to lie, now, would you?" Jax tried to keep a straight face but couldn't. He burst out laughing.

"Ha ha," Pops retorted. "Who is coming?"

"The guys who stopped by this morning to help us," he said.

"That was something, all of them showing up like that. Are you guys like the brotherhood now?" Mia wiggled her brows.

He chuckled. "We don't have a name like you and your friends do." But he couldn't deny he liked that they considered him one of them now. He liked the comradery and the friendships he'd established with each individual, and the group as a whole. He liked being part of something, even if it was a group of friends who got together for a beer once in a while, who played a game of pool at Donahue's, who hung out together and watched the game, or listened to live music on the patio.

"That's not twelve." Pops's voice pulled him from his musings.

"I'm sure Layla's sister, Zara, will be there, too," Mia said. "She's in town for the holiday weekend. And Piper will be there with Cooper. She's my younger sister and Cooper's fiancée."

"I look forward to meeting her," Pops said.

"What about Abby and Elle?" Jax asked.

"They might stop by later, after the Coffee Palace closes for the day." Mia turned down the next row of cars. "And there's you, me and Pops of course."

"Oh, there's an open spot." Jax pointed to the space a short distance away on the right.

"Perfect." She pulled in. Glancing in the rearview mirror, she said, "Pops, you let us know when you want to leave. I don't want you to get too tired."

Lord, Jax adored her caring heart.

"I promise." Pops crossed his heart. "But I have to warn you, I'm looking forward to getting out of the house for a while."

"That's good." Mia grinned. She killed the engine and hopped out.

Jax met her at the rear of the vehicle. He extracted the wheel chair from the trunk and helped Pops get in.

They started toward the restaurant.

"Hello, Alex." A tall, thin woman with gray hair stepped up beside them.

"Hi, Donna," Pops said. He introduced Jax and Mia and gave a subtle gesture for them to give him some privacy.

"I seemed to have lost my phone." Jax patted his pockets. "Mia, can you help me search for it in the car?"

"Sure." She couldn't hide a smile. "No problem. We'll be

right back. Has Pops got a girlfriend?" she asked when they were out of earshot.

"I don't know." Jax waggled his brows.

His phone buzzed when they reached the car. He pulled it from his pocket and glanced at the incoming text.

"Something wrong?" Mia asked. "You have a frown on your face."

"I just got a text from SmartCare. Someone is available to watch over Pops. They want to set up an interview for Tuesday morning to make sure the person is a match."

"That's a good thing, right?" She looked unsure.

Yes. No. Lord, he was so confused.

Mia wrapped her arms around his neck. Rising on tiptoe, she brushed her lips over his. "We both know me watching Pops was only supposed to be for a week or so."

She was right. He should be happy. So, why wasn't he? It's not like he was going to stay here indefinitely. He needed to get back to New York. To his life. To saving his career.

"This will be good for both of us." A huge smile formed on her face. "I can concentrate on Pops's en suite conversion and get started on the designs for Abby's tea house sooner. That's huge for me. I have two clients. Two! I'm not even in business yet. Can you believe it?"

He loved her passion and excitement. "I'm really proud of you."

"You are?" She was looking at him as if she couldn't believe it.

"Yes. You have such skill and talent. I know you can make a go of this."

The smile on her face was pure joy. Seeing it filled him with happiness.

"Thank you for encouraging me to take this chance. I can't tell you what that means to me."

"I told you before, I've got your back." He kissed her again, because he needed to.

"Yes, you did. And like I told you, it goes both ways. You need anything, I'm your girl."

"I need this." He pulled her close and felt her body melt against his.

"I'm happy to oblige." She batted her eyelashes.

"Having someone else care for Pops won't change anything between you and me." It was a statement. Not a question.

Her brows rose. "I hope not."

"Good." With one final kiss, he eased away from her.

She moved and leaned against the rear of the car. That's when he spotted the couple getting out of their vehicle a few feet away. His parents were here.

Maybe they wouldn't notice him.

They stopped midstride and stared at him.

Was that hurt on their faces? He couldn't tell from here.

They averted their gazes, and instead of walking by him, they turned and went the other way.

Shit. What was he supposed to do now?

"Would you like some unsolicited advice?" she asked.

Jax blinked. "Huh?"

She gestured to his parents.

"Do I have a choice?" The women he'd dated in the past just said what they wanted and didn't care if he wasn't interested in hearing it.

Her brow furrowed. "Of course you do. I'll keep my mouth shut if you tell me it's none of my business, and I won't be offended or mad."

He liked that she gave him a choice. "I'm all ears."

"Go and talk to them," she said. "Tell them how you feel."

Jax stiffened. He couldn't. What was he supposed to say?

"I hate to see you suffering like this." She kissed his cheek.

"Maybe things could be different if they understood how what they're doing affects you."

He wished that were true, but nothing had changed over the years. It's why he'd left. It's why he stayed away.

"What's the worst thing that can happen?" she asked.

Nothing will change.

He'd have the same problem he'd always had.

And…he'd be no worse off than he was right now.

Jax swallowed hard. What did he have to lose?

Nothing.

He couldn't go on like this indefinitely.

He wasn't an eighteen-year-old kid anymore. He was a grown man, and he couldn't keep running away from this.

Because that's what he'd been doing these last twelve years. He'd bolted from New Suffolk the day after high school graduation, and he hadn't stopped running since.

It's why he'd gone to Africa, northern Canada, even Antarctica—anything to get away.

Time to man up and do what needs to be done. His gut twisted.

He hadn't known what to say all those years ago. Truth be told, he still didn't.

Jax remembered his parents' surprise visit a few nights ago. He cringed. He needed to deal with this once and for all.

But not here, in a public place. And not now. He'd call them tonight. Extend an olive branch. *And see what happens next.*

"I'm here if you need me." Mia smiled.

He did need her. Wanted her by his side.

The love thing remained to be seen, but wanting her with him…

Yeah, that's a resounding yes.

The thought should have terrified him. Would have just a

few short weeks ago. He would have bolted again—like he always did—as fast and as far away as possible.

Jax wasn't terrified.

He knew he didn't want to run anymore.

Chapter Nineteen

Mia held Jax's hand as they raced into the Coffee Palace at seven thirty on Monday morning. The torrential rain that had started around midnight last night wasn't slated to ease up until sometime tonight.

Too bad neither of them had an umbrella.

Her hair and clothes were plastered against her like a second skin. "I look like a drowned rat." She wiped the water from her face with her wet hands.

"What are you talking about? You're gorgeous." Jax dropped a quick kiss on her lips.

Hearing him say that never got old.

"You're pretty hot yourself." She waggled her brows.

They stepped into the short line in front of the counter.

"Is it my imagination, or are people staring at us?" Jax said in a hushed tone for her ears only.

Mia shot a covert glance into the dining room, then leaned close to Jax. "Yep. They're staring. The redhead over there—" she made a slight nod to her left "—is Mandy Crawford. She's the PTO president. Her daughter and Kiera play together all the time. The blonde sitting two tables to the right of Mandy is Lisa Hawkins. She's one of the room mothers that helped out in my class last year."

"Who's the middle-aged woman standing over there?" Jax

pointed to his right. "The one with the long jet-black hair with the sour expression on her face?"

Mia let out a loud snort. She couldn't help it. "That's Kristin Campbell, Kyle's admin."

She'd once called all of these women and many of the others who sat here gawking her friends. "And if the finger-pointing is anything to go by, some of them are talking about us too."

"Maybe we should get out of here?" Jax suggested.

Mia sighed. A few weeks ago she would have been mortified to be the subject of local gossip. She'd always done her best to give the gossips nothing to talk about.

They'd had a field day when word got out about Kyle's affair with Oriana, and Kyle and Mia's subsequent divorce.

She'd been devastated when her so-called friends had turned on her.

Now Mia couldn't care less.

If there was one thing she'd realized over the past couple of weeks, it was that the people who gossiped about her were never her friends, and her true friends accepted her and didn't judge. They didn't try to force her to be someone she wasn't.

Layla, Elle, Abby, Piper and Zara were her true friends. They'd encouraged and supported her through the tough times.

"No way." She wouldn't allow anyone to make her feel like she was doing something wrong, because she wasn't. Mia grinned. "They're just jealous because I'm with a hot, sexy guy, and they're stuck living their mundane lives," she whispered into his ear. "They secretly wish they were me, so they could have mind-blowing sex instead of the same-old, same-old."

Jax laughed so hard she thought she could see tears in his eyes.

"What's so funny?" Elle asked.

"Nothing," Jax deadpanned.

Mia let out a loud snort.

"Okay." Elle shot them a whatever glance. "What can I get for you?"

"Two large coffees, black," Mia said. "And a couple of your pastries of the day, whatever they might be."

"That'll be the apple cheesecake tarts," Elle said. "It's a new recipe I'm trying out. I want to use it for the afternoon teas once we start those. You'll have to let me know what you think."

"Oh my God." Mia's mouth watered as she imagined the tasty treats. "They sound divine."

"Maybe you'd better make it four," Jax said. "Two separate bags please."

"Coming right up." Elle rang up their order, and Jax paid.

Elle filled two large to-go cups with aromatic steaming coffee. "Here you go." She handed them their coffees and two white paper bags containing their pastries. "Are you guys doing anything later today?" she asked.

Mia shook her head. "Piper and Cooper canceled their barbecue this afternoon, so I'm going to finish up all that I can on Pops's first-floor bedroom remodel, and Jax is going to edit some photos."

"Too bad there's no paint bar at Piper's gallery tonight. That would have been a fun thing to do."

"What's a paint bar?" Jax asked.

"It's a bar that has artists come in and instruct patrons on how to create a simple painting," Mia explained. "Customers can drink wine and eat snacks while they paint. It's a fun night out."

Elle chuckled. "Even for those of us who don't have an artistic bone in our bodies."

Jax nodded. "I've never been to one, but I know what you're talking about."

"Piper does that at her gallery on Monday nights to help bring in more business," Mia said. "She's also going to trial an art camp during the day for a couple of weeks during the summer."

Jax's expression turned thoughtful. "I like that idea. That's thinking outside the box."

"It is," Mia agreed.

"Unfortunately, neither option will do us any good this evening."

"No. Her gallery is closed tonight due to the holiday. You can always join us later if you want," she offered.

"Yeah. Mia's girls are coming home tonight, so we're all going to have dinner together," Jax said.

We. Yeah, she liked that.

"Thanks, but I think I'll pass. I was looking for a little more…excitement."

Mia laughed. Dinner with her girls was anything but exciting. At least, not the kind of excitement a single person would be looking for. She shot a glance at Jax. He didn't seem to mind including Aurora, Brooke and Kiera into the mix. He fit right in with their little family right from the start.

"But you guys have fun," Elle said. "Take care."

"You, too," she called.

The wind howled as they exited the Coffee Palace and made a mad dash for their cars, parked behind each other on Main Street a short distance away.

"See you at Pops's in a half hour," she called as she jumped inside her vehicle.

Jax blew her a kiss and slid behind the wheel of his Porsche.

Mia arrived home a few minutes later. Twigs and small branches littered her lawn from the storm. She knew what she'd be doing tomorrow. It would probably take her an hour or so to rake up the debris. More if there were downed branches in the backyard as well.

She pulled her car into the garage and hopped out. After

grabbing her items from the Coffee Palace, she opened the door that led into her kitchen.

She set the bag and the coffee on the island counter, then she pulled out a tart and bit into the sweet goodness.

"Yep. As good as I'd imagined," she said to the empty room.

With her coffee, she walked into the family room and peered out the window while she sipped. The wind was really howling now, and was it possible that the rain was coming down even harder than before? She wasn't sure.

A branch fell from the maple tree in the backyard. It wasn't large enough to do any damage to the roof.

Thank God.

Damage to the roof was the last thing she needed right now.

Mia walked into Pops's kitchen later in the afternoon. Taking a mug from the cabinet, she filled it with the coffee she'd set to brew a few minutes ago.

"Hey, there." Jax walked into the room. "Is there enough for me?" He gestured to the pot.

"Of course." She grabbed another cup and poured. "Is Pops awake? He might want a mug as well."

Jax shook his head. "He's sound asleep in his chair."

"How's the editing going?" she asked.

"Good. I got a lot done. I'll tackle the last few pictures later tonight. Are you sure you don't mind coming over here for dinner?"

"Not at all." She smiled and waved off his concern. "It's much easier for me to bring the girls over here than for you to try to get Pops over to my place with this weather."

This is nice. On the surface it might seem unexciting, but with Jax it wasn't. She liked talking with him and sharing her day.

"What about you?" he asked.

"I've finished everything I can in Pops's new room for now.

We'll need to remove the common wall between the bedroom and what will become the new bath, but we won't do that until the end of the project. That way Pops can still use the bedroom without having to deal with the construction while Nick and his crew work to transform the other space."

Jax nodded. "Make sense." His cell buzzed. He pulled it from his pocket. "I need to take this."

"Okay." Mia glanced at her watch. "I need to head home now. Kyle will be dropping off the girls any minute."

"See you later." Jax pressed a kiss on her lips and connected the call.

Mia stepped outside and popped open her umbrella.

The torrential downfall of the last sixteen-plus hours had diminished to a heavy rain.

She spotted Kyle's Audi sitting in her driveway already.

She jogged across the street and stopped on her way to the front door.

Kyle's window opened and he scowled. "You're late."

Was he kidding? "It's one minute past four."

Both of the back doors opened, and her girls piled out.

"Mommy!" Kiera came running over to her and threw her arms around her. "I missed you so much."

Mia clamped her arms around her and dropped a kiss on her head. "I missed you too, sweetie."

"I missed you too, Mommy." Brooke stood with her hands on her hips. "But can we please go inside? It's raining out here."

Mia laughed. "Of course." She released Kiera and strode to the front porch. Tapping the code on the keypad next to her door, she pushed it open wide when the lock released. "Okay, everyone inside. Quickly. Shoes off at the door so you don't track mud in."

Aurora, Brooke and Kiera raced through the door.

"Mia. A word, please." Kyle's voice made her jump. She hadn't heard him come up behind her.

"What do you want?" she asked when her heart stopped racing.

"Can I at least come inside so we can get out of this mess?" He stuck his hand out from under the umbrella he held and flicked off the rivulets of water.

"Fine." She walked inside and waited for him to follow. "What is it?"

"Mommy, can we watch TV for a little while?" Aurora called from the kitchen.

"Sure, honey. Go ahead."

The girls ran toward the back of the house.

Kyle's brows knit together. "The television is in my office."

He might have commandeered the single-story addition put on by the previous owners as his space when they'd moved in, but he didn't live here anymore. "It's a family room now. What did you want to talk about?"

"Right." A discomfited expression appeared on his face. He shoved his hands in his front trouser pockets. "There is something we need to discuss."

"Okay." Mia arched her brows. "Are you going to tell me what it is, or do I need to guess?"

Kyle opened his mouth to speak, but stayed silent when the girls started screaming.

"What's wrong?" Mia raced into the family room.

Her mouth fell open when she spotted the half inch of water pooling on the floor in the right corner of the room.

"Look, Mommy," Kiera said. "It's raining inside."

Her gaze darted to the ceiling. Sure enough, a thin stream of water oozed from a cereal-bowl-sized spot on the ceiling that was saturated and bowing out.

"Oh, for crying out loud, Mia, don't just stand there." Kyle hurried to the broom closet and grabbed a five-gallon pail she kept there. He rushed over to where the water was coming in and set the pail beneath it.

She jerked into action. "Okay girls. No television right now. Mommy needs to clean this mess up. Go upstairs and play in your rooms."

Her daughters seemed to grasp the gravity of the situation, because they didn't argue.

"Bye, Daddy." Aurora said. She gave her father a hug.

"See you later." Brooke gave him a kiss and raced off to follow her sister.

"Bye-bye." Kiera followed.

Mia turned and was about to leave when Kyle spoke.

"Where are you going?"

"To get the Shop-Vac from the basement so I can clean up this water."

"How did this happen?" he asked. "Didn't you just replace the roof?"

"I didn't have a chance yet."

He frowned. "But I thought you were going to do that in the spring. You knew the roof needed to be repaired when you bought me out last winter. It's why you got the house for less money."

"I've had other priorities." Why was she explaining? She didn't owe him anything.

"Mia, you should have come to me if you needed the money. I would have helped you."

She had to give him credit. He did care and concern well, but she knew him for what he was—a master manipulator— and she wouldn't fall into his trap again. She snorted. "I doubt that."

"My daughters live here. Their safety is paramount."

"Save it. We both know this house is not unsafe."

He pointed to the ceiling. "That looks like it's going to cave in any minute."

Unfortunately, he was probably right, but Mia wasn't about to admit that. "Don't worry. I'll keep the girls out of this room until the ceiling is fixed." Mia peered outside. The rain had stopped. *Thank God.* She'd load her daughters in the car and head to the home and garden center to purchase a tarp that would cover whatever damage the storm had caused. Maybe Shane could help her put it up? It would be easier with two people. If not, she'd take care of it herself.

All those years working for TK Construction when she was younger were paying off bigtime these days.

She'd have to cancel dinner with Jax and Pops tonight, though. Her heart sank.

"I'd be happy to have Aurora, Brooke and Kiera stay with me until the repairs are made. That way you don't have to worry about them getting hurt if something happens."

Mia remained calm. "I'm not worried."

"I know you want what's best for them."

"The girls will stay here. With me. They'll be fine." She was done dealing with him tonight. "It's time for you to leave."

"Mia," he began in his placating tone. "Think about our daughters' safety."

Mia grabbed her phone from her pocket.

"Who are you calling?" Kyle asked.

"The police."

"Okay, okay. You win. I'll go now. We can have our discussion later." Kyle headed out.

There was a knock on her door a moment later.

She went to see who it was.

"Hi, Jax." She gave him a quick peck on the lips once he stepped inside.

"What's up with Kyle? He looked mad. Is everything okay?"

His look of concern warmed her heart. "We're fine. He'd said he wanted to talk to me about something." Mia frowned. "But he never did." Instead, he'd harassed her. "We got sidetracked when the girls started screaming about all the water inside the house."

Jax's brows formed a deep V. "Huh?"

"The storm caused some damage to the roof in the family room addition we put on a few years ago." Mia motioned for him to follow her.

"Crap," Jax said when he saw the damage.

"Yep. That pretty much sums it up," Mia agreed.

"How did this happen?" Jax asked.

"I'm not sure. Maybe something hit the roof and loosened some of the shingles. It was pretty windy last night and this morning. At least, that's what I'm guessing." A thought occurred to her. "You know, I'll check the security feed from the cameras Mom and Shane insisted I install after Kyle moved out last year. I kind of forgot I have them. They're a bit overkill, if you ask me."

"No they're not. I like knowing you and the girls are protected."

His words warmed her inside and out. "I don't think there's a hole. There would have been a lot more water on the floor if that were the case. And I definitely would have noticed it when I came home this morning, before I headed over to Pops's place."

Mia turned to face Jax. "I hate to do this, but I'm going to have to cancel dinner tonight. I need to get a tarp to cover the damaged part of the roof until I can repair it. But first, I need to get this water vacuumed up before someone slips and falls. Thank goodness we used luxury vinyl planks." She crossed her fingers. "Hopefully the floor didn't sustain any damage."

"What can I do to help?" Jax asked. "How about I go to the store for you? The last thing you need is to pile the girls in the car and bring them with you. Or I can stay here and watch them if you want to go out and get what you need. I can vacuum up the water while you go."

He was willing to watch her girls for her. Mia's heart did a crazy little flip. "You really are a sweet, considerate man." She dropped a quick kiss on his cheek. "Thanks, but you need to take care of Pops. Bill doesn't relieve you until eight tonight."

"I think he can stay on his own for the thirty minutes it will take you to get to the store and back."

Mia shook her head. "Bring him over here, if that's okay with him. It's not raining now, so it shouldn't be a problem using the wheelchair. He can stay with me while you go to the store."

"You've got it. I'll grab takeout for you too, so you don't have to worry about making dinner."

"Perfect. They love burgers and fries."

"I'll put an order in at the diner."

"You're the best." She kissed his lips. "Thank you for having my back."

Jax grinned, and everything inside her went all soft and mushy.

Mia couldn't deny the truth any longer.

She was one hundred percent, head over heels in love with Jax Rawlins.

What the heck was she going to do now?

Chapter Twenty

Jax jumped out of Mia's SUV and strode across the parking lot toward the entrance to the home and garden store.

The sun was now shining bright in the early evening sky. If it weren't for some downed branches and twigs littering the ground, you'd never know a storm had blown through.

He thought about Mia's roof. Talk about bad luck. Even worse was having her ex there when she found the problem. Kyle was none too happy about it, if the look on his face was anything to go by.

Once inside the store, Jax found the aisle containing the tarps and picked up the one Mia wanted him to buy.

He checked out and exited the building. Jax spotted Nick hopping out his truck as he approached the car. "Hey, Nick. What's up?"

Nick extended his hand and Jax shook it. "Not much. Just picking up part of Mia's order for Alex's house. The store can't deliver until late in the day tomorrow and I want to get started early. I should be there by nine."

"Pops is usually up no later than seven, so it's no problem."

"How is Mia?" Nick gave him a speculative glance. "You two looked like you were having fun at Layla's."

Since Nick had spent the afternoon with them, Jax assumed Nick was looking for verbal confirmation that he and Mia were together. They hadn't flaunted the fact, but they hadn't hidden it, either.

He wasn't about to kiss and tell. "Yes. It was a lot of fun. Your band was great."

Nick sighed. "I get it. You're not gonna tell me anything. That's fine. I wouldn't, either, if I were in your shoes." He held up his hands in front of him. "But you can't blame a guy for asking."

Jax grinned. "Gossipmonger."

Nick let loose a chuckle. "Small towns and all that. So, what are you doing here? I gotta tell you, you're the last person I thought I'd run into."

"Just picking up a tarp for Mia's roof," he said. "The storm earlier caused some damage."

"Oh, man, that sucks. You need some help getting the tarp up?" Nick asked.

Jax shook his head. "No. We got it. I called Shane. He's going to meet me back at her house in half an hour. He and Mia will get the tarp up and I'm going to watch the girls while Mia is busy." He glanced at his watch. "I'm going to grab dinner for them and we'll kick the soccer ball around in the backyard until she's done."

"Wow." Nick's brows winged up. "I'm impressed. Look at you doing the dad thing."

Him? A dad?

No friggin way.

"Here you are." Mia walked into her kitchen. "What are you doing in here all by yourself?"

He'd needed a few minutes away. Time to think. His head was still spinning from running into Nick earlier. "Just cleaning up after dinner." He brandished the last plate as he set it in the dishwasher.

"You don't need to do that. I can take care of it later," she said.

He smiled, although he wasn't really feeling it. "It's no trouble. Were you and Shane able to get the tarp up?"

"Yes. It was much easier with another person. Thanks for giving him a call."

He rinsed a glass and set it in the dishwasher. "You're welcome." She was always doing things for everyone else. He was glad he could do something to help her, even if that something was to call her brother to help.

Fixing things wasn't exactly his jam. He'd tried working with Shane at TK Construction one summer in high school and decided rather quickly that it wasn't for him. He was going to stick to taking pictures for a living.

"Getting dinner for the girls while Shane and I worked was above and beyond." She walked over and dropped a kiss on his lips. "I really appreciate it."

"It was nothing. All I did was pour some juice and hand out the meals I'd purchased." The truth was, he liked helping her. He liked spending time with Aurora, Brooke and Kiera.

But being a father? Sweat formed on his brow and Jax's hands shook as he picked up another dish. How the hell was he supposed to do that? He had zero experience.

It's not like he had a role model he could look to.

His father hadn't been around much when Jax had been growing up. He was always gone on business trips. Birthdays, sports games, heck, he'd even missed a few Christmases.

Dad's work had always been more important to him than Jax ever was.

So yeah, he didn't know how to be a father.

Time for a subject change. "How bad was the damage to the roof?"

"Not too bad. A few of the shingles got broken off, leaving a small portion exposed. We were able to cover the damaged area quickly. I'll make the repairs tomorrow so that it's weather tight again."

"Hey, sis." Shane walked in the room. "Wow. Look at you."

He gestured to Jax and the mostly full dishwasher. "I never thought I'd see the day."

"Ha ha." Jax couldn't hide his grin. "Don't you need to leave?"

"Actually, I do," Shane said. "Got a hot date with my fiancée tonight. I'm going home to change, and then I'll head over to The Sea Shack to pick her up."

"Have fun," Mia said. "And thanks again."

"Anytime." Shane kissed Mia's cheek. "You up for a guys' night at Donahue's sometime this week?" he asked Jax. "I'll see if the others want to join us."

Jax nodded. "Sounds good."

"Okay. I'll shoot a text out tomorrow and see when everyone can make it."

"I'll walk you out," Mia said to Shane. To Jax, she added, "Be right back."

He finished cleaning up while she was gone. When Mia returned, he said, "Pops and I need to get going too."

"All right." Mia frowned. "Is everything okay?"

"Yes." *Lie, much?* Because yeah, he'd just told a whopper. "I want to get all my questions in order for the meeting we have with the person SmartCare is sending over tomorrow. And I need to finish editing my photos. I have a meeting with my agent tomorrow afternoon." At least that much was the truth.

Of course, he'd left out the part about meeting with his parents tonight after Bill came to stay with Pops.

His father had called when Mia and Shane were fixing the roof and had asked him to come over at eight, so that's what he was going to do. His stomach flipped like a fish out of water.

"No problem." She smiled. "I'll see you tomorrow after I drop the girls off at school. Only two more weeks and they're out. I can't believe another school year is done."

He wanted to ask her what she was going to do then, but

he didn't. "See you tomorrow." He pulled her into his arms and held her tight, savoring her closeness.

Why couldn't they just stay like this forever? Everything seemed perfect when he held her like this.

"Mommy," Brooke called. "Kiera stole my stuffed animal and won't give it back."

"Jax, can you please bring me some water?" Pops said.

Because it's not just the two of you, that's why. It's much more complicated than that.

Jax couldn't do it. Could he?

"I'll see you in the morning, Pops." Jax waved as he headed toward the front door. "Make sure you listen to Bill."

"You do know I'm a grown man, don't you?" Pops grumbled.

He huffed out a laugh. "Yes, but that doesn't stop you from getting into trouble, now does it?"

Pops gave him the evil eye. "Don't worry. I'll be on my best behavior."

"You do that." Exiting the house, he strode down the driveway to the sidewalk that lined the street. He arrived at his parents' house two minutes later.

He stood at the front door for a moment. His insides jumped and jiggled. What was he so uptight about? He could do this.

An image of Mia's smiling face flashed into his mind.

I'm here if you need me, she'd told him.

She'd be there for him if everything went south the minute he walked inside. Her big heart was only one of the things he adored about her.

Yes, he could do this.

Jax stared at the door. Should he knock and wait until one of his parents answered, or maybe just open the door and go in, like he did at Pops's house? What was the protocol when you'd been gone more than ten years?

Knock and wait for them to answer, it is. That was the safest course. Jax rapped on the door.

His father appeared in the entry a moment later. "Well, what are you doing out there?" He clapped Jax on the shoulder. "Come in. Come in."

That was a good sign. He released the breath he'd been holding and walked inside.

Jax peered around the space. "Wow. The place looks great." He wasn't sure what he'd expected to find when he walked inside, but the light walls and patterned area rugs gave the space a homey feel.

"Jackie, darling." His mother walked into the room wearing an apron. She walked over and kissed his cheek. "It's great to see you. Please, sit down." She gestured to the love seat and matching club chairs in front of the fireplace.

"Great, thanks." He smiled and sat in one of the chairs. Yes, this was going better than he'd anticipated.

"I'll get you a glass of wine," his mother said.

His father sat in the other chair. "The boy probably wants beer," his dad countered. He looked at Jax. "I'm right, aren't I?"

"My Jackie is more refined than that. He wants wine. Don't you, sweetie?"

And here we go again. Jax sucked in a deep breath and counted to ten, and counted ten more for good measure.

"I don't want anything, thanks." He made a concerted effort to keep his composure. "Please, Mom. Just sit down."

"Let me get the appetizers I prepared. I'll be back in a jiffy."

"He asked you to sit down," his father interjected in a casual tone. "He said he wants to talk to us."

"I'm sure my baby doesn't mind if I get the food first. Am I right, Jackie?" his mother asked.

Dad chuckled. "He's not a baby. The man is thirty years old, for crying out loud."

"Enough." Jax stood and started pacing across the room. "You need to stop." He made sure to modulate his voice so he came across calm, cool and collected. He wouldn't let them derail this meeting before it got started.

"Stop what?" his mother asked.

Jax halted midstride and turned to face them. "This constant bickering when I'm around. Making me feel like I have to choose one of you over the other. You've been doing it for as long as I can remember."

His parents stared at him as if he'd suddenly sprouted a second head.

"What are you talking about?" his father asked.

Could they really not know?

"The constant quarreling," he said. "Every time you call me, it's to complain about something the other one did."

"Okay, maybe I like to vent once in a while," his mother responded.

"You can drive me a little crazy at times," his father said to his mother.

They both laughed.

Were they kidding? They acted as if their squabbling was no big deal. Jax shook his head. Had he fallen down the rabbit hole into an alternate reality?

"You make me feel like I have to choose one of you over the other."

They were staring at him again.

Maybe he had lost his mind. It sure felt that way.

"I'll go and get the appetizers and wine now." His mother rose.

"Beer," his father corrected her. He rose and clapped Jax on the shoulder. "You like beer. I'm right. Go ahead, just admit it."

"How would you know? You were never around when I was growing up. You don't even know me. Never made an attempt. It was like you were some long-lost uncle who dropped in every once in a while and brought me presents." Jax didn't yell or accuse. He was beyond that.

"Now see what you've done." Mom glared at Dad. "It's okay, Jackie."

He jerked his gaze to his mother. Working hard to keep the anger from his voice, he said, "Please don't call me that. I asked you to stop a long time ago."

"Well, what am I supposed to call you?" Mom looked bewildered. "That's your name."

"His name is Jax." Dad flashed a smirk. "Says so on his birth certificate."

Mom placed her hands on her hips. "I like Jackie better." She turned on her heel and strode into the kitchen.

Dad gawked at him, but didn't say a word.

Goddamnit. What was he supposed to do now?

Mom returned a moment later with a small platter of appetizers in one hand and a bottle of wine and three glasses gripped in the other.

She placed everything on the coffee table and sat in one of the club chairs. Hands resting on thighs, she peered up at him. "Let's discuss these issues you have with your father." She sent his dad a smug smile.

Dad's gaze narrowed as he looked at Mom. "He's got just as many problems with you. More so probably."

Jax held up a hand. "Please stop."

They continued as if he hadn't spoken.

"I was here. You were not," Mom retorted. "Jackie knows the truth."

"Oh, please." His father rolled his eyes. "I'm surprised you even noticed. You spent day and night at the country club with your uptight, snobby friends. Is it any wonder I stayed away as much as possible?"

"How dare you?" Mom jumped up from her seat.

"I dare because it's true," Dad retorted. "I worked long,

hard hours to pay for that country club membership, and the babysitters. Because someone had to take care of him. Yeah, some mother you turned out to be."

"Don't start acting all pious. We both know you'll never be up for father of the year."

Enough was enough. Jax strode toward the door. He was out of here.

"Where are you going?" his father asked.

"We haven't finished our discussion," Mom added.

He stopped when he reached the door. "I'm leaving." He was done.

Jax turned to face them.

"Neither of you have ever loved me. I don't think you know how. You're too consumed by your hate for each other."

"That's not true," Mom said. "You don't know what you're talking about."

"Yes. It is." They weren't capable of loving anyone. He finally understood.

Chapter Twenty-One

Mia walked into the Coffee Palace the next morning.

"Hey." Elle motioned for her to come over to her side of the counter. "How's it going, Mia?"

"Great." She pasted a bright smile on her face. *Fantastic. Phenomenal, even.*

Liar.

Yes, she was. She was anything but fine. Jax was withdrawing from her. He'd told her everything was great, but she knew it wasn't. She could see it in his eyes.

Had he guessed what her feelings were for him?

Probably.

Lord, how could she have allowed herself to fall in love with Jax when that was the very last thing she wanted?

Talk about lessons not learned.

Really, you'd think this last year and a half would have taught her to guard her heart. *Nope. Nada. No siree.*

She'd totally ignored the warning signs and fallen hook, line and sinker at the first opportunity.

What fool does that?

You, that's who.

Idiot, idiot, idiot.

"Do you want your usual today?" Elle asked.

She shook her head. "Just the coffee, please. I'm not really hungry." Who could eat when your stomach was jumping and jittering all over the place like a bag of popcorn in the microwave?

"Everything all right?" Elle frowned. "You don't look all that well."

Mia sighed. "Yeah. I've just got a lot on my mind right now."

Elle nodded. "I heard about the storm damage to your roof. That really sucks."

"It wasn't that bad." She could make the repairs quickly and for not a large sum of money. *Thank God.*

"Hey, sis." Piper walked up beside her. "What are you doing here? I thought you usually head over to Alex Papadopoulos's house as soon as you drop off the girls at school."

"That's right," Elle said. She handed Mia a large cup of steaming coffee.

She picked up the cup and inhaled the invigorating aroma. "I wanted to give them some space this morning. They're interviewing a potential daytime caregiver, someone who can cover the full twelve hours." That, and she was avoiding Jax at all costs. How was she supposed to face him feeling the way she did?

How had she gotten herself into such a mess?

Jax is a great guy, that's how.

A really, really, really great guy.

That was the trouble.

"What'll you have, Piper?" Elle asked.

"A large coffee and one of those chocolate cupcakes." Piper pointed to one in the display case with an obscene amount of frosting heaped on top. "Does this privacy you're giving Jax and Alex mean you have time to sit and catch up? I have a few minutes before I need to head to the gallery."

"Yeah, sure." Mia glanced at Elle. "We're going to grab a table."

Elle nodded. "Okay. Enjoy." She handed Piper her order.

Mia led the way to a table for two in the middle of the restaurant. She sat in the chair on the right, and Piper grabbed the one on the left.

"So…how are things going with you and Jax?" Piper asked. "It looked like you two were having a great time together at The Sea Shack the other day. You were all smiles."

Mia nodded. "It was a lot of fun." She had been with Jax. How could it not be?

"Things are good with you two?" Piper pressed.

"Sure." Another lie.

Her cell buzzed. Mia glanced at the incoming text and frowned.

"Is something wrong?" Piper asked.

Her brow furrowed. "Jax just texted me. Mom and Ron Turner are at Pops's house. They want to talk to me."

"What about?" Piper ate the last of her chocolate cupcake and wiped her mouth with her napkin.

She shrugged. "I have no idea."

"Well, TK Construction is doing the build-out for Alex's project, and Mom and Ron do own the company, so it must have something to do with that."

"Maybe," she agreed. "But Ron and Mom don't usually get involved with every TK project, do they?" They hadn't when she'd worked for the company, but she'd left seven years ago, when Brooke was born.

"Mom was definitely hands-on when TK did the renovations for my art gallery." Piper chuckled.

Mia laughed as she stood and grabbed her coffee. Her mother had been instrumental in setting Piper up with Cooper by having Cooper do the renovations on Piper's space, even though Piper and Cooper were practically sworn enemies at the time. "Yes. And you got a fiancé out of the deal, but I don't think a setup is in the cards for me. Not if Ron's there, too."

"True," Piper agreed.

"Besides, you don't need a setup. You've already got a man."

"Jax is not my man." Her heart ached as she said the words. Mia shook off the disappointment.

"Oh yes, he is. That man is crazy for you."

Even if that were true, he wasn't interested in a relationship. He'd made that abundantly clear.

Piper rose and dropped a few bills on the table for a tip. I have to get going. "Call me later. I can't wait to hear all about your meeting with Mom and Ron."

"Will do." She gave Piper a quick hug.

"Say hi to your man from Cooper and me." Piper grinned.

Mia shook her head, but she was smiling. "Bye, sis."

They stepped outside. The bright sun was shining in a clear blue sky.

"It's going to be another top ten day here in New England," Piper said as she headed toward the gallery. "Take care."

"You too." She strode to her car.

Mia drove the short distance to Pops's house and hurried inside.

"Mia." Pops grinned at her from his recliner.

"Hi." She dropped a kiss on his cheek. "I heard my mother and Ron are here." She looked around, but the living room was empty other than the two of them.

"Jax is showing them your handiwork in my new primary bedroom. They loved your new bathroom design. Of course, what's not to love? It has everything I could want for now and for the future." Pops winked.

She turned toward the hall that led to the new primary bedroom.

"Hold on a second," Pops said. "There's someone I want you to meet. Charlie, can you come into the living room for a minute, please?"

A tall man with curly blond hair, who appeared to be in his midtwenties, appeared a moment later.

"This is Mia. She's my interior designer and my neighbor, and your predecessor," Pops said.

Charlie extended his hand, and Mia shook it. "It's nice to meet you. Alex told me a lot about you. I have some big shoes to fill now that you're focusing on turning the bedroom and den into a first-floor master suite."

Mia turned her attention to Pops. "Ahh, that's sweet." To Charlie, she said, "I guess the interview went well then. It's nice to meet you, too. If you'll both excuse me, I need to see why my mother and her business partner are here."

She walked through the living room, down the short hall and into the bedroom. "Hi, there," she said as she opened the door.

"Oh good. You're here." Jax looked relieved. "I was just telling Jane and Ron about your plans, but you can do a better job than me. I'll leave you to it."

"Thanks, Jax," her mom said.

"You're welcome." He strode out of the bedroom and closed the door behind him.

"So." Mia glanced from her mom to Ron and back to her mom again. "What's going on?"

"I didn't realize you did the design work on this renovation when you contacted me last week," Mom said. "It wasn't until I was talking with Nick this morning that he mentioned it. How come you didn't tell me?"

"It wasn't exactly a secret. I…" *Needed to make sure it came out the way I wanted before I mentioned anything.* "Guess I was a little nervous."

"We really like your design, both for the bedroom and the proposed en suite," Ron said.

Mia smiled. Happiness bubbled up inside her. "Thanks."

"Is this a one-off thing for you?" Her mother eyed her curiously.

"It was supposed to be a one-off," Mia admitted. "At least

for now. You know I'm not in a position to give up my teaching job."

"But you've agreed to come up with some concepts for the new tea room at the Coffee Palace," Ron said.

"How did you know that?" Mia asked.

"Cooper mentioned it," he responded.

Piper must have told Cooper. "Yes," she agreed. "I should be able to get the preliminary designs to Abby and Elle in the next few weeks." Mia shook her head. "Why the interrogation? What's going on?"

Instead of answering her question, Ron asked another one. "Is teaching your true passion?"

What did that have to do with this project? "I like teaching…"

Mom smiled. "I sense a *but* coming."

"It's not my dream job."

"What if you had more clients who wanted to retain your services?" Ron asked.

"We want you to come work for TK." Her mother's words came out in a rush. "As a designer."

Her brows knitted into a deep V. "But TK is a construction firm."

Ron nodded. "We want to expand. We have a lot of clients who inquire about home design, and every time they ask, we have to refer them to someone else, which means we lose out on additional work. We'd love to be able to offer that service."

"We could offer you a full-time position with a salary and benefits." Mom flashed a hopeful smile. "And you'd be able to set your own hours, so you can work around the girls' schedules."

She could be there for her kids. No day care needed. Mia's mind whirled.

"We thought this salary would be fair compensation to

start. You'd also get a commission for each job you bring in."
Ron handed her a folder with an offer letter.

Her eyes widened, and Mia had to work to not let out
a squeal of pure delight at the figure she saw on the page.
"It's…" Amazing, fantastic. Financially, she wouldn't have
to worry. "A great offer. Are you sure about this?"

Ron and Mom burst out laughing.

"We wouldn't have made you the offer if it wasn't a good
business decision," Mom said.

"We've seen what you're capable of." Ron made a gesture
with his hand that encompassed Pops's new bedroom. "This is
great, and what's better, Alex loves it. If we needed more proof,
all we'd have to do is look at your home. You've done amazing
things with it. You have a keen eye for the details that matter.

"Think about it." Ron tapped a finger on the folder she still
held in her hand. "And get back to us in a few days. I hope
you decide this will work for you."

"Honestly, we would have made this offer a long time ago
if we'd known you were interested." Mom pointed to the plans
for Pops's bathroom lying on top of the desk in the far corner
of the room.

Ron nodded. "It would be a win-win for all of us, and we'd
love to have you back."

"I don't need to think about anything." This offer was even
better than owning a business. It eliminated the financial uncertainty, and it allowed her to concentrate on the part of the
business she loved best. "This is what I've always wanted to
do. I'll take the job." Mia threw her arms around both her
mother and Ron. So much for professionalism. "I can't thank
you enough."

"It's about time you started making your dreams come
true," Mom said.

"I know your father would be happy." Ron kissed her cheek.

"It was always his hope to have you work with him. I'm glad we could finally make his vision come true."

"Me too." Mia grinned, but her eyes were a little misty.

Ron turned to Mom. "We should probably get going. Nick will be here any minute, and I'm sure he and Mia have things to discuss." To her, he said, "I'll have HR call you sometime in the next few days to work out the details."

Mia opened the bedroom door. "Thank you again. Both of you."

She stepped out into the small hall and walked them the short distance into the living room and to the front door. "I'll see you later."

"Goodbye, dear." Mom gave her another hug and a kiss on the cheek.

"Take care, Mia." Ron did the same as her mother.

They stepped outside, and Mia closed the door.

"You look happy." Pops eyed her curiously. "I take it everything is still a go with my renovation project?"

Mia grinned. "Oh yes. Definitely. Do you know where Jax is? I have some news I want to share with both of you."

"Does this have anything to do with why your mother and her business partner came here?"

She nodded. "Yes. I want to tell both you and Jax at the same time. You are never going to believe my luck."

"He's upstairs," Pops said.

"Okay. I'll go get him."

She climbed the stairs two at a time and knocked on the door of the bedroom Jax was using as his office.

He appeared a moment later, cell glued to his ear. "Hold on a second." Jax hit a button on the phone and lowered it from his ear. "What's up? Is everything okay?"

"Yes. Sorry. I didn't realize you were on the phone. This can wait. Come down when you have a minute."

"I will. Gotta go for now."

"No problem," she said.

With a little wave, he closed the door.

She returned to the living room and found Nick and his crew waiting.

"We're ready to get started," Nick said.

This is it. Her first design project for someone other than herself. Mia's heart beat faster than a race horse galloping at top speed.

The faint sound of chimes filled the air. Mia peered up from the color swatches she was studying and listened. Was that the front doorbell ringing? She couldn't tell with the deafening sound of the table saws cutting in the background.

Exiting the former den, and closing the door to lessen the loud noise, she walked into the living room. Pops was still sitting in his recliner, although now he sported a pair of headphones and was watching TV. There was no sign of Charlie.

The chimes played again. Mia hurried to the front door and opened it. "Hi. Can I help you?" she said to the woman who stood on Pops's front porch dressed in a trendy blue blazer with matching shorts, a white button-down shirt and stiletto heels.

"Yes. Is Jax Rawlins here? I'm Cate. His agent," the woman said.

She might have guessed this woman was from New York City. People in New Suffolk usually didn't wear haute couture.

"Of course. Jax is upstairs. You'll have to excuse the noise. We're renovating inside. Please come in, and I'll go and get him."

"No need." Jax appeared by her side. To Cate he said, "Please come in. This is Mia."

"It's nice to meet you," Mia said and extended her hand to the other woman.

"You too," Cate said.

"You remember my grandfather, right? He came to one

of my shows in the city earlier this year." Jax pointed to the recliner.

Pops removed the headphones. "Hi there."

"It's nice to see you again." Cate gave a little wave. "So this is why you left so suddenly." She pointed at the crutch lying on the floor beside the chair.

"Pops took a nasty tumble down the stairs," Jax said. "I've been helping out while he recovers."

Cate nodded. "Ah… I see."

"I'm doing much better, thanks to my boy." Pops grinned.

"I'm glad to hear that." Cate turned to face Jax and beamed a thousand-megawatt smile at him. "I've got huge news for you. Pack your bags. You're going home."

Chapter Twenty-Two

Jax's gut twisted.

No, dammit. He didn't want to think about leaving. "What's going on?"

"Yeah," Pops added. "We all want to know."

Cate grinned like a Cheshire cat. "I've had several conversations with the Breitenberg gallery over the last couple of weeks."

Jax's jaw dropped. "Are you serious?" He couldn't have heard her right.

"I am." Cate's excitement filled the room.

"Sounds like you hit pay dirt," Pops said.

"Congratulations," Mia added.

"Don't get too excited." Jax shook his head. "Breitenberg has never been interested in my work before." Jax shot Cate a quizzical look. "What's changed?"

"*You* have." Cate let loose a soft chuckle. "More to the point, the images you're shooting have changed."

Jax couldn't deny that either. He wasn't interested in shooting the raw, edgy animal images he used to. He wanted to capture something more inspiring, powerful.

Like the beauty of the sea drenched in the first light of a new day. The heartwarming cheerfulness of seals frolicking in the chilly waters.

Feel-good images.

They reflected his current state of mind.

"I told them about your new work," she said.

Jax's brows drew together in a deep V. "But you haven't seen any of my new photos yet."

"You did send me your Victoria Falls images," Cate responded. "Gunther loved them."

"But they're not my latest work," Jax insisted.

Cate waved off his concern. "So why don't you show me your new stuff? Is there somewhere we can go for lunch?" She gave him a pointed look. "Four hours is a long way to travel."

"A Zoom meeting would have been fine with me. You're the one who insisted on making the trip."

"Yes, well, I wanted to deliver my news in person."

And make sure he was on the right track. She might not have said the words out loud, but he knew what she was thinking. He couldn't blame her. He'd been unsure of a clear direction in recent weeks.

But all that's changed. He glanced at Mia. *At least as far as my career goes.*

"Okay. Let me grab my tablet so I can show you the new images I've captured while I've been here." *You wanted different, and that's what you're going to get.* He grinned. The truth was, he couldn't wait to show her. "I'll be right back."

She smiled. "I look forward to seeing them."

Jax hurried up the stairs two at a time. After grabbing the tablet from atop his makeshift desk, he returned to the living room. "Do you want to see them now?"

"Let's wait until we get to the restaurant."

"All right." Jax walked over to Mia and dropped a kiss on her lips. "I won't be long. We can talk about what you wanted to tell me earlier when I get back."

"Sure," she said.

"See you later, Pops." Jax waved.

"Good luck," Pops said.

He opened the front door and gestured for Cate to precede

him. "We'll take my car." He opened the passenger door for her and waited until she'd settled in before closing it. After walking around to the driver's side, he slid behind the wheel.

"Where are we going?" she asked.

"How about French fusion?" he suggested. He backed the car down Pops's driveway and headed into town. "The restaurant boasts a Michelin star chef. She earned three during her time at one of the finest establishments in Paris and another here at her own place."

Cate nodded approvingly. "Sounds wonderful, but I have to ask what she's doing in a town like this, with such extraordinary credentials—no offense to New Suffolk, of course. I mean someone with that kind of talent could cook in New York, or San Francisco, or any other major US city. What made her settle here?"

Jax slanted a quick glance in Cate's direction. "She likes it here." There was a lot to like, as far as he was concerned. He remembered his meeting with his parents. Jax sighed. *And some to dislike.*

"It's a cute little town and all, and I do like the close proximity of the beach, but I can't imagine there's any nightlife."

Jax snorted. "It's not Manhattan, that's for sure." *Thank God.* "But we manage to have fun."

Cate shot him a skeptical glance. "If you say so."

He let out a deep belly laugh. "I do."

Jax pulled into the parking lot of Layla's place a few minutes later.

"The Sea Shack?" Cate gawked at him. "Is this some kind of joke? If so, I can tell you, I'm not in the mood."

Jax pressed the key fob to stop the engine and held up his hands as if he were surrendering. "I'm not kidding. This restaurant is run by one of the top chefs in New England. Layla's food is fantastic. Don't let the name fool you." He exited the vehicle and walked around to open Cate's door. "Come on. You're going to love it, I promise."

A hostess seated them at a table for two overlooking the ocean.

"This is nice." Cate peered around the room and glanced at the twinkling fairy lights. "And the views are spectacular." She gestured out the window.

"I told you you'd like the place." Jax propped his arms on the table.

A server approached. "Are you ready to order?"

"Can you recommend anything?" Cate asked.

"If you're looking for something light, our Niçoise salad is a warm weather favorite. The chef makes it with pan-seared tuna. It's served with a fresh baguette and whipped butter."

"Yes." Cate's eyes lit with delight. "I'll have that."

"I'll have the Sea Shack Burger," he said when the server turned her attention to him. "Medium rare, with fries."

Cate ordered a glass of white wine, and he asked for a domestic beer.

"Okay." The server smiled. "I'll go and put your orders in and be back with your beverages."

"Thank you." Cate smiled. She turned her attention to him when the server disappeared. "So, what do you think of my news?"

"It sounds like an interesting opportunity." He still wasn't convinced it would come to fruition.

The server returned and placed their beverages on the table.

"It's more than an 'interesting opportunity.'" Cate made air quotes with her fingers. "Aren't you even a little excited?"

He lifted his glass and drank some of the beer. "I'm cautiously optimistic. We've been down this road before, and it ended in disappointment." He wasn't going to get his hopes up. How could he when Cate hadn't even shown Gunter Breitenberg any of his new work? "How did this all come about?"

Especially at a time when many galleries weren't even interested in showing his images.

"I told you; Gunter loved your Victoria Falls photos."

Jax eyed her skeptically. "And he's willing to give me a show based on that?"

"Well, no." Cate shook her head. "But he does want to see your new images."

The server appeared again and placed their meals in front of them. "Can I get you anything else?"

"No, thank you." Cate smiled. "This looks delicious."

"I'm all set," he said.

Cate sliced a piece of seared tuna and lifted the fork to her mouth. "Mmm. Fantastic. You were right about this place."

Jax grinned. "New Suffolk is not as backwoods as you think."

"Well," she arched a brow, "that remains to be seen."

Jax lifted his burger and bit into the juicy meat. "I can see why this is such a big hit." He wiped his mouth with his napkin. "Man, is it good."

"So…" Cate tapped her fingernails on the table. "We have a meeting with Gunter tomorrow."

"Okay." He bit into his burger again. Maybe he could go to the meeting and come back as soon as it was over. He'd have some time before they scheduled an actual show. Breitenberg was booked months in advance.

Yes. He could do this.

Cate glared at him. "You're doing this on purpose, aren't you?"

Jax shook his head. "What are you talking about?" He dipped a fry in the house-made ketchup and popped it in his mouth. Layla had added a hint of curry. *Delicious.*

"Keeping me waiting while you sit there dripping in beef. Come on. Don't keep me in suspense any longer." She motioned for him to hand her the tablet he'd set on the table beside his plate.

"Sorry." He'd been lost in thought and forgot. Jax wiped his hands and passed the tablet to her. "The images are already queued up."

Cate scrolled through the images slowly, taking time to study each one. Her expression remained neutral and gave nothing of what she was thinking away.

Jax wasn't sure how much time had passed when she finally looked up.

"So?" he said.

"From a technical perspective..." she began.

Jax's shoulders sank. "You don't like them."

"That's not true. I like them a lot."

"Then what's the problem?" he asked. "And don't try to tell me nothing is wrong. Not when you start the conversation talking about the technical aspects of my work."

"All right, fine." Cate set the tablet on the table and trained her gaze on him. "Seals playing in the water. It's not you."

"You wanted a change." His words dripped with accusation. "That's what you got."

"Change, yes, but these are a complete departure from the raw, edgy style you're known for." Her brow furrowed. "Sunrises? I mean yes, the colors are stunning. And the light rays reflecting off the powerful waves..."

Inspirational. Like anything is possible. That was what he'd experienced when he shot the pictures.

"What's going on with you?" She picked up the tablet again and scrolled through a few images. "Now, *this* is you." She turned the tablet and showed him one of the Victoria Falls photos. She turned the tablet toward her again and swiped a few more times. "And this one."

Jax nodded. He'd captured the massive iceberg images on

a trip to Alaska two years ago, when he'd done the photo-shoot of a lynx.

"Different than the animals you usually photograph, but edgy and raw, just the same."

Jax sighed. "Bottom-line it for me."

"You need more of these." Cate pointed to the Victoria Falls image and the iceberg image. "Come on, Jax. This is your *career* we're talking about. Do you really want to give up everything you've worked for?"

No. He didn't.

"It's time to stop messing around with frolicking seals and sunrises—no matter how glorious they are—and get back in the game."

She was right. No matter how much he wanted to deny it.

"I'll postpone the meeting with Gunter, but I need you to do what you do best. Get me the kind of images Gunter will be pleased with."

He gritted his teeth. If he knew what Gunter wanted, he would have captured those types of images years ago. The man had eclectic tastes. Jax's raw, edgy style should have fit right in with the types of work Gunter displayed at his gallery, but they didn't.

"You have until next week," Cate finished. "Can I count on you to come through?"

"Yes." Bile swirled in his stomach and burned a path up his throat.

Mia barely heard the quick knock over the loud din of the saw. She jerked her head toward the door in time to see Jax walk in. "Can you excuse me a moment?" she asked the man she was speaking with.

"Sure." The plumber nodded. "I'm all set." He brandished the drawing in his hand. "I'll get started on running the pipes."

She nodded. "Good. Let me know if you have any more questions." Mia strode over to where Jax stood.

"Can we talk for a minute?" His grim expression spoke volumes.

A heavy weight settled on her chest, making it hard to breathe. She already knew what he was going to say. It didn't take a genius for her to figure out he was leaving. His agent had all but announced it earlier. "Sure. Let's go outside." She didn't want to have this conversation in front of the other people milling about in here.

"I'll be right back," she called to Nick as she followed Jax out of the room.

With Pops at his rehab appointment, the living room was silent as they passed through.

Jax opened the front door and gestured for her to precede him.

She stepped onto the front porch and turned to face him. "You're leaving," she said, making sure to keep her voice void of the storm of emotions swirling around inside her.

Jax nodded.

Mia blinked away the moisture that had gathered in the corners of her eyes at his confirmation. *Dammit.* She'd promised herself she wasn't going to get upset. Yet here she was, about to burst into tears.

"I have to go as soon as Pops gets back," Jax said.

"That soon?" She glanced at her watch. Pops's appointment was already done, and the rehab center wasn't that far away. He'd be back any minute now.

"I have a flight to Iceland out of JFK later tonight."

Her vision blurred. Mia gritted her teeth. She wasn't going to do this. They'd agreed to a no-commitment, fun-while-it-lasted affair. The fun had come to an end. Just because she'd broken the rules, and had fallen in love with him, didn't mean Jax had fallen for her in return.

He wasn't a relationship kind of guy. He'd warned her.

You didn't listen.

Deep down inside, she'd hoped against all odds that he'd change his mind.

Foolish, foolish, foolish.

"When do you think you'll be back?" The words escaped from her mouth before she could stop them.

Lord, what was wrong with her? She didn't want to make this uncomfortable for him. He wasn't a bad guy.

He was a *great* guy. That was the problem.

"I'll be back in New York next Tuesday. We have a meeting with Gunter Breitenberg the day after that."

She'd been wondering when he'd return to New Suffolk, but it didn't even seem to be on his radar. That spoke volumes to her. "Sounds like you'll be tied up for a while."

"Yeah." He looked at her, and oh God, was that pity in his eyes?

Her gut twisted, and everything seemed to cave in on her. Their time together had definitely come to an end.

Mia sucked in a deep breath and got herself under control. She wouldn't beg him to stay. "Good luck, Jax." She forced herself to smile. "I hope everything works out for you."

She walked back inside with her head held high.

A sob escaped her lips as soon as the door closed.

Chapter Twenty-Three

Mia's cell rang as she placed her dirty glass in the dishwasher. After drying her hands, she extracted the phone from the back pocket of her shorts and glanced at the caller ID. Her sister. She connected the call. "Hi, Piper. What's up?" Her voice sounded bright and cheery. At least, she hoped it did. She was feeling anything but.

She missed Jax. He'd been gone now for ten days, eight hours and—Mia glanced at her watch—twenty-three minutes. Not that she was keeping track.

Instead of getting better, the ache in her heart grew worse with each passing hour.

And how pathetic was that?

Seriously pitiful.

"Do you have the kids tonight?" her sister asked.

"Not for the next few hours. They're having dinner with their father, but they'll be home by eight." At least, they were supposed to be. Kyle hadn't spoken a word to her when he'd arrived to collect them a few minutes ago. A welcome relief, as far as she was concerned.

Actually, the entire week and a half had been quiet. He hadn't spoken to her once since the evening her roof had been damaged.

The repairs had been minor, and she'd made them herself.

That reminded her, she still needed to check the security feed to see what had caused the damage.

"I'd love to get together for a glass of wine if you're free. I haven't seen you in over a week."

That's because she'd been keeping a low profile. Mia hadn't even patronized the Coffee Palace. She wasn't up for answering questions about her and Jax. The truth was, she hadn't told anyone she and Jax were over. When Piper had called a few days ago and asked about Jax's sudden departure, she'd acted like it was no big deal. And burst into tears as soon as the call had ended.

Mia sucked in a deep, calming breath. "Tonight's not good." The last thing she needed was for Piper to see her waterworks up close and personal. "I've got a bunch of things I need to get done."

"Are you all right?" her sister asked.

Tears welled in her eyes. "Yes. I'm fine." She prayed Piper wouldn't hear the quiver in her voice.

"Okay. Talk soon."

Mia scrubbed her eyes with the back of her free hand. "Absolutely. Bye." She ended the call.

She finished tidying the kitchen. What was she going to do now? Working on Pops's renovation had kept her busy these last few days, but they couldn't do anything more until the vanity and shower were delivered.

Mia walked to the refrigerator and peered inside. The thought of food made her sick to her stomach.

The doorbell chimed a short time later, and she frowned. She wasn't expecting anyone. Mia strode to the front door. Piper, Layla, Abby and Elle stood on her front porch.

She was about to leave the door unanswered when her sister called out, "You know we can see you through the front window, don't you?"

Mia glanced at the picture window to her right. Piper and

Layla waved from outside. She sighed and opened the front door. "Ladies, this really isn't a good time."

Four pairs of eyes stared at her.

"We know something is wrong," Elle said, her voice full of compassion.

Abby nodded. "You haven't stopped in for coffee since Jax left."

"I've been busy. That's all," she countered.

"Your cheeks are tearstained," Layla said.

Piper gazed at her. "I heard the sadness in your voice when we talked a few minutes ago."

Moisture gathered in her eyes again. "You guys better come in." She'd start ugly crying any second now.

"Oh, sweetie." Her sister threw her arms around her and hugged her tight.

The dam burst.

Mia wasn't sure how long she wailed for, but she was exhausted when she came up for air.

"Come on. Let's sit down and you can tell us what happened." Piper guided her to the sofa, and they both sat. Layla did too.

Elle and Abby took the two chairs opposite the couch.

Mia looked at her friends. "It's over. Jax and I are done."

"And you don't want to be," Abby said. It was a statement, not a question.

Mia shook her head. "I don't have any choice."

"I don't understand." Elle shot her a questioning look. "Did you guys have a fight? Is that the reason Jax left?"

"No. He really did have to leave for work," she said.

Layla's brow furrowed. "Maybe it's just me, but I still don't see the problem."

Her shoulders sagged. "It wasn't supposed to get serious. Neither of us wanted that. But…"

"Oh my God." Piper's eyes bugged out. "You're in love with him."

Mia's shoulders slumped. "I don't know how it happened."

Layla flashed a knowing smile. "It just does, honey."

"Trust me, Layla is right," Piper agreed.

"Does Jax know how you feel?" Elle asked.

She shook her head. "How am I supposed to tell him when he made it clear from the start that he wasn't interested in a relationship?"

"He might have told you that," Abby said, "but the Jax I saw with you at Layla's place when we all gathered to hear the live music seemed pretty smitten with you."

Piper nodded. "Shane told me Jax went all domestic the night he came over to help you put the tarp over your roof. That doesn't sound like a thing a guy would do if he was only interested in a fling."

"Maybe he feels the same way you do," Abby posed.

Mia shook her head. "Why wouldn't he say anything?"

Piper gave her a curious glance. "What if falling in love scares him the way it does you?"

Mia was about to dispute her sister's statement, but Piper was right. She was terrified of ending up brokenhearted again. Not because Kyle had broken her heart. She might have thought that at the time, but the truth was, she'd never loved him enough for that to happen.

Losing her father all those years ago... Mia pressed her fist to the center of her chest. That was the real reason she was afraid. Her heart squeezed. She couldn't go through the loss and heartbreak that came with loving someone so deeply and losing them again.

Except...

That's exactly what was happening. Letting Jax go hadn't stopped the heartache. It had made it worse.

"It's frightening to put yourself out there," Layla said. "Believe me, I know. I was afraid to open my heart again after what I went through with my ex, but I'm so glad I did, because I couldn't be happier."

"I feel the same way. I fought my feelings for Cooper tooth and nail. And look how that turned out." Piper waved the third finger on her left hand. The diamond caught the light shining in through the picture window. The stone sparkled, as if emphasizing her point.

Mia flashed a watery smile. "I remember."

Piper locked her gaze with hers. "You helped set me straight."

Mia laughed. "I did, didn't I?"

Her sister linked her hands with Mia's. "And I will always be grateful for that."

"Tell him how you feel," Abby encouraged her.

"I agree," Elle said. "You owe it to yourself to see if you can find a way to make your relationship work."

"Take a chance, Mia. Love is worth the risk," Piper said.

Mia sucked in a deep breath. Could she do it? Could she open her heart to love?

"Come on, Jax." Cate approached the bar. Grabbing his hands, she pulled him to his feet. "This is supposed to be a celebration, not a funeral. We finally did it."

Yes. The meeting with Gunter Breitenberg the day before yesterday had been great. Better than great. He'd loved the images Jax had captured.

Cate had been right about the trip to Iceland. Not only had Gunter offered to showcase his work next week, he'd booked another exhibition for a month from now.

Once word got out, the Arte Loft and several other prestigious galleries in New York City had requested shows.

His career was back on track, and he was sitting pretty. He should be on top of the world. So why wasn't he?

"Come on. Let's have some fun before you get on another plane tomorrow," Cate said.

That was another problem. He wasn't interested in leaving again so soon, but he needed to if he was going to take more photographs for all of the upcoming show requests.

"Everyone's on the dance floor. You need to be there, too," Cate insisted.

"I'm not really in the mood." Jax returned to his seat.

"Your friends are expecting you to join them."

Jax glanced at the group gyrating on the platform a few feet away. He couldn't call any of those people friends. Heck, he didn't even know most of them. They were just here for the party he was throwing.

How sad was that?

Pretty sad indeed.

"You go ahead," he said.

Cate shook her head. "Suit yourself." She walked back to the dance floor without a backward glance at him.

Jax strode to the club exit. Outside, the warm evening air surrounded him. No cool ocean breeze here, he thought as perspiration clung to his skin.

What he wouldn't give to be dressed in a pair of board shorts and a T-shirt, sipping a cold beer and playing a game of pool right about now.

No, dammit. Why was he thinking about New Suffolk? His time there was done.

He slipped off his jacket and folded it over one arm. With his free hand, he flagged a cab. He slid inside when it pulled over. Jax gave the driver his address.

The cabbie stayed silent as he drove the short distance to Jax's Manhattan loft.

His cell rang just as the driver pulled up in front of his building. He answered without glancing at the caller ID. He didn't have to. It was Pops's ringtone. "Hi, Pops. How's it going?"

"Things are great here. My new bathroom is coming right along. Another week or so and it'll be done."

"That's good." Jax paid the driver and hopped out of the cab.

"Mia—" Pops began.

"I don't want to hear about what's going on with Mia," he warned. His heart gave a painful thud. He missed her, dammit. More than he believed possible. "We're over. Done."

"I know. I know. I was just going to say how much I like her design. I mean, the computer-generated images were fantastic, but the real thing is turning out even better than I expected."

Oh hell. "I'm sorry." Jax sighed. Of course Pops was excited about his new bathroom. Yet here he was jumping down his throat because he mentioned Mia. He was the one with the problem, not Pops.

Jax stepped inside the high-rise and strode to the elevator bank. "I'm glad it's turning out so well. I hope that means you'll be happy sleeping on the first floor." He stepped into the waiting car and rode to the penthouse level.

"Oh, I know I will. Mia—"

His gut twisted. How was he supposed to forget her when Pops kept talking about her all the time?

Don't blame Pops. You're the one who can't stop thinking about her.

He could have sworn she'd had some feelings for him. Okay, maybe not love, but something they could build on, but she'd sent him on his way without a second thought about what they'd shared.

Not true. She'd asked when he'd be back. He knew she meant back to New Suffolk, but he'd deliberately misunderstood the question.

Face it, you left because you were afraid of what would happen if you stayed.

It was true. His departure had nothing to do with his career or any of the other rationales he'd invented. He'd used those reasons to justify getting the hell out of Dodge.

He'd left for one reason and one reason only. He was head over heels in love with Mia.

He broke out into a cold sweat just thinking about it.

I don't do relationships.

How could he when he was terrified that the person he loved couldn't or wouldn't love him back.

When your parents couldn't love you...

Jax sighed. He'd convinced himself that it was better to leave New Suffolk behind than risk opening himself up again to the pain and suffering he'd experienced with his apathetic parents.

How's that working out for you?

Not good. Not good at all.

Jax stepped out of the elevator and into the small hall. *Time to turn the conversation to safer ground.* He unlocked the door and stepped inside. "How's your physical therapy going?"

"Good. Got my follow-up appointment with the orthopedist a week from Monday. I should be able to ditch my crutch once and for all."

He smiled and dropped down on the sofa in his living room. "That's great news, Pops. Maybe you can come visit. I have another show at Breitenberg next month."

"That sounds great. Speaking of photos, you ought to see some of the pictures Aurora has taken lately. She's really mastered the use of light. Well, as much as an eight-year-old can."

He'd taught her how to do that. He wished he could teach her more. He liked working with her more than he'd anticipated. She needed someone to nurture her talent. *Not gonna happen, so you might as well forget about it.*

"Oh, and Mia brought me to Kiera's soccer practice. You should see her go," Pops continued. "She's a little spitfire."

His little spitfire.

No, no, no. Dammit. He needed to stop this.

"Hold on a minute. There's someone at the door," Pops said. "Bill, can you get that?" he called.

"Who's visiting you this late at night?" he asked.

"It's Kiera, Aurora and Brooke," Pops said.

Jax's eyes widened. "Mia's daughters are there?"

"Yes sir. Mia too. She brought chocolate-chip cookies over for dessert."

Mia and her girls were at Pops's house? Now? *No way.* "It's almost nine. Aurora, Brooke and Kiera go to bed by eight thirty."

"They did." Pops paused for a moment, and continued with, "But now that school's out, they go to bed later. Come over here. Give your Pops a hug and a kiss."

He heard indiscriminate voices. "They're really there?"

"You'd better believe it. Just because you were stupid enough to walk away from them doesn't mean I am."

He wasn't stupid. Was he?

No, dammit. You're not.

"Oh, who's this?" Pops asked.

Jax's brow furrowed. He heard another muffled voice. This one was distinctly male. Was someone there with Mia?

"Nice to meet you, Sam," Pops said.

Who the hell is Sam? He was about to ask when Pops spoke again.

"Yes, yes. Go ahead into the kitchen. I'll be there in a minute."

"What's going on?" Jax growled. "Who is this Sam character?"

Pops let out a loud belly laugh. "Why do you care? You and Mia are done. You said so yourself. Although I can't figure out why. I've never seen you as happy as you are with her. And Mia…she adores you."

He *was* happy with her. Happier than he'd ever been. And

Mia... Pops was right. She might not have said the words, but she'd showed him how much she cared. With her support and encouragement, with her sweet kisses and tender touches.

The way she'd made love with him.

Oh God. What an idiot he'd been. She wasn't going to reject him. She loved him as much as he loved her.

"What did you expect her to do?" Pops sounded like he was talking to a moron. "Sit around and wait for a man who's made it abundantly clear he's not interested? That's not fair to her. She deserves better. Maybe that's Sam."

"No!" Jax wanted to be that man.

So what if his parents couldn't love him? That didn't mean he was unlovable.

Pops had shown him that. He was everything a son could want in a parent. Kind, loving supportive. Pops was everything Gary and Francine weren't.

Pops hadn't just loved him. He'd shown Jax how to love.

Why hadn't he seen that before now?

He'd been stuck in the past. Focused on what he lacked instead of what he had.

We can't change the past, but we don't have to allow it to affect us for the rest of our lives. Mia's words echoed in his brain.

He could and would choose a different outcome.

He wanted to love Mia and have a life with her. He wanted to be a father-figure to her daughters. In New Suffolk. With his friends. With Pops.

"You'd better smarten up, son. And make it quick. If you don't, you're going to lose Mia forever. I gotta go now."

The line went dead.

Message received. Loud and clear. He wouldn't screw things up again.

He'd do whatever was needed to win Mia back.

Chapter Twenty-Four

The doorbell rang as Mia carried her overnight bag down the stairs. "I'm coming," she called. "Hold on a minute." Piper was way early. Her train to New York City wasn't supposed to leave for another hour.

Mia's stomach jumped and jittered. She was really going to do this. She was going to show up at Jax's doorstep and tell him she was madly in love with him.

Now that she'd decided to do it, Mia was actually excited, although Lord knew why. There was still a chance he could laugh in her face.

Stop it. That's the fear talking.

It was screaming at the top of its lungs.

But she wouldn't allow it to ruin what might be possible for her and Jax. Piper was right. Love was worth the risk.

She set down the suitcase and opened the door. "Hey, sis. You're—" She stopped midsentence. Piper was not the person standing in front of her. "What are you doing here?" Her expression turned grim.

"I wanted to talk to you," Kyle said.

"I'm busy. Now is not a good time." Mia started to close the door, but stopped. She had something more to say. "And by the way. The house isn't unsafe anymore. I made the repairs."

"I'm not surprised. It's not like there was a lot of damage to the shingles."

Her brows shot up. "How would you know? You never saw the actual damage."

"Oh, ah…" He looked like a deer caught in bright head-lights. "I mean… I guessed. There wasn't a lot of water that came through."

"You were freaking out because you thought the ceiling might cave in from all the water."

"Well, ah…" He rocked back and forth on his heels. "I guess I was wrong."

Her gaze narrowed. "It was you, wasn't it? You caused the damage to my roof, not the storm. I should have known. There weren't any big branches in the yard."

"I don't know what you're talking about," Kyle protested.

Mia opened the security app on her phone. She called up the feed for the backyard cameras from the night of the storm.

Fast forwarding through the footage, she gritted her teeth when a man wearing a rain slicker appeared. He grabbed the ladder she kept stored along the back of the house, set it to access the right corner of the roof and climbed to the top. "Actu-ally, I should let you know that the house is super safe now."

Kyle's brow furrowed. "What's that supposed to mean? You're not making a lot of sense."

"I had a security system installed."

"That's great. When did you do that?" His tone was casual, but his worried expression gave him away.

"Right after you moved out. So…" She pursed her lips as if she were thinking about how long ago that was. "About a year ago."

His eyes bugged out.

"Which means I captured the culprit who *broke off* the shingles on my roof, causing thousands of dollars of damage." Mia turned her phone so he could see himself in the act. "I'm calling the police, Kyle. You've gone too far this time. You vandalized my property."

Kyle went into full panic mode. "No. Please. Don't. I'm so sorry. I'll pay you back. Every single penny."

"Damned right you will. Why'd you do it? Do you hate me that much?"

"No." He shook his head. "I love you, Mia. So much. I was… mad. I wanted you back, but you flaunted Jax in my face. I was—"

She held up a hand to stop him from saying the rest. "I don't want to hear your pitiful excuses." She'd heard enough of it over the last few months.

"Jax is gone now. I even understand why you had a fling with him."

Her eyes widened. "Oh really?" Now *this* she had to hear.

"You wanted to get back at me for the Oriana thing."

"Wow." Mia shook her head. He really had no clue. "Just wow."

"It's all right. I forgive you," Kyle said.

Bitter laughter bubbled up inside her. "You…forgive me?" She couldn't believe the gall of the man. "Let me make this perfectly clear, so even you can understand. There isn't a snowball's chance in hell of us getting back together again. Ever."

"But I love you," he insisted.

"I'm sorry. I don't love you." She lifted her phone again.

"You don't want to call the police," he said. "Think about it, if you have me arrested, I won't be able to pay child support while I'm in jail. What will you do then? You don't make enough money—"

"You're pathetic." She punched in the number and waited for the call to connect.

Kyle ran to his car as her call was answered.

Mia reported the crime. The officer assured her they'd pick Kyle up for questioning. She thanked him and ended the call.

"Hey, Mia." Piper stepped inside the house. "What was

that all about?" She gestured out the door. "Kyle was in such a hurry he almost plowed into me."

Mia shut the front door. "Don't ask." She didn't want to explain everything now. "I think I'm going to head to the train station a little early."

Piper grinned. "You go, girl."

"Remember to pick up the girls from day camp at three o'clock. And show your license," she added.

"I will. Don't worry. We'll be fine. I'm looking forward to spending the evening with my nieces. I don't get to see them nearly enough."

Mia laughed. "We'll see if you feel the same way after twenty-four hours together."

Her doorbell chimed again.

Piper's brow furrowed. "Are you expecting someone?"

"No. I swear to God, if that's Kyle—" Mia jerked the door open with more force than necessary.

Her mouth fell open.

It couldn't be. Her eyes must be playing tricks on her.

"Hi, Mia." Jax beamed a thousand-megawatt smile at her.

No trick. He was really here.

Jax glanced at Mia. Why wasn't she saying anything? Worse, why was she just staring at him as if he was an abomination of some sort?

Piper appeared behind Mia. "Oh my God!" she exclaimed. "Don't think you're going to need me after all." She squeezed by Mia. "Hi, Jax. It's great to see you. Bye." She gave a little wave as she hurried to her car.

Jax dragged his attention back to Mia. She was still staring at him, and she still hadn't spoken a word.

Shit. Maybe he'd been wrong about her feelings for him? Maybe he shouldn't have come?

No. Mia loved him. He was sure of it. And he loved her.

Jax cleared his throat. "Can I come in, please?"

She blinked as if emerging from a trance. "Yes. Of course." Mia stepped aside and allowed him entry.

At least she wasn't telling him to get the hell out of here.

"What are you doing here?" she asked.

She sounded perplexed more than angry. He'd take that as a good sign. Hell, anything was better than her just staring at him.

"I'd like to talk to you." His heart beat so fast he thought he might pass out.

"Umm…okay." She didn't take her eyes off him.

Jax sucked in a deep breath. "Mia."

He'd rehearsed what he was going to say to her more than a thousand times since Pops's call last night, but he couldn't remember a single word.

Start with the obvious. "I've been such an idiot."

A ghost of a smile formed on her face. It gave him hope and the courage to continue.

"You mean the world to me." Jax stepped closer to where she stood. They were only a few feet apart, but the distance seemed like miles. "You're everything I could ever want. All I could ever need."

Her smile grew brighter. He moved closer, resisting the urge to close the distance and scoop her up in his arms. He didn't want to rush things.

"I love you, Mia. With all of my heart." The words spilled out of him. "I should never have left without telling you that. I'm praying that it's not too late to tell you now."

"No. No, it's not." She launched herself into his arms. Her smile banished the loneliness inside him and filled him with light and hope. "I love you too."

She *loved him*. Jax's heart soared. He wrapped his arms around her. He wanted to hold her close and never let her go.

"I was afraid to tell you how I felt." Her voice shook with emotion. "We agreed we weren't going to get serious."

"A lot of good that did us." He laughed. Happier than he'd ever been. "I think I've been in love with you for a long, long time." *He'd* made her off-limits more than Shane ever had. To protect his heart. He didn't need to do that anymore.

"You have?" Mia stared at him, a stunned expression on her face.

He gave her a sheepish grin. "I didn't realize it at the time, but that's the real reason I jumped at the chance to be with you when you propositioned me all those months ago."

Her eyes danced with delight. "It's the same for me. I had more than just a passing crush on you in high school. I think I always knew it was something more…but I was too afraid to risk my heart. Losing my father hurt so much. I didn't think I could go through that again."

"My parents—" he began.

"I know." She brushed her lips over his. "Did you ever talk to them?"

"I did. I finally figured out that they're the problem, not me."

"I'm so sorry." She kissed him again. "I know how much you wanted a relationship with them."

"I'm okay. It's their loss. Not mine." He'd finally realized that. "I have you. Aurora, Brooke and Kiera. And Pops. My family of choice." He wasn't alone anymore. This lone wolf was now part of a pack.

"I like the sound of that." Mia grinned.

He did too. "Does that mean you'll tell Sam to hit the road?" Jax held his breath and waited for her answer.

Mia's brow furrowed. "Who's Sam?"

"The guy you brought over to Pops's house last night," he said.

She looked at him as if he'd lost his mind. "I didn't bring anyone to Pops's house last night. I wasn't even there."

"You and the girls didn't bring chocolate-chip cookies over to Pops's place at nine last night?"

She shook her head. "Of course not. The girls were in bed at eight thirty."

Pops made the whole thing up. To make him come to his senses, no doubt. And he fell for the ruse, hook, line and sinker. *Thank God.* Jax doubled over with laughter.

"What's going on? What's so funny?" she asked.

He told her about Pops's call.

Mia laughed. "I'll have to remember to thank him."

"Me too." His expression turned serious. "I can't imagine what would have happened if he didn't intervene."

"We'd be having this conversation in Manhattan." Mia pointed to her suitcase. "I was on my way to the train station when you arrived on my doorstep."

His eyes widened. "You were?"

Mia laughed. "Looks like we both came to our senses at the same time. Speaking of Manhattan…"

Jax looped his arms around her waist. "Did I tell you I bought a place in New Suffolk?"

Her eyes bugged out. "You did *what*? But your life is in the city."

He shook his head. "Not anymore. I want to live here. In New Suffolk."

"But your career—"

"I've decided to make some changes there." He'd had a long conversation with Cate this morning about what he wanted moving forward. He couldn't say she was thrilled about what he'd proposed, but she'd accepted what he'd had to say. "I'm going to cut back to six major shows a year, and maybe a few smaller venues, like your sister's gallery. That will allow me to be home more. Which is what I want. I'm also going to start shooting the kinds of pictures that inspire me." Like frolicking seals, and gorgeous sunrises, as well as the types of images he'd taken in Iceland, because they'd inspired him as well.

"Jax…you don't have to give up everything you've worked for, for me. We can find a way to make it work."

"That's not necessary. This is what I want. Turns out I really like living here. I've got great friends." Real friends who were there for him. He looked forward to returning the favor. "Pops is here. And of course, there's this gorgeous brunette that I'm madly, deeply in love with…"

Mia grinned. "Tell me about this place you got."

"I made an offer on the old toy store in town this morning, and Loni accepted. I want to use the downstairs as a studio. I can edit my photos there, and I was thinking I might even try my hand at teaching photography when I'm not traveling."

"I think I know a young lady who'd be interested in being your first student."

Jax beamed a wide smile at her. "I plan to live upstairs. At least for now."

"No more hot sex in a hotel room?" Mia grinned.

"Can't have the gossips talking about my best girl, can I?"

"I told you, they're clearly just jealous of me." She gave him a look that sent a jolt of electricity sizzling through him. "How could they not be when I have you."

His chuckle turned into a gasp when Mia slid her hands under his T-shirt.

He closed his eyes as she stroked her palms over his chest. His shoulders.

"I have some career news, too." Mia twined her arms around his neck and dropped a kiss on his lips. "I accepted a job as a home designer with TK."

He smiled and nuzzled her ear. "That's why your mother and Ron came by that day, isn't it?"

She let out a soft groan when he pressed his lips to the pounding pulse at the base of her throat. "I was going to tell you, but things went a little haywire for us after they left."

Yes, they had. But they'd straightened everything out now.

"Mia." He cupped her cheeks with the palms of his hands and gazed into her eyes. "For the longest time, I trudged through life each day, but never really lived. Then you came along and now my gray world is filled with vibrant colors.

"You are everything to me, and I'm a better man because of you.

"I am so lucky to have found you. Thank you for choosing me, loving me."

"Oh, Jax." A single tear ran down her cheek, but she was smiling. "You are the best thing that has ever happened to me and I am so blessed to have you in my life.

"You are my favorite hello and my hardest goodbye." Her smile turned misty. "The one I've been searching for all my life, and the only one I want by my side."

He lowered his forehead to hers, marveling at the joy and happiness bubbling inside him. "I love you with all my heart. Now and forever."

She smiled and his heart filled to bursting point. "Looks like you're a relationship kind of guy after all."

Jax grinned. "With you, definitely."

* * * * *

Catch up with the previous titles
in Anna James's miniseries
Sisterhood of Chocolate & Wine

A Taste of Home
A Deal with Mr. Wrong

Available now,
wherever Harlequin books and ebooks are sold.